VENGEANCE AT PURGATORY

OTHER BOOKS BY J. B. SISAM

Divine Providence

Grace: What's So Amazing About It?

Thinking Forward 90-Day Journal

A Jacob Creek Novel | BOOK 1

VENGEANCE AT PURGATORY

J. B. SISAM

LIVING LIGHTS
PUBLISHING

Minneapolis, Minnesota

Vengeance at Purgatory
© 2019 by Jason (J. B.) Sisam

Publisher's Note: The characters and events in this book are fictitious. Any similarity to real persons, living or dead, is coincidental and not intended by the author.

Cover and page design by Living Lights Media
Cover copyright © 2019 Living Lights Publishing

Published by Living Lights Publishing / Sisam Enterprise
P. O. Box 43732
Minneapolis, MN 55443

Scripture quotations taken from the New King James Version®. Copyright © 1982 by Thomas Nelson. Used by permission. All rights reserved.

Scripture quotations are taken from King James Version (Public Domain)

ISBN: 978-0578511214 (*print edition*)

Printed in the United States of America
10 9 8 7 6 5 4 3 2 1

VENGEANCE *AT* PURGATORY

WELCOME HOME

Repay no one evil for *evil*. Have regard for good things in the sight of all men. If it is possible, as much as depends on you, live peaceably with all men. Beloved, do not avenge yourselves, but *rather* give place to wrath; for it is written, *"Vengeance is Mine*, I will repay," says the Lord.

— *THE APOSTLE PAUL*

CHAPTER ONE

Six years since his father's murder, Jacob took his family back to Purgatory, Wyoming. The former Reverend died in a mining accident, and he answered the call to become the new Reverend.

He looked behind into the covered wagon at his wife and daughter. Virginia laughed at something and he strained but couldn't figure what his wife, Sarah, said. He focused his attention back to the purple-hued mountains that rose in the distance. Ten years prior, he left Purgatory to attend seminary, to get away from his drunk and abusive father. Now dead, his father no longer bothered him. After the funeral, Jacob stuck around for two months helping Momma cope with running the family ranch. Jacob had his seminary degree in hand and the decision to go back home began. The two-horse team pulling the wagon slowed their canter as Jacob pulled back on the reins. They had one good day of travel ahead and needed to break for camp soon; the animals needed a break.

Jacob looked behind him again and his gaze landed on their earthly belongings. Amazing how one wagon held their whole life, heading out with nothing but a prayer and faith that God would guide their journey. The sun dipped behind the mountains, igniting the sky in brilliant shades of reds and oranges. It was time to settle for camp.

"Jacob, do you think we should break for camp soon?" Sarah said, poking her head through the canvas.

"I was just thinking that. We should get another hour in before breaking for camp. I don't like sitting out in the open." He slapped the reins. "I'll try to find cover soon, we'll build a nice fire and eat grub. How's that sound?"

"Sounds great."

Sarah moved out of sight into the wagon and Virginia giggled again at Sarah. Virginia, he loved that girl more than life itself. Her infectious laugh, light hearted manner, and easy company became the joy of his heart. The day she entered the world brought him more joy than all else life offered. Not that marrying Sarah was a bad day, by any means, but Virginia filled his heart with pride.

At twenty years old, he fell in love with Sarah. The other young ladies in Purgatory paled to Sarah's charm. Both their fathers were ranchers, and the two met at a young age. Momma considered Sarah a girl's-girl and after her parents died in an accident, Sarah came to live with Leonard and Momma. She didn't care for dirty things, and she didn't care for the life of a rancher. Little did Sarah know she'd marry a farmer turned preacher at the young age of nineteen. Nothing, not even the slightest hint showed that Jacob fell hard for her. Course, growing up, Jacob didn't speak much; his father tried to encourage him to speak up, be a man, and stop being such a Momma's boy. Despite doing his father's will, the abuse never ended, especially when his father came home drunk. Jacob understood his mother coddled him when things got rough, but when Sarah came into the picture and lived with them, Jacob desired to be himself, away from his father's watchful eye. Despite his shortfalls, Sarah made a wonderful wife and an even better mother.

The first thing on his list: ask for Sarah's hand in courtship. His infatuation for Sarah overwhelmed his senses, but once he'd pulled his belt up and grabbed his courage by the horns, he asked her to court him.

She said yes.

The sun continued its dip behind the horizon. This would have to do. Jacob commanded the team of horses to slow to a halt, and once they stopped, he pulled the brake back and hopped down. Sarah and Virginia climbed their way out the back.

"Here, let me help," Jacob grabbed his wife's hand and helped her to the ground, then went to lift Virginia out, but she insisted trying herself. "Okay, have at it," he laughed.

Virginia disappeared into the wagon and with a quick run and jump, she landed with a thump. She giggled, "I did it!"

Jacob patted her on the head then unloaded the packed food. He loaded a few cans of potatoes, beans, and canned meat into a satchel. He pulled out dried beef–preferring it to the metallic taste of the canned stuff–then set them on the ground, next to a large boulder. "Virginia, come help your mother with these cans while I work on a fire."

Virginia ran over. "Yes, Sir." She grabbed the satchel and heaved it over to Sarah.

Jacob's mouth watered as the fire quickly cooked their simple meal into a stew. Sarah scooped food onto waiting tin plates, then passed them out to her family. "How long before we reach Purgatory?" she asked.

"We should be there sometime tomorrow," Jacob said

between bites. He noticed that Sarah worried they made the wrong choice by going back to Purgatory. He set down his plate, "It'll be okay. There's nothing to worry ourselves about. Besides, the man who killed my father is dead. They hanged him before we left."

Sarah knelt next to him and cupped his hands, "That's not what worries me."

"What, then?"

"I'm worried nobody will care. People change, Jacob. Your father was not evil, I get it. He died because he made a bad choice. He should never have taken that money," she looked away, "What if we aren't accepted and we fail? What if all they see is your father, not you?"

There it was. One thing he understood about Sarah, she didn't like change and detested when people talked about her behind her back; hated it even more when they talked about Jacob's family with disdain. They would see Leonard, not Jacob. They took a risk going back to Purgatory and Jacob understood his wife's reservations, but one thing was clear, God called them back to Purgatory.

Jacob wasn't his father. His father, Leonard, needed the money to pay the bank the rest of the Creek Ranch mortgage as they struggled to keep the place going. Leonard took money from the wrong person and they demanded payment. They collected with a lead bullet. A rumor circulated that a man named Gabriel Grant, a local businessman, shot his father. The Judge cleared Grant's name and hanged another man for Leonard's death, yet somewhere deep inside, Jacob had his reservations concerning the businessman.

Jacob shoved the thoughts aside. "God has our back. No weapon formed against us shall prosper." He knelt down next to her, "It doesn't matter what happened prior. We are Creeks.

We move forward and we let no one steal this moment. And if they run us out of town, we'll just move and the mission work will continue."

The answer looked to satisfied her. She looked up, "I love you. You know?"

Virginia, pretending to eat, popped her head up and said, "I love you too, Papa!"

"I love you too, little one," Jacob laughed and reached for his plate again for another bite.

CHAPTER TWO

SITTING BEHIND the large mahogany desk he purchased from a businessman from India, Gabriel Grant stared at the open financial ledger. He accounted for every person in payments owed but one person, Joanna Creek. For nearly six years the widow paid her late husband's debt, but she had paid nothing for nearly six months. Flapping the book closed, he leaned against the chair and fingered at his mustache. How should he approach Joanna for payment? It wasn't like the Miner's Lodge brought in a lot of cash flow for Gabriel's enterprise in Purgatory.

Joanna's husband had borrowed nearly two thousand dollars when the bank turned him down to pay for some cattle, with the promise of returning every dime when he sold the cattle. The problem being, Leonard Creek failed to pay and Gabriel collected the debt with a lead bullet. He pushed back from the desk and gathered his top hat, coat, and gloves.

Moira, his wife, stood in the doorway. He pulled at her hand. "Tell the staff I want my evening meal when I return."

He knew she'd ask where he was headed and she did not

disappoint. "You're leaving? Now? But it's so late, my dear, you never run the business this late at night."

"That's enough. Tell the staff my instructions, I'd hate to put someone on the street because you failed to do as I say." Moira's gaze fell to the floor and Gabriel lifted her chin. "Look at me when I speak."

"I'm sorry, dear."

"That's better," he grabbed his cane and walked out of his study.

The head butler saw him coming, stood, and opened the door, "I'll call the carriage house, sir." The staff would see him coming, but the head butler would make sure they were to gather his horse so that Gabriel would be ready to leave the moment he walked up to the building.

After mounting his horse, he took off toward Purgatory to speak with Joanna Creek. Thirty minutes later he approached the Miner's Lodge, which stood just at the edge of town, across the street from the Mayor's office, a position he would soon control. He pushed the thoughts aside as his equine trotted up the street to the Lodge.

As usual, Joanna rocked in a chair which sat on the tiny porch. A tradition most in town had come to expect. If anyone wanted to know what happened in Purgatory, they'd pay Momma a visit. Momma, a term of endearment that stuck, and Gabriel could see why. As sweet and quiet as she was, you'd always mind your manners when she was around. If you cursed, she'd put you in your place and tell you a passage from the Bible. She was a good Christian woman.

"Mr. Grant. What brings you to my Lodge this late into the day?" Momma stood and pulled a shawl around her broad shoulders. Her feet settled on the porch as she smoothed the dress around her body and then checked her nearly pitch black hair, which sat balled up on her head in a simple bun.

"I've come to see you."

"Come in, come in. I have tea on, if you'd like," she said as her short plump body pushed through the door.

"I shouldn't be long."

Gabriel tied off his horse and followed her into Lodge. Several men milled around and their dirt-covered faces seemed black as midnight. Their eyes were so white they looked like hard-boiled eggs set against a black tablecloth. He loved the sight of dirty men, because sooner or later, they would have to pay him their share of gold.

"I hope you boys found something today."

Their egg-like eyes stared back, drilling into Gabriel like a miner's pick axe. "Just so you can have your cut, I bet," one man said.

"That's enough, Eli. Go wash up before dinner. Mr. Grant and I have business to discuss."

"Whatever," he said, pushing past Gabriel with a slight nudge of the arm.

She motioned to her tiny kitchen and offered him a chair. Refusing, he pulled out a piece of paper and a pair of spectacles. "Mrs. Creek, I was busy doing my books this afternoon when I realized that you haven't made any payments my way in the last six months." He pulled off the glasses, "What I'm wondering, after everything you've been through—losing your husband, your son going away, and your struggling farm— why you would choose now to stop paying me the money your family owes?"

Without missing a beat, Joanna looked at him and began kneading dough that sat on the table. "Mr. Grant, I understand your sentiments for the money my late husband owed you, but we were not under any agreement. The night you took my husband's life, your exact words were, 'Joanna, I'm terribly sorry about your husband, but he chose his path and it cost him his life. I consider his death payment for all monies owed.'

"Now, did you, or did you not tell me that or was it a piece of fibbing, Mr. Grant?"

Gabriel couldn't argue against the woman. She was correct, he gave her a waiver on all money owed. The lead bullet paid the debt. But something interesting happened, she paid back the debt without ever being asked. That one gesture made his deal void. And now, he was here to keep her end of the bargain.

"Now," she continued, "despite all the water under the bridge between us, I consider you a good man, Mr. Grant; however, the Lodge needed the money and I had to take care of my boys, here—notwithstanding needing a few supplies for my son and his family when they arrive tomorrow." A smile played her lips, "They're moving back, and I couldn't be a happier woman."

Gabriel just looked at her with little to say. His words halted by one thought: Jacob Creek. The boy was coming home and Joanna used money to buy extra supplies just for her family? That money should have been paid to him first. He ran a few fingers through his hair, carefully laying out in his head what to say next and what he said surprised even him. "Mrs. Creek, since you took it upon yourself to pay back your husband's debt, my original offer became void. Your family now owes the full amount of over one thousand dollars for the loan I gave Leonard."

"You do what you must, but I will not pay you another cent until I deem it necessary." She buried her hands deep into the dough, "Right now, I'm making some honey oat bread for my family and I would appreciate some space. I agreed to pay you back because it was the good Christian thing to do. Now, that'll be all, Mr. Grant."

He plopped his hat back onto his head, "Mrs. Creek." He walked out the door and pulled at the reins of his horse. The gall of the woman. She paid because it was the Christian thing to do? And now she's refusing to pay because, what, because her family was coming to town? The moment Jacob arrived, Gabriel would make sure he would introduce himself and let the boy know who owned the town and to whom his family owed the debt.

He mounted the animal and dug his heels into its ribs. First, he'd go home and eat dinner; then he'd pay Jacob a visit when they arrived tomorrow.

CHAPTER THREE

W HEN DAWN broke, they ate a small breakfast of roasted barley and beans. Jacob chased them with coffee and packed the wagon. A day of travel sat before them. If they got moving, they could make town by day's end. Jacob scanned the horizon with a compass and determined to keep moving south-west.

Jacob lifted Virginia after Sarah climbed aboard, "All set?"

"All set!" Virginia said.

"Great," he climbed aboard and slapped the reins. The team of horses tugged at the wagon as Jacob clicked his tongue and the trip to Purgatory began. He stared ahead at the purple-hued mountains and prayed to the Lord.

Thank you, Father, Maker of heaven and earth and all that is within it. I bless your Holy Name. We embark on a journey that will change the course and direction of our family for generations to come. I know you've called me with a holy calling and have set me apart for your mission in Purgatory.

I ask, by your grace, that you comfort my wife. Give Sarah grace to know the people of Purgatory as you do. Allow her to see the children of this town as her own. Let the people accept your humble servant as we do this mission you've called us to carry out.

There is none righteous, no not one—but I ask that you grant me grace in showing your kindness to those who've wronged my family and have caused my mother to be an outcast in her own town.

He finished praying as the wagon lurched forward. Pulling hard on the reins, Jacob brought the team to a stop.

"Jacob? What happened?" Sarah called as he hopped down.

"I think an axle broke."

Jacob crouched underneath, hoping the horses stayed put. Sure enough, grease oozed where the axle broke at the right wheel. He should have purchased a new axle before leaving Utah. He had attended seminary in southern Utah, which was a much-needed break from everything that happened in Purgatory. His father owed someone money and then was shot over a two-thousand dollar debt. As much as Jacob loved his father, cheating someone out of money was never a good idea. Leonard had borrowed as much money as needed to make life easier. The world doesn't work that way; if you borrow money, you're expected to repay what's owed. Leonard Creek never understood that concept, and it got him killed. Jacob was two years into seminary when his father died.

It doesn't matter if you're a good man; a simple poor choice affects how society views your actions. All they'll ever see is a cheater, swindler, and a liar. Jacob wanted to change the image of his family in Purgatory.

He wanted to help vindicate his mother by helping the town see he wasn't Leonard Creek. And if taking over Purgatory's church and the schoolhouse became the ticket to making it a reality, then so be it. Now he beat himself up for not buying an extra axle. Normally he'd have an axle underneath the wagon. Not this time. Jacob threw his hat. It smacked the dirt and a small cloud of dust to rose. He plopped to the ground.

"Jacob? Was it the axle?" Sarah called.

He looked up at his wife as concern filled her eyes. "Yup, and we're stuck. I don't have another one."

"How are we getting to Purgatory?"

Jacob looked at the wheel again. Maybe he could find a way. There had to be another way. Axle or not, he would get his family to Purgatory. They had saddles and Jacob could ride back for their belongings tomorrow. Unfortunate, as their whole life was shoved into a wagon. Several chests and wooden boxes filled the canvas-covered wagon.

God, I need help here.

He stood, dusted his slacks, and grabbed the saddles out of the back, "Guess we have little choice. It's this or we spend the day here hope'n someone comes along."

Sarah frowned, "What about our things?" She looked at Virginia, "And what about Virginia? She can't ride that long on horseback."

Jacob agreed it'd be tough for three people riding on two horses. He lifted the first saddle and brought it to the front of the wagon before returning for the second. "We'll be just fine. The Lord will guide us. We'll just stop more often for a rest."

It took a few minutes to unhook the horses and saddle them. He had Sarah grab a few saddle bags with enough food for the day's journey and told Virginia to gather a few things. Jacob jumped into the back and secured everything with tarps. He looked at his rifle and snatched it up.

"When will you fix the wagon?"

Jacob took Virginia to Sarah. "I figure we'll get to town and I'll check in with the blacksmith to see if he has a spare axle. Then I'll head back out to fetch our belongings." Jacob slid the rifle into the scabbard and mounted his horse, "I see no other way."

CHAPTER FOUR

THERE SAT Purgatory on the horizon, a small yet booming mining town in southern Wyoming. It lay west near the banks of the Encampment River with the Purgatory Gulch mines to the east. The town buzzed and Virginia sat up, squealing in delight. "Are we here, Daddy?"

Jacob smiled, "Yes we are, my dear. This is your new home."

It had been six years since he stepped foot in Purgatory. The only problem with the bustling town was the constant revolving door of miners who came in droves, worked for their gold, then traveled north toward Saratoga or west to Sunrise on the other side of the territory. Trains didn't come into town often, and when they did, they would bring another fifty men looking for a quick turnaround in fortune.

Jacob saw the Livery stable at the edge of town and would have to remember it on his way out. He needed a new axle and a couple men to help with repairs. Someone should be around to help him out.

They continued their descent into town and Jacob noticed

the glancing eyes peering out from under hats and bonnets. Some looked unsure of the newcomers, while others tipped their hats as they rode past. But it all seemed so unsettling. He knew there'd be people wondering why he returned and he didn't blame them. When he tried to visit them, the man who killed his father, Judge Talbert, turned him away and refused to allow Jacob any closure. Now, it had been six years since the hanging and his father's choices still haunted him, not because he loved the man who emotionally abused him, but for closure. Jacob tried to put it all behind him. This was his town now, and Leonard Creek was long dead and buried.

Jacob had worked hard to become a minister. He and Sarah left Purgatory for Salt Lake City after being newly married and he decided it was time to leave his childhood home. In the years since, he had made a good life. He shifted in the saddle. Funny how fate seems to rear its ugly head. Now they're back to take over the church, in a town filled with bad memories, and the feeling that God okayed the whole thing. Two months ago, Jacob received word from his mother that the previous minister had died in a freak mining accident. Shame it happened, but mining remained a dangerous job and people died all the time from accidents. The story was that an explosion rocked the south side of the mine and killed the Reverend. Those present said he would've died with little pain.

Jacob clicked his tongue to urge the equine forward. The far side of the town housed the miners in a tiny building that crammed men into small quarters. Momma ran the tiny lodge, cleaning and cooking for each miner and treating them like royalty. Jacob figured there'd be twenty to thirty men crammed in for the night, which would make it impossible for his family to sleep there. Far as he knew, a family friend, Bill

Erickson, ran the ranch outside of town, about a two-hour ride. Bill moved into the ranch with Momma's blessing after she opened her Miner's Lodge in town.

Several men walked in and out of the local tavern as they passed. Some nodded and others stared. A minute later they pulled up to the Miner's Lodge. It was good to be home.

Jacob dismounted, then hoisted Virginia down, followed by offering Sarah his hand.

"Well, this place hasn't changed, has it?" Sarah said, straightening her dress.

Jacob looked around. Not a soul. Mother would be alone. "Nope, it sure hasn't."

"Lands, is that my Jacob?" Momma's voice shot through the door. Jacob could just make out her figure before she stepped into the sun.

"Momma," Jacob said.

"And praise be, this must be little Virginia," Momma stooped down and offered Virginia a flower from a flower pot that sat near the door.

"Hello, Grandmother," Virginia smiled and accepted the flower, "Thank you, it's beautiful."

Momma hugged Sarah and then gave Jacob a kiss and hug. "It's so good to see you all," she walked back to the door and motioned inside. "Come, come; I have a kettle on and some freshly baked bread."

They walked into the dark lodge. The walls were clean, and he wondered if Momma wiped everything down daily. Miners were filthy and, thinking back to his last time in town, they arrived black as coal from the mines. Momma had 10 baths all ready to go when they arrived back. Each tub held one man. It would take several minutes for each man to wash, dry and change, and Momma made sure hot food awaited them after their cleaning sessions.

She motioned toward the small table in a little area with just enough room for Momma. There was no way they'd be able to stay. The place was nice, but damp, dark, and small. She set a small plate of hot bread on the table with honey and butter, "The coffee's hot, otherwise I have water."

Jacob gave Virginia and Sarah a slice of bread and honey, then proceeded with his own. "I'll be fine with some water. It's been a long morning ride," he said, then took a bite. How long had it been since he'd had Momma's bread? "Anyone at the Livery Stables these days? I need a new axle for the wagon."

Momma continued to watch Virginia eat. She seemed mesmerized by her granddaughter. Without looking up at Jacob, she sipped her coffee before continuing, "I think someone is there. Not sure who. Course, he could be down at the ranch helping Mr. Erickson get the herd ready for pasture." She looked up. "How's the bread, sweetie?"

Virginia smiled, "It's delicious. Thank you."

"You're welcome, my dear." She focused on Jacob's eyes, "What happened to the wagon?"

Jacob recounted how the axle broke the previous day. They had traveled for two weeks and just a day's journey out from Purgatory, it snapped like a twig. He picked up his hat and fixed it on his head. "I'm heading to the Livery. You two stay here with Momma and I'll fetch us a new axle." The chair vibrated as he slid back and stood, "Momma, thanks for the water and bread. Sarah, I love you." The two kissed, "I'll be back soon."

Jacob walked outside, mounted his horse, and edged it to

the other end of town, back toward the Livery Stable. As he passed the Tavern, a voice called out, "Jacob Elliot Creek."

A slight smile crept over his lips. He stopped and there stood, Missy Cartwright. The second most beautiful woman in Purgatory. She made the best darn soup in town and Jacob would have to come by for a bowl. Mother hadn't approved of their friendship, but that hadn't stopped Jacob from befriending her years ago.

"Hello, Missy."

Her red velvet dress hung on her otherwise petite body. She wore a simple apron which suggested she took a break from cooking or serving the local patrons. She brushed her auburn hair from her eyes. "What brings your sorry butt back to Purgatory?" he watched as she dug her fists into each hip.

"We're here to take over the church. Sarah will be the new teacher in town."

"That right? You have a minute to chat with an old friend?"

Jacob wished he could. "Sorry, Missy. I've got business at the Livery," he paused, "Anyone there today?"

She waved it off. "Fine, fine. But you must come by for some soup one of these days." Missy scratched her head then continued, "I think Freddy is working there today. If not, he's out at Creek Ranch helping Bill."

Jacob laughed, "All right, I'll take your word for it," he said then kicked the horse and continued down the street toward the Livery. The doors sat wide open and white smoke billowed out, filling the air. Someone was working. Maybe this Freddy fellow could help him with an axle. He dismounted and tied off the horse. The clicking of Jacob's boots notified the owner of his presence. A small wire-framed man looked up from an anvil. A glowing horseshoe pulled up with him, and he tossed it into a nearby bucket. The water spat and boiled off the metal, leaving a faint steam trail to rise from the bucket.

"Can I help you, Mister?" the words huffed out of the man as he flipped his hammer onto a workbench.

"As a matter of fact, I'm in need of an axle. My wagon broke down yesterday."

He wiped his hands on a cloth that hung nailed to the center post. "Name's Franklin, c'ept everyone calls me Freddy," he extended a hand.

"Freddy, call me Jacob."

"Jacob. Let's see if I have an extra one lying around here. Where ya from?" Freddy walked toward the back of the barn.

"We're originally from Purgatory, been away for ten years, but came back to take over the church."

Freddy threw several scraps of wood onto a nearby pile. His voice remained distant, "Poor fella, they said the Preacher died in a mining accident. Terrible thing to happen to a nice guy." A few more pieces of metal and wood flew and landed near Jacob's feet. "They say someone killed him in the mines, though there's no proof, he got into it with Gabriel Grant and next thing ya know, he's dead." Freddy's head poked up and he scratched it, trying to find his lost axle.

"I know the name," Jacob pushed Gabriel from his mind—not now—and wondered if there was an axle worth using here.

"Wanna come back here? I found it. A little dinged up, but she'd get the job done. I must reset the cotter holes, but it should get your wagon back to Purgatory just fine. Once we get it back, I can help you fix it up proper."

Jacob joined him, then helped lift the axle onto a nearby wagon and pulled it back to his main fire pit. "This should work. Looks decent enough."

Freddy smiled, "Good. I'll reset the cotter holes, they look a little rusted shut. Should take me by tomorrow to get the job done."

"Any chance you can get it done by today?"

Freddy shook his head, "I'm not sure. Any reason it can't wait?"

Jacob frowned, "All our belongings are still in the wagon, and it's about a good day's journey outside of town."

"Tell ya what. Give me until tomorrow to get this fixed. I'll head out there to meet you tomorrow. Your family can stay with mine if you'd like."

"I appreciate the gesture," Jacob said. "Deal, but my family will stay at Creek Ranch while we're in town. It's my mother's place."

That comment lit up Freddy's face. "You're Jacob Creek? It all makes sense now. Your Momma told me ya'll be com'n to town. Didn't know you'd be the Preacher around here."

Jacob walked toward the door and smiled. "Thank you again, Freddy. I'll see you out by Encampment River, half day's ride West."

He waved, "Alrighty, Preacher. By cracky."

CHAPTER FIVE

AﬆFTER FINISHING with Freddy, Jacob stopped at the Tavern to take Missy up on her soup. How long had it been since he'd stepped foot inside? At least five years ago when he traveled to Purgatory to check in on Momma. She'd been sick for weeks and had needed someone to run the Lodge while she recovered. That's when he met Missy. She was short, auburn-haired, and had an attitude to match the fire in her cinnamon eyes. As long as you behaved yourself, she let you stay in the Tavern, but the moment you caused a scene, she'd kick you out on your butt.

He pushed aside the two chest-high doors, and they clattered behind him as he stepped into the Tavern. Someone played the piano, which sat near the back and sang out of tune. He wouldn't be using them for Sunday's hymn sing. Several round tables cluttered the small floor, and at least four sets of poker games were in progress. Jacob's head spun from the smoke-hazed room. He thought better of coming into a place of sin. He glanced around the room. Where was Missy?

"Jacob Creek," Missy waltzed up behind him. Now he

noticed her red velvet and black lace dress that whooshed around her waist. It highlighted her curvy features and when he looked into her eyes, he realized just how beautiful she was. After she kissed him on the cheek, her perfume arrived and wafted over him. The room's smokey smell began to fade.

"Missy Cartwright. How are you?" He took off his hat and tossed it onto the hat rack by the door. He leaned in and kissed her cheek.

"I'm doing mighty fine, Jacob. Come, have a seat. I'll get you some soup; it's on the house."

"Thank you," Jacob pulled up a stool and sat down at the bar. Its mahogany frame stood around four or five feet off the floor and his feet just touched the ground. A mirror lined the back wall, with rows of whiskey and other spirits arranged on each shelf that protruded from the mahogany backboard. A couple of men sat around him. Neither looked up nor paid attention to Jacob.

Missy arrived with a bowl of soup and placed in front of Jacob. "Can I get you anything to drink? It's on the house."

"Beer," he said as he bit into soft chicken and potatoes. The creamy broth warmed his dry throat and settled his growling stomach.

Missy filled a mug and handed the foamy drink to him. "It's nothing fancy like what you'd see in Salt Lake City. We don't have coolers for it."

"That's fine," he took another bite, "Soup's good, thank you."

"So you're here to be our new preacher, Mr. Creek?"

Jacob wiped his mouth, "Sarah and I are here to take over the church. We heard the Reverend died in a mining accident."

The people around Jacob quit talking. Missy leaned over the counter and lowered her voice. "We don't talk about it."

"Talk about what?" came the familiar voice of Gabriel Grant. Jacob turned and met the man's eyes. His dark brown eyes met Jacob's. Gabriel had a peppered VanDyke comb, which curled at the tips. His long jacket hung from his shoulders and a black top hat sat on his head. He extended his hand, "Jacob Creek?"

Jacob stood and shook Gabriel's hand. The businessman took the stool next to Jacob and laid his hat on the counter. "Mr. Grant."

"Don't embarrass yourself, call me Gabriel," he turned to Missy, "I'll have whatever he's having." Gabriel flicked a nickel on the counter. "I hear rumors you're in town to start that church up again," he frowned. "Shame the other preacher died. It was a very tragic accident."

Missy promptly set the beer before Gabriel and walked away.

"Isn't that right, Missy?" Gabriel said.

She wiped a spill on the counter without looking up, "Yes."

"Now, get back to work, I don't pay you to chat with clients."

"So what brings you to my fine establishment, Reverend?" Gabriel leaned back against the wooden stool.

"I figured that I'd take time and get to know some parishioners, and I've known Missy for a few years."

Gabriel hissed, "You realize, son, that this is a drinking establishment, do you not?"

He could tell he wasn't welcome. "I did, yes. I don't think it isn't too much of a stretch to see the parishioners taking a drink at the local tavern. Heck, I even have my beer." Jacob took another drink, then stood, "May I get everyone's attention?" He stood with his back to the bar, "My name is Jacob Creek and I'm the new reverend in town. My wife Sarah and I would like to invite you all to service on Sunday morning this weekend."

Gabriel stared at Jacob, "You're the same, Creek. Your father was Leonard Creek, was he not? Your mother, Joanna?"

He'd already figured it out. That didn't take long. "Yes, sir, he was. I grew up here in Purgatory, married here. Sarah and I moved away for a short time so I could attend seminary. And now we're back to take over the church."

"You realize that your father owed me a sizable amount of money?" He took a single shot of whiskey, grinning, "and I do believe he never paid me. Now, I think it'd only be fair if you'd rightly pay me for what he owed me." He swigged back another gulp, "Isn't that right, folks?"

The words stuck in the back of his throat thick as glue. "I, um…" he turned to Missy. "Could I get some water?"

Before she could answer, someone in the crowd shouted, "Yeah, the trough the animals drink out of." The place unloaded a boisterous roar of laughter. A few cheers and clinking glasses echoed off the walls.

The whole room spun. What happened? This was to be a simple meal and cordial introduction! He grabbed the brass pipe on the bar to keep from slamming on his face.

Click, click, click.

A gun!

Jacob gazed down the long end of a .45 caliber gun attached to Gabriel's gloved hand.

"Now, Mr. Preacher Man, I'd say this be a good time to leave."

"Gabriel, stop it," Missy yelled. The place went quiet.

Everyone watched with bated breath. What would Gabriel do?

Gabriel lowered the hammer and holstered the weapon. "Missy, get the man some water." He raised his glass, "Go back to your drinks, this is a saloon," he cackled before slurping his beer.

Jacob stood and gathered his hat, "I think I'll leave. Good-night." He walked out the door and grabbed the pole. Bile formed a lump somewhere deep in his throat. Stupid. He punched the wall. Something grabbed his throat and squeezed. Jacob swallowed over the lump and fought throwing up.

Gabriel Grant hadn't changed. For years he'd harassed Leonard for Creek Ranch. To think his father took a couple thousand dollars from him seemed inconceivable, and the Judge had hanged another man for Leonard's death. Did Gabriel kill his father over a matter of a thousand dollars? If that were the case, things were just getting started. Maybe coming back to Purgatory was a bad idea.

CHAPTER SIX

THE NEXT day, Freddy rode out to help Jacob fix the wagon. It wasn't a hard fix. They had to remove every-thing from the wagon to hoist it up to change out the axles. Freddy brought along three other men to help lift. The job took a few hours, and it was off to Creek Ranch with their earthly belongings.

When he arrived, Sarah busied herself setting everything into the home. It wasn't a large house, but it had everything a family of three needed. A living area, stove, and two bedrooms. Virginia's room wasn't a bedroom, more of a loft that overlooked the lower portion of the house.

Bill, who had just moved out of the main house and into the Mother-in-Law shack next door, helped lift the crates and chests out of the wagon. Grateful for the help, Jacob heaved his own down. Jacob had known Bill since childhood, and he became a good friend and confidant to his Momma after Leonard's death. When Momma moved into town to start her Lodge, he took over the ranch and maintaining its integrity.

Outside of seminary, being a rancher was all Jacob knew. The ranch was home, and Momma made sure the home was ready by replacing the stove before they arrived. She had a new outhouse built. Good thing too; the old one practically fell over when you shut the door.

A few chickens ran in front of Jacob as he carried several bags inside. That gave him an idea. Sarah always fixed the best fried chicken. He stepped outside and asked Bill to fetch a chicken and prepare it for Sarah.

Jacob grabbed a few logs from the front porch and shoved them into the stove, stoking the fire. He walked over to a nearby chest and opened it. He bent over and pulled out his Bible. Sarah had given it to him the day they accepted him into Seminary. He relished the memory. Hard to believe that was ten years ago.

Jacob sat down in the rocker and picked up an old image of his father. His father would be dead six years now. "I wish you were here to see this. See the man I've become."

Sarah wrapped her arms around his neck and kissed him from behind. "He would have been proud."

"He would have been, but he wasn't the best father one could ask for." Jacob set the image down and opened the Bible.

"But he loved you."

"In his own way."

She kissed him. "Okay, you study. Tomorrow's coming faster than you think. We want you to be ready for your first sermon."

Jacob kissed her back. "Okay, Mrs. Creek. Go make our food now."

After she left, he thought back to the night before. Gabriel had rubbed him the wrong way. Maybe he should see Mr.

Grant tomorrow following the service. Sarah wouldn't like that much, but Jacob figured the man needed to understand that pushing him around wouldn't gain him any favors.

What's the use? He looked at the fire spinning inside the stove. Would it only stoke the fire? Grant already figured Jacob a pushover; maybe he was, but threatening and then laughing about it wasn't a fast way to make a new friend. He'd seen plenty of men like Gabriel Grant in Salt Lake City. Those business-type investors. They only care about one thing, the bottom dollar. If something didn't make a profit, it didn't benefit them and they moved on. Most businessmen didn't waste their time with small fry like Jacob. But why did Gabriel threaten? He wasn't expecting them to pay his father's debt, was he?

Jacob looked down at the Bible on his lap. The worn pages fell open to Romans 12:19: *Dearly beloved, avenge not yourselves, but rather give place unto wrath: for it is written, Vengeance is mine; I will repay, saith the Lord.*

It caught him by surprise. Jacob sighed and stared at the passage open in front of him. *Lord, what are you asking me?*

Maybe he better leave well enough alone. Gabriel proved his point, and Jacob got the message loud and clear: he was not welcome in Purgatory.

After dinner, Jacob looked out the window as the sun dipped below the horizon. It felt good to be back home.

"Are you coming to bed?" Sarah asked.

She'd finished her work, and he realized how late it was. Jacob closed his Bible and placed his journal on top. "I'm coming." He peeled off his shirt as he walked into the bedroom. Sarah was already in bed and he closed the curtain behind him, shutting out the rest of the house.

Jacob crawled into bed as Sarah snuggled up to his back.

He said, "I love you."

"I love you too, Jacob Creek."

He closed his eyes and envisioned standing before his new congregation. That was the last he remembered.

CHAPTER SEVEN

The rooster woke Jacob from his sleep. It was Sunday morning, the Lord's Day. Jacob sat up and rubbed the sleep from his eyes. Sarah was already up. His stomach growled for the breakfast Sarah prepared while trying not to wake Virginia.

Jacob wondered what it must be like for her. Being uprooted from her friends in Salt Lake City, dragged south to a small mining town to take over a church. Virginia knew no one. She was starting over. It was fine for both him and Sarah; they knew people; they had Bill and Momma. Virginia had no one.

He pulled on a pair of pants and slipped into his boots. "Good morning, Dear," he said, waltzing into the kitchen area.

Sarah stopped what she was working on and smiled. "Good morning, Love," she pulled out a cup and poured some coffee.

Jacob's heart melted. He remembered the day she walked down that aisle. Standing at the front, he knew there were people in that little church, but he only saw Sarah. She became his strength and his right hand.

She handed the cup to Jacob, and he quickly kissed her before she whirled away back to the stove. He then took in the deep coffee aroma before taking a sip, "Thank you."

"Breakfast should be ready soon. Are you ready for today?"

"I think so. I was up late last night pondering this morning's message."

She stopped cooking again, "And what message is that?"

"You must come to church and find out, Mrs. Creek," they both laughed.

Virginia said, "You guys woke me up," before waltzing into the kitchen past Jacob.

"Hey, little miss. You're not thinking of saying hello to your Mother before me, are you?"

Virginia whirled around. She let a coy smile play her lips, "Why, I would never think of it."

"Hey," Sarah said.

She threw her arms around Jacob. He bent and she kissed his scuffed face, "Good morning, Pa."

He kissed her head, "Good morning, dear. Now go help your mother."

Sarah handed Virginia a basket, "Fetch me some eggs."

"Yes, Ma'am."

Jacob followed her out the door. He checked in with Bill as he didn't get the chance the day before. He squinted in the morning sun. The birds sang and the sound of hammering jostled their little tune. He stepped into the sun.

The morning dew clung to the ground as the air pebbled his skin. It was a beautiful day. Just cool enough so you'd enjoy some good, hard work. Jacob walked to the fence on the south side of the barn.

Bill Erickson hoisted a beam into place and grabbed his hammer.

Jacob's crunching books distracted him for a moment, "Nice morning to do some good work."

Without looking up, Bill said, "Sure is. Wanted to get these finished before heading for church." Bill grabbed another nail and hammered it in. He set the tool down, took off his gloves, and offered a hand.

Jacob took it, "How long has the fence been like this?" He said, looking at the broken fence.

Bill wiped a handkerchief across his brow. "Boy, as long as I can remember. I repaired the fence on the east side last year, but behind the barn doesn't get a lot of attention." He wiped his forehead again, "Most of the cattle stay on the south side of the ranch. Figured I'd fix that first."

Jacob couldn't argue with the logic. Bill had taken over maintaining the Ranch. Five or six years of neglect damages buildings. The fence got the worst treatment by weather. He should remember to help Bill with the repairs. Jacob had all week to help Bill, but right now, he had to think about the community of Purgatory. They needed a minister.

The church maintained a weekly Bible study, but had no one with any seminary or ordination for ministry. He applauded the fact they wanted to keep their little church going, and without a shepherd, the flock had nowhere to go. It was Jacob's intention of making sure the people had someone to guide them in their spiritual faith.

Jacob asked, glancing at the barn, "How is the status of the barn?"

"Oh, I'd say it needs a little attention, but the horses seemed to be fine this morning. There's a hole in the roof. I plan on getting to that later this week." Bill hopped onto the new fence. "She holds."

They laughed.

"Sounds good. Don't work too long, Sarah's fix'n some breakfast then it's off to Purgatory." Jacob patted the man's knee, "Why don't you join us for some food?"

Bill picked up his hammer and toolbox, "I think I'll go clean up."

"Sounds good." It was time to eat and Jacob couldn't handle his stomach's rumbling any longer.

CHAPTER EIGHT

AFTER BREAKFAST, Jacob loaded the wagon and set off
for Purgatory. *Lord, O God, I pray now you'll give me the
words of wisdom to speak this morning to your people. I don't feel as if
I'm the man you've called for this job. I ask your Spirit give me a deeper
understanding to who I am in you.*

Once they arrived, Jacob helped Virginia down and
offered his hand to Sarah.

"Are you ready for this?"

He clung to his Bible, "I sure hope so. I believe it's God's
will."

"Then you'll do just fine. It's tomorrow I have to worry
about."

The church was typical for a small mining town, with
white double doors and an arched window above them. A
sleek cross sat perched atop the steeple. The washed paint
looked old and cracked, crying out for some fresh paint.

He took Sarah by the hand, walked up the steps, and into
the building. The roof peaked high over their heads. Ten pews
that held 40 people faced the front altar. A pulpit sat in front

with a cross etched into the wood, with a larger cross sitting near the table of remembrance.

Jacob walked to the front, taking in the view. He ran his fingers across the pulpit's finish. The power of God's spirit rested on his shoulders as a lightning bolt of energy rushed through his spine. This was his church, it would seat his congregation as they listened to him preach. The thought toppled him over. Sure, he'd given several sermons in Salt Lake City as a pastor's assistant, but this was different; this was his church.

Sarah stopped half way up the aisle as she held onto Virginia's gloved hand. His wife's dress spun at her legs and laced in the back. Sarah's hair pulled tight against her head with several pins securing her flowered hat. The sun radiated in from the windows and accentuated her feminine features. A lump formed in Jacob's throat at the sight of his wife. How did he ever deserve such a wonderful woman?

They'd been through it all together. She stood by his side when he decided it was time to go to seminary and train to be a minister. She followed him to Salt Lake City to the seminary where they raised their daughter; then when the Lord called, they followed him back here to Purgatory. The town held both good and bad memories and Jacob focused on the good ones.

Yet, the night before at Missy's Tavern left a bruise. Gabriel Grant needed to understand that, even though his father owed the money to Grant, Jacob wasn't responsible for the payment.

That ended the day his father died.

After taking in the view, Sarah said, "You okay, dear?"

The question pulled Jacob from his thoughts. He smiled and made his way back to Sarah. He caressed her face with his thumbs, "I'm fine. I think this church'll do."

She smiled, "I agree. After service I want to look at the schoolhouse next door. I want to make sure there are enough slate boards and chalk for the children. If not, we should talk to the General Store owner to see if he'll open for a few supplies."

"I think that's a good plan."

The clicking of boots to wood caused Jacob to turn around. A young family walked in. The little girl couldn't have been much older than Virginia. They'd be friends. She needed some kids her age.

"Good morning, Reverend," said the man.

"Good morning. Name's Jacob Creek. I'm the new Reverend…" he stopped himself. "Guess you already knew that," Jacob shook the man's hand.

He laughed and took off his hat, "Ma'am."

"Hello," Sarah said.

"We heard the church was open today. I was in the tavern when Gabriel threatened you. Sorry that happened. He's a rough guy around here. Owns half the town. But not to worry, he doesn't like new people anyway. Stay out of his way, and you'll be fine. Name's Joe. We'll be your most faithful attenders, as long as I'm not out-of-town helping some rancher run cattle. Also, if you need anything, I run the local Mercantile in town."

Sarah exchanged a smiling glance at Jacob, who said, "Thanks, we'll keep that in mind. Well, I hope you enjoy the service. I look forward to getting to know you kind folks."

"Likewise, Reverend."

As the place filled up and the singing began, Jacob stole a look around the tiny church. There had to be around thirty people. They packed the place. He figured it'd taper off after a few weeks. Jacob was a novelty a man who took over because they had no one else to be their Reverend.

Jacob took his seat on the tiny stage as Bill led the tiny congregation in a couple songs.

When the singing ended, Jacob opened the Bible. He swallowed over a lump in his throat. "Good morning," he cleared his throat, "Guess you all figured that I'm your new Reverend."

A small amount of laughter ripped through the room.

"It's an honor to meet some of you and I know God has some great things in store for you and this town. I was reading in the Gospel of Matthew and came to understand something we forget about. Jesus was not only God, but he was fully human. Every man who followed Jesus understood that he was special and that he brought a message of peace and prosperity."

Jacob saw each person listened to each word. That was good. Maybe they'll warm up to him sooner than he thought. He glanced down at the Bible and thumbed its worn pages and continued, "God in his mercy gives us grace and gives us freedom. When we look at the Beatitudes of scripture, we see it is the meek that will inherit the earth. We shouldn't be proud or haughty. We should look out for our fellow man."

Sarah smiled and nodded her approval. He couldn't help and smile back. This was their life now. They handled the spiritual well-being of the community. And if a message of peace would help, then that's the message he'd bring.

After the sermon, Jacob ended with another hymn and then proceeded to the front steps of the church. As each parishioner filed out, he took each hand and thanked them for coming. The one person he hoped would have been there—if anyone needed to be in God's house—it was Missy. He decided to stop by in the morning and invite her to the next service.

Virginia waited by the wagon. Jacob warmed as the sun illuminated the red in Sarah's hair. He closed the doors and breathed a sigh of relief. No one booed him off stage and everyone said thank you. For that he was grateful. Jacob bounded down the stairs and hurried to the wagon after everyone had left. He lifted her up and offered his hand to Sarah, who had just returned from checking out the school house.

"I think everything's in order. We should have enough slate boards. I hope all the children bring their own Bibles, we don't have many. I have 10 primers at home and another 15 here, so that shouldn't be a problem."

Jacob jumped up and settled on to the bench. He unwrapped the reins and slapped them against the horses, "I'm glad. Should we go home?" he asked.

The wagon lurched forward.

It was time to go home.

CHAPTER NINE

IT WAS the first day of school. Jacob had just dropped Sarah and Virginia off at the schoolhouse. Sarah figured he was heading into town to talk with the locals and get a feel for the town. Still, she couldn't believe it'd been ten years they left Purgatory. In some ways, it felt like the same town; in others, it felt new.

The town boomed with new people, miners, and those looking for gold. It wasn't uncommon in Wyoming to see these towns pop up and die off. Purgatory was different. The town stayed, and the miners kept coming. To Sarah, that meant more families and more children to teach.

She walked into the tiny schoolhouse which sat next to the church. It held only twenty students. Each township had their own schoolhouse, and this was the only one in the Encampment River area near Purgatory Gulch Mines. She was told by Charlotte Jennings, the exiting teacher, that she'd have only twelve students. As it stood, Sarah would have about one in each grade.

Virginia found a seat near the front by Sarah's desk and

plopped into the chair. "Can I have this one, Mommy?" Virginia said, running her hands across the surface of the desk.

She bent down and kissed her daughter's cheek, "Yes, my dear." Sarah made a note of where her desk sat compared to Virginia's. "And since you're this close, you can be my helper." She tapped the desk with a finger, "How's that sound?"

Virginia let out a yelp and hugged her mother. "I love it. Thank you!"

Soon enough, children piled into the worn building. Each found their seat after giving Sarah an apple. She'd never seen so many apples on one desk before. Enough to bake a pie.

The desks were arranged in three rows of five. Her desk sat near the front and to the right, leaving just enough room for the chalkboard and the American flag to her left.

"Hello, children," Sarah said. She picked up a piece of chalk and wrote her name on the board. "My name is Mrs. Creek."

The room remained silent.

"This is when you say, hello, Mrs. Creek," she instructed.

After a brief silence, they responded in a jumbled noise.

"There, that's much better," Sarah glanced the room over and counted eleven children. She grabbed a stack of primers. Handing them to Virginia she said, "These are your primers. You'll be using this and a Bible each day you're here." It seemed as if only a few had a Bible. "How many of you do not own a Bible? Please raise your hand."

Six children raised their hands. Guess her work was just getting started. The question, how to buy some Bibles?

"Okay. Today, you can share with your neighbor and I have an extra one that someone can use," Sarah pulled one from the top drawer and handed it to a young boy who looked only ten, "There you are. I will need this one back, okay?"

He said nothing and pushed the Bible off his desk. It clattered to the ground with a thud.

Sarah reached down for it and slapped it back on his desk. "This is for you to use today. I will need it back, okay?"

"My Pa said Bibles are for wussies. So I don't need one."

So, she had a sarcastic one. Sarah wouldn't put up with back talk. "As long as you're in my class, you'll be using a Bible and a primer. I expect you to come to class with a Bible, and if you don't, I will provide one for you."

The boy crossed his arms, refusing to acknowledge her.

"I'll take your silence as an agreement. Good. Now, what's your name, young man?"

"Felix Grant."

"All right, Felix. I want everyone to stand up and place their right hand over their heart."

Each child stood and proceeded with the instruction.

In unison they all mumbled along, "I pledge allegiance to the flag of the United States of America, and to the Republic for which it stands, one nation under God, indivisible, with liberty and justice for all."

"All right children, you may sit down and open your primers to the first page." She took a breath and continued after the children opened their books, "Today, we will be looking at the letter A. I need someone to tell me a few things that start with the letter A."

Each child pulled out their slate boards and wrote suggestions as they arose from the group. Sarah was pleased. Other than the behavior from Felix, the children complied and listened to her teaching.

She taught for the next hour before giving them an

assignment to complete. Sarah wanted each child to write several words she needed them to learn before the next day.

Sarah watched the hands of the clock on her desk strike high noon. She closed her primer and stood. The day had gone well so far. "As soon as you're done with your writing, we will break for lunch and then play a few games outside to clear your heads."

One by one, they set their slates down and grabbed their lunch bags. Some had bread and fruit, others had dried beef. Sarah opened the door to the building and allowed everyone outside to eat under the large oak. The bright sun warmed her face. She unfolded a large blanket under the giant oak and sat down.

It was quiet and everyone ate their lunch in peace. Some children chatted while others sat alone. Sarah bit into an apple. The skin split and juice exploded on her tongue. The sweet and tart puckered her lips. It was good. She took another bite and leaned against the tree. The tranquillity and peace to her heart at the awe of God's creation. Sarah loved the outdoors.

Virginia's voice broke the silence, "Give it back!"

"It's mine and you can't have it."

"Give it back!"

Sarah stopped chewing and looked around for Virginia.

"If you want it so bad, take it from me."

Sarah saw Virginia lunge forward to grab something from Felix's hand.

He whipped his hand back and Virginia fell. "You're too slow," he laughed.

Sarah was up, "You two stop that now."

Felix looked up, smiled, then kicked Virginia.

Sarah watched in horror as Virginia's head snapped back and her daughter fell once more.

She ran toward her daughter, who lay sprawled on the ground. "What's wrong with you?"

Virginia cried against the pain. Her cheek was red and swollen, with tears streaking down her dirty face. Sarah picked her up and held her close, asking again, "Felix, what is wrong with you?"

The boy just stood there. "She deserved it. She took my bread," he said, then bent over and picked up the dirty piece of bread.

Sarah snatched it from his hand. She recognized it. It was the loaf she baked the night before. "I know my bread. I baked it. This is Virginia's lunch." She threw the piece on the blanket. Turning back to Felix, "Now, I advise you to pack up your things and go home. I will be by later to speak with your father."

Felix snickered, "Doubt that will do any good," he smiled something sinister, then said, "Good luck."

"Pack up now and leave," Sarah grabbed Virginia's hand and led her to the blanket to get a better look at her face.

The girl sobbed in Sarah's arms. Did this boy's parents not teach manners? You never hit a girl. Ever! She pulled out a handkerchief and wiped the mud off Virginia's bruising cheek. Jacob would have a field day with this. There's no way he'd let it slide.

They'd only been in town for two days and Virginia had already made an enemy. She didn't need this. She didn't ask for it. Sarah felt guilty for dragging her away from Salt Lake City. Virginia was happy there. She had friends and people who cared for their whole family. Now, she was taken away from all that and brought to a small mining town. A town which held no meaning to the girl.

Sarah figured Jacob would give a piece of his mind to Gabriel Grant. It need not matter the history between the two men, but the children need not be bickering and fighting. Sarah sighed. This was not how the first day was supposed to go.

One of the other girls neared, "Are you okay, Virginia?"

Virginia looked up and wiped another tear. Her face now blackened. "I'm okay."

"Guess we should have warned you about Felix. He's got a real temper," the girl looked around, contemplating if she should continue. "He's the reason the other teacher left us. We liked her, but Felix's Pa wouldn't have a teacher telling his boy what to do," she looked at the ground, "I hope you don't get forced out like Ms. Jennings."

Sarah felt a lump form in her chest, which sat on her like a log. This was not a good situation. Gabriel Grant didn't seem like the type to give up and for that, she feared his retribution for letting Felix go home halfway through the school day.

She looked up at the sun and prayed a silent prayer, then bent down and folded her blanket. "Okay children, let's go inside."

CHAPTER TEN

JACOB BOUND up the walk to Gabriel Grant's house. The righteous indignation burning in his chest hadn't subsided since he learned of Felix kicking Virginia's face in. *You don't lay hands on women and children.* Jacob had every intention of making Gabriel understand his son needed to learn that lesson. A father who would let their son do such horrible things to a girl rattled Jacob's mind.

Sarah touched his back as he knocked. She meant well, but fire raced through his nerves. Raised voices inside reached the door as it creaked open.

A slender woman stood in the doorway. A tight bun coiled beautiful black hair atop her head. She wiped her hands on a red apron hanging over her green dress that accentuated her feminine features. "I assume you're the Reverend and Mrs. Creek."

"They are, let them in," Gabriel snapped.

"Howdy, Ma'am," Jacob said, removing his hat and stepping through the door into their large red-brick home.

"Come in, come in. I have just boiled some water for tea."

She started down the hall, then stopped, "Oh, where are my manners? I'm Moira."

Jacob nodded, "Nice to meet you. This is my wife, Sarah."

"Hello," Sarah said.

Jacob had never been in a house this large. He stepped into the hallway. Dark mahogany wood lined the walls and long red velvet curtains adorned each room's doorway with brass grommeted rings. Jacob saw a dark cherry wood couch covered in the same red velvet sitting to his left. His eyes followed the long hall to the right and saw what appeared to be a sitting room at the far end.

Gabriel Grant walked from an adjacent room. "Reverend Creek. Please follow me into my study. Moira, give Mrs. Creek some tea and don't interrupt us." He motioned to the room he left and Jacob walked through the double doors.

The large room rose to a high vaulted ceiling. Several wooden walls were lined with cherry bookshelves. Someone filled every shelf with many books, collections, and encyclopedias. Gabriel's desk sat in the room's middle. Its carvings were ornate and bold. Two curved chairs sat in front of the desk. Each leg curved down to a claw gripping a ball like a gargoyle. He rounded one chair and sat in its green upholstery.

Gabriel waited, then sat behind his desk. He leaned forward on his elbows, "So, Reverend. I hope you're not upset about the other night?"

"I'm sure everyone had a few too many beers that night."

Gabriel opened a box to his right. He pulled out a cigar. After clipping the end, he held it over an open candle. "That's not what I meant. I hope you weren't upset over our little chat." He puffed some smoke, "I wasn't drunk. I don't like people who steal from me and never pay me back."

Did Gabriel assume he owed his father's debt? The man

had held a gun to his face. His father was dead, and Momma told him he shouldn't even owe a silver dollar, that the debt was canceled.

"We're not here to talk about my father," Jacob cleared his throat, "We're here to talk about your son's behavior in school today."

Gabriel blew more smoke, "I'm all ears, as they say." He leaned back and puffed the cigar, sucking on it like a prized peppermint.

"Your son not only threatened my daughter, he kicked her and bruised her cheek." Jacob had to swallow against his anger, "I don't think it's right that a boy should ever feel the need to hit a girl. That's not the respect I would teach a son."

Leaning forward, Gabriel set the cigar down. As he folded his fingers, each bone popped. "Mr. Preacherman—I think I'll call you that—I was under the impression that your bully of a girl threatened my boy. Now, never in my life have I heard of a girl stealing something as a loaf of bread from a defenseless boy."

Jacob opened his mouth to speak but nothing came out.

The man rose, placing his palms hard on the desk, "I would never raise a boy who wouldn't defend himself. So, if he hit your girl, she deserved it," he said, before sucking once more on the cigar. "Sometimes a lesson needs to be taught to the women folk in our lives." He narrowed his face, then blew smoke into the air, "Tell me, you've never spanked your school teacher wife, have you?"

Jacob's throat went dry with a burning heat. He stood and straightened his jacket, then tried to clear his throat, "Mr. Grant, to assume I've raised a brat of a child is an awful assumption. My wife baked that bread earlier and had given it to our daughter. Your son, Felix, kicked her face in and I'd be more than happy to bring her over to you, tomorrow, to see for yourself."

Gabriel let out a laugh and sat back down. He grabbed his cigar and puffed once more. "Preacher, calm down. I know my boy hit your girl; otherwise, you wouldn't be here." He pulled out a leather-bound book from the drawer and tossed it onto the desk, "Tell you what. If you pay me what's owed by your family, I'll call my boy in here and give him a whoop'n while you watch."

Jacob wasn't about to acquiesce, "Where would I even get that kind of money? By all intents and purposes, the death of my father canceled that debt."

"True. But that's a lot of money and I could just take your Mother's lodge as final payment. But because of the miners and the business they bring me..." he laughed again, "It is, after all, my enterprise that runs this crap hole of a town. This place would go under if it weren't for my innovations and investments." Gabriel spread out his arms wide, "I'm a god here. I own everyone and everything."

Jacob had heard enough, this was ridiculous. To pay that kind of money, he'd have to sell most of his cattle, a barter he wasn't willing to negotiate. But what does one do with a man who doesn't care about the actions of his child? Jacob's father would have beat an apology out of him for disrespecting a girl, let alone hit. It was the only good thing his father taught him.

"Mr. Grant, I don't want to assume that you've already spoken with your son. But I would encourage you to at least tell the boy to behave himself," Jacob exhaled. "If he doesn't shape up, you'll be teaching him from this office. Do I make myself clear on the matter?"

Gabriel ground the cigar into the ashtray and stood, "Perfectly."

Jacob walked through the door and straight toward the home's double-door entrance. "Sarah, we're leaving," he called.

He waited by the door as she sauntered down the hall. "It was nice meeting you, Moira. Let's grab tea again."

Moira smiled, "I would like that a lot."

Gabriel stood between the study doors. His glare shot cold shivers down Jacob's spine.

Jacob turned toward Moira and tipped his hat, "Mrs. Grant."

"Reverend," she said.

Gabriel said, "I'll be seeing you around, Reverend."

Jacob didn't acknowledge the man as he and Sarah walked down the stone steps to their wagon. He helped his wife up, then checked the horses. Satisfied they were secure, he hopped up, released the brake, and slapped the leather reins. "Heya!" The wagon lurched forward toward home.

CHAPTER ELEVEN

"THAT MAN had the audacity to come into my home and tell me how to raise my boy!" Gabriel slammed his fist on the desk.

Moira stood there unmoving. Her face turned white as Gabriel paced back and forth like a caged animal. And he sure appeared like one.

He understood one thing: Jacob Creek had to go. It no longer mattered about his late father. All that mattered to Gabriel was Jacob Creek. He threw the cigar box lid open and snatched one up. He rolled it around his fingers and smiled. "You realize, Moira, this cigar is like the good Reverend. He's slim, tall, and can burn." Gabriel picked up the cutter and slid the tip of the cigar through the hole. "The Reverend messed with the wrong family." He snipped off the end. It rolled and bounced on the desk before leaving a trail of tobacco in its wake.

"I don't understand the problem. Sarah and I had a nice chat, and you two seemed polite." She crossed her arms, "And besides, you already beat the boy for what he did."

Gabriel puffed smoke into the air. He considered his next words. It would seem prudent to let things be. The boy deserved a beating and got the message to leave Virginia alone. But there was that issue of being owed money from the Creek family he couldn't leave alone.

He drew another drag, letting the smoke linger in his mouth before exhaling. "Moira, the boy got what he deserved. The Reverend needs to understand that I run this town, not him, and not his God." He crossed the room to a bookshelf and pulled out a ledger. "You don't question me, woman. I love you and respect your opinion, but this time you're crossing a line." He slapped the book closed after not finding what he looked for. "Now, I have work to do. Leave me in peace."

Moira nodded her head and walked out, closing the curtains behind her.

He watched her walk through the door and down the hall. Gabriel grabbed another book from the shelf. Leafing through the pages he found where he noted giving one thousand dollars to Leonard Creek on July 1, 1868.

Gabriel remembered the day. He finished buying out the Purgatory Gulch Mines, which sat east of town. It was a large land deal that gave him an edge in the community to invest in local establishments. People came to him for loans because he owned the local bank. It wasn't unheard of until Leonard Creek came along.

The bank threatened foreclosure on his family farm, so, he came asking for a personal handout. Gabriel hated giving handouts. It seemed petty and was unwelcome. Loans cost him money. Money was not a luxury, it was a commodity. The more he made, the more people wanted to borrow.

The problem with Leonard: he was a struggling rancher

and the town drunk who never paid on time. After begging, Gabriel gave in. He knew Creek Ranch produced some of the best cattle he'd seen and had the best grazing land. Yet, Leonard never bought more cattle to sell. So, he gave Leonard a second thousand dollars to settle with the bank, after Moira convinced him it was the right thing to do.

It stopped the foreclosure. The issue was that Leonard hadn't told Gabriel he only owed the bank five hundred dollars, and the rest of the money went for those cattle investments. More than likely, Leonard spent the money on spirits and gambling at the Tavern, of which he was a local fixture.

Gabriel threw the ledger on the desk and sat. He picked up the cigar and drew smoke into his mouth, then blew it out. Watching it roll and spiral, he knew it was time to send a message. The Creek family owed money. It wasn't a handout anymore, it was robbery. Leonard Creek stole the money and never paid. After being confronted, Gabriel threatened retribution if he didn't ante up.

After months of trying, Gabriel shot Leonard in the head. It shut the drunk up and it settled the debt, at least that's what he told Joanna Creek. Joanna, for several years, tried to pay little bits of the loan at a time. She desperately tried to own up to her late husband's debt. Then, six months ago, her small payments stopped.

As a millionaire, he didn't require the money, and he didn't need it. That was until Jacob came back into town. His arrival brought each emotion back and Gabriel knew they should pay the debt. That's why he stuck a gun in Jacob's face the other night. Seemed fitting.

The one thing he didn't take into consideration was Jacob's righteous indignation against Felix. The man had the audacity to confront Gabriel on the ethics of raising a son.

Jacob didn't even have a son. Sure, you don't hit a girl, Gabriel knew, but you don't tell a parent they're wrong either.

The seething anger grew in Gabriel's throat. His face flushed hot. Jacob Creek would pay what's owed or pay the same consequences. It was a matter of principle. One man owed, died, and now Jacob owned his father's estate. Sure, Bill Erickson ran things while the Creek family lived in Utah but that changed nothing. Joanna and her son, Jacob, had a debt that needed paying.

It wasn't polite to go after a widow. She had no money. But Jacob, if he was running the ranch, he'd have to sell off cattle and then he'd have cash to spare. The math excited Gabriel. If Jacob sold 250 cattle, that would leave him financially well.

Gabriel figured the average steer cost around $7 per hundredweight. If an 800-pound steer would cost around $55–simple math–Jacob could walk away with nearly $5,000 in profit after paying each man their wages. Take away what's owed, that left the preacher just under $4,000. Yet, you figure in six years of interest owed...Gabriel would just demand it all.

The question that plagued him was, how do you encourage a man to sell off his livelihood? Everyone understood your worth was in the cattle; the more you had, the wealthier you became. No one had more cattle than Gabriel Grant. He owned more land, had more workers, and owned several mining companies in the area. He alone brought more wealth to the lower portion of Wyoming than anyone else he knew.

Maybe he needed to sleep on it. The morning would bring a new idea, but he had to work through the logistics, and it might work.

For now, Gabriel had a Mayoral campaign to worry about.

The election was in about a weeks time and he knew there was no contest—he'd win.

He leaned back in his chair and thumbed the corner of his desk. He'd ride out to meet Jacob tomorrow, then off to talk the good folks of Purgatory into voting for him.

CHAPTER TWELVE

T HE NEXT morning, Gabriel rode out to the Creek Ranch. It was time to confront Jacob on his own property. It was a risk, yes, but needing to drive home the point that money owed was money owed, was enough to take the risk. If he could convince Jacob to sell off his cattle ranch, he would cancel the debt, and Jacob could come work for him on his ranch and could keep his little church too. It seemed like a good deal and Jacob should take it. But the question of how much Jacob knew or if Joanna told her son anything worried him.

The sun beat down on his oil-slicked jacket that weighed like iron on his shoulders. His top hat rose high and made Gabriel appear taller. As he rode onto the property, he noticed not a single cow grazed on the land. This was a ranch, was it not? If so, where were the cattle?

The ranch had a barn, chicken coop, a garden, a large house, and what appeared to be a small tool shack. Two men worked on a fence near the east side of the barn. A chicken ran past his horse, causing the animal to spook. Gabriel steadied her. "Easy girl."

The two men stopped working and looked his direction. The Reverend set down his hammer and wiped his brow, then walked in Gabriel's direction.

Gabriel dismounted and tied the horse to a nearby fence. He straightened his coat and tie.

"Mr. Grant, what brings you all the way out to Creek Ranch?" Jacob said, taking off his gloves.

"Nice place you've got here, Reverend," he said, offering his hand.

Jacob stuffed his hands deep into his pockets. "What brings you out this way?" He pointed at the fence, "Needing some honest work? I've got plenty."

Gabriel felt stupid keeping his hand out, so he put it on his hip. "I'm hoping you and I can talk. Come to an arrangement."

"They need no arrangements, and you're not welcome here," Bill piped in.

Annoyed, Jacob placed his hand on Bill's arm and said, "Can you let my wife know we have company? Have her put on some tea."

Bill sighed and turned toward the house, leaving Jacob and Gabriel alone.

Jacob looked into his eyes, weighing what to say next, "Talk, Mr. Grant. I have a lot of work to do."

Gabriel pulled from his saddle pouch a set of documents and handed them to Jacob. "You'll find within these documents my request to take as payment your cattle and livestock. I've already talked with the bank and they mentioned it would repay the monies owed by your family." He pointed to the fifth page. "These documents just need your signature and consent to proceed," he said while looking around for a moment and thought the ranch would make good grazing land. "The documents are just a formality. I'll even let you keep the cattle on the land and care for them. Though the sole right to sell them would be mine."

Jacob scanned the paperwork. The thoughts racing through his eyes made Gabriel giddy. His lower lip curled as his tongue played each tooth. Jacob continued turning each page and then looked at the signature page.

Jacob's blue eyes set in stone. He glanced up and tossed the documents to the ground. "Mr. Grant, if you think I will put my family's livelihood at risk by giving you our security, you're mistaken."

"Reverend, let's think about this for a moment," he picked up the papers, "These don't put you at risk. I'd be taking the risk. Your cattle could be damaged goods. I'm trying to give you a way out of this mess." He stretched out his hand over the land, "If you give me your cattle, it will pay the debt in full. No more mess, no more arguing. Everyone wins."

Jacob kicked dust and watched it swirl. "You win, Mr. Grant. You came into town, bought up the place, and now demand I give you my family's farm?" Jacob pointed to the house, "How do you think I'll be able to pay the debt owed on this farm? Without cattle to spare, you're leaving our family destitute. And the Almighty knows full well that a church cannot pay a minister its weight in gold."

Gabriel sneered at the Reverend's hot indignation. Didn't his God provide all his needs?

"Preacher, I know you're feeling bad about all this. In fact, I'm willing to pay you your weight in gold. I'll give you $200 a month. Now, I consider that a fair wage to earn. Not even

Freddy, the Blacksmith, makes that much cash. Shoot, I bet he makes around $80 a month."

The Reverend bit his lip and held out his hand, "I appreciate the offer, but our family isn't selling our cattle. This ranch has always maintained itself in the community. We even provided for the Union Army during the war. This ranch means everything to us. We're not selling. And unless you have something else to say, that'll be all."

Gabriel ignored the gesture. He slipped the papers back into the saddlebag. Grasping the reins, he hoisted up into the brown leather. "Reverend, you're making a big mistake. Oh," he pulled out a small button and flipped it at Jacob, "I'm running for Mayor, and I'd love your vote come election day."

Gabriel clicked his tongue and edged his animal around Jacob.

"Mr. Grant, you are no longer welcome on my property. Come here again, harassing me, I will talk with the Sheriff."

"This is not the last time we will talk." He turned hard on the reins and circled his horse around Jacob again. "You don't want me as an enemy, Preacher. I'm trying to give you a way out and I suggest you take it.

"Goodbye, Mr. Grant."

"Suit yourself," Gabriel kicked his animal hard. He looked back to watch Jacob stare him down. This would not be the end. It was time to get help, and he knew just who to call.

The horse's trot made his mind wander about putting the Preacher in the ground. His old man deserved a piece of lead and the Preacher wasn't far behind. He passed a lone steer grazing on some grass. Guess they had some cattle. Gabriel slowed the animal and pulled out his Colt .45. He tightened his grip on the cold steel and pulled back the hammer. He armed the gun with three clicks.

He would enjoy this.

He squeezed the trigger, and the gun fired. The bullet struck the cow. It staggered, then collapsed to the earth with a thud.

Gabriel watched the smoke swirl out of the barrel before holstering the weapon. A small trail of blood leaked from the wound in the animal's head. That should teach him a lesson. He'd own the cattle, even if he had to take every last one by force.

It would be minutes before Jacob showed up with Bill to examine where the shot came from. It was time to get out of Dodge.

Kicking the horse hard, Gabriel took off toward Purgatory. Let this be a lesson. You don't mess with Gabriel Grant. It was time for war, and Gabriel had every intention to not only start the war, but finish it.

CHAPTER THIRTEEN

JACOB DISMOUNTED his horse and crouched down to examine the dead steer. Bile hit his throat, and he swallowed hard against the forming lump. He poked at the animal. A single bullet and the steer was dead. He looked at the hills to his left and right. The trees obscured his view, and he saw nothing. Jacob's only guess was that Gabriel Grant had shot the animal.

He had just finished setting in a fence post when the shot rang out across the field. One of the ranch hands found the animal and had ridden to tell Jacob.

Jacob squeezed his brow, nose, and chin. He rose and secured his hat. "You had to kill one of my cows, didn't you?" he mumbled.

"Sir, what would you like me to do?"

"Rope it up. We'll butcher it and prepare it," Jacob grabbed the saddle's horn and mounted the horse. He pulled a gun from his belt, "Here, take this. If anyone comes by wanting to take him, shoot them."

The ranch hand took the gun and fastened it to his belt. "Thank you, sir."

Jacob circled his horse once. "You can use the spare wagon in the barn. I'll send Bill with it." He looked at the gun, "Be careful."

"I will. Make sure Bill brings a hoist. It'll make the job easier to lift her into the wagon."

Jacob nodded then took off toward the ranch. Gabriel Grant had quite the nerve. It was incredulous to think Jacob would hand over one thousand dollars. He hardly knew a man who owned that much in cash.

As it was, Jacob was scraping by. He already planned on taking out a loan from the bank to pay for some new cattle to try to get the Ranch up and running. Now, with Gabriel breathing down his neck on the monies owed, money Momma told him they no longer owed because Gabriel had Leonard killed to satisfy the debt, Jacob didn't know if the bank would even pay out.

Gabriel wouldn't want that transaction to go through, and that was the other problem: Gabriel Grant owned the bank.

Jacob banked his horse down the small hill that overlooked the ranch. This was his favorite spot. The trees opened to the pasture below and there, in the clearing, sat Creek Ranch with the whole ranch laid out before him. To the east sat the barn, a chicken coop next to it, and the house on the western edge of the clearing, next to some pine trees.

Creek Ranch was not the largest in the area. Jacob knew Gabriel held that title. And that was the other thing bothering him. If Gabriel Grant had all this money, why come after him for it? Gabriel could make that amount of money in a week. The Grants were not hurting.

He led the horse down into the pasture and slogged his

way back home. Seeing the new fence, he noticed how nice it looked. Bill had done a remarkable job with tending to the place. After tying up the horse, he walked to the barn for a chat.

Bill busied himself hammering out a horseshoe. Jacob watched the red glow dim as Bill hammered away, casting red flecks into the air before their light dissipated like a firefly's glow. He set the shoe into a bucket of water and the water popped against the metal's heat. Bill looked up, "Sorry, Jake, I didn't see you there."

Jacob laughed, "No worries."

"Gabriel kill anything?" Bill asked, knowing the next answer.

Jacob removed his hat and tossed it to the workbench. "He killed one cow. A single bullet to the head."

Bill shook his own head, "That man has real nerve. Why not just rope it and take it home? That one head is worth at least fifty dollars."

"I don't know how to stop him." Jacob pulled against his belt buckle, "and with him running for Mayor, he'll be even more dangerous." He looked at the button he pulled from his pocket, disgusted, he tossed it into the fire.

Bill placed a hand on Jacob's shoulder, "You're the preacher. Maybe you should ask God for some wisdom. We both know Gabriel will not stop until you pay him what's owed."

Jacob frowned. He found a stool and sat. Leaning forward on his elbows, he said, "God has been so quiet." He sighed, "I thought I heard him. I brought my family back to Purgatory to start our lives. Now, Gabriel Grant threatens to take it all away. Everything I've worked my whole life for."

"Maybe this is God's way of getting you to trust him. God's in control. He knows the end from the beginning."

Jacob looked up and smiled, "When did you become an expert on the Bible?"

Bill laughed, "Just been listening in church and reading the Good Word." Bill stood and replaced his gloves, "My shoes have gone cold. Thanks." He pulled it out of the water and threw it back into the fire.

"When you're done with that, head out to the north pasture and take the wagon. We need to load that steer up and get him butchered. I don't want that meat going to waste."

Bill pulled the shoe out and tossed it back into the bucket. The water spit and spat. "I'll head there now."

"Thank you."

"Remember, God's in control. Let him fight your battles."

Jacob walked through the door into the house, where Sarah was preparing the evening meal of potatoes, carrots, and a healthy cutting of roast beef. The aroma of caramelized onions and garlic wafted over him. He welcomed the salivating smell.

He threw his hat and jacket onto a hook. It had been a long day. Gabriel had crawled under his skin, taking up residence and mocking him. Jacob hated every second that Gabriel dug into his soul.

"I'm sorry, my Dear," Sarah said after contemplating her words.

"I don't get it. How could my father be so stupid and ask for a handout? I understand he was strapped..." He let the thought linger in the air.

Jacob grabbed his Bible and sat. "I've worked my whole life in honor of this book. Now, that faith is wavering. It's hard to trust a God I cannot see to fight a battle I feel I'm about to lose."

Sarah stopped cooking. After wiping her hands, she let the apron fall over her blue flowered dress. She was anxious. The events of the past week weighed on her. Even though she was concerned for him, she always remained supportive and understanding of each decision. This last one worried her, and Jacob felt bad.

Kneeling next to him, she cradled his hands. The softness of her skin smoothed his inner turmoil. Jacob exhaled and let his body relax as she leaned in and kissed his hands. She worked her way up his arm and kissed his neck. Gooseflesh rippled across his back as she caressed his face and lightly kissed his waiting lips. He pressed into her embrace and allowed his senses to dissolve into the passion that warmed his body.

Once she pulled away, she bit her lower lip and tossed him a smile, "I love you."

His breath came up short, "I love you, too."

Sarah picked up his dropped Bible and placed it back into his hands. "This book is the very Word of God. You know how much I love you, and I just showed that passion to you." She pointed back to the book, "He loves you even more and he will fight your battles. Don't give up hope. God's got this."

Jacob felt tightness grip his chest again. The uncertainty crept back into his mind and then subsided. Jacob knew she was right. She was always right. And that's why he'd married her ten years ago.

"The battle is the Lord's and he will give you the wisdom you need to fight." She stood back up and dusted off her wrinkled apron. "Gabriel Grant won't win. I have an unwavering faith in you. God has called you for such a time as this." She tossed him another smile, "Don't screw it up."

Jacob watched her meander back to the stove to check on the roast. He looked out the window as the sun dipped behind the horizon. The reds and oranges ignited the sky with fervor and his trepidation melted away as the Lord spoke.

Trust me, I know what I'm doing. Be strong and of good courage; do not be afraid, nor be dismayed, for I am with you.

He recognized the passage. It was from the sixth book of the Bible, Joshua. Joshua was a man thrust into authority after his master Moses had died. He was uncertain and afraid of how to lead the Children of Israel. It seemed an impossible task. And the threat of the Canaanites served as a reminder he was only human and facing an impossible fight.

The sun disappeared and the first stars poked the sky with light. The fight ahead with Gabriel Grant would not end soon. There had to be another way. There had to be something Jacob could use to get Gabriel off his back regarding the thousand dollars.

It looked as if the sun began its climb again. The orange glow became brighter. That's when the shouting reached them. It was Bill. He was yelling about something.

Sarah dropped her pan, and the potatoes spilled out. One rolled in Jacob's direction, thumping against his foot.

"Jacob! The barn!" Sarah screamed.

CHAPTER FOURTEEN

FIRE SHOT into the sky as smoke blended with the night, blotting out the stars. Jacob ran into the building as fire crawled up the center posts, igniting the hayloft above.

Jacob coughed as the thick black smoke burned his lungs. Even though he doused his clothes with water, the heat burned against his skin, and with each passing moment, it felt as if his hair would ignite.

The horses, still in their stalls, thrashed against the raging inferno, squealing for a way out.

He barely noticed Bill behind him. "We've got to get the animals out," Jacob yelled above the fire's roar.

"Jake, we don't have time. This place is coming down."

"I'm not letting them die."

Jacob grabbed the first stall door and swung it wide. The frightened animal balked at Jacob's grasp. He swatted the animal's hind to get it moving.

Bill roped the animal's neck and led it outside.

He grabbed the second door. Searing heat shot through his hand when he touched the metal hook, burning his palm.

Jacob swung the door wide and roped the second animal as Bill returned.

"Jake, we've got to go." A non-supporting beam fell to their left. It knocked over an empty stall, igniting the hay. Smoke filled the barn as the fire licked the third stall.

"Okay. We'll go."

Jacob looked back at the stall. Bill's horse thrashed against the heat and smoke. For a second, he could hear the horse scream in pain as the stall erupted into flames. He wanted to go back to see if the animal was still alive, but he knew better.

The crackling fire intensified as they neared the barn's entrance. Jacob jumped to the right as another beam fell, exploding into several amber pieces.

Several burning coals fell and hit the horse. The animal's rear legs kicked against Bill's leg, then shot through the door, away from the fire. Bill fell inches from the fallen beam. Jacob ran back. He grabbed Bill's arm and helped him to his feet. The big man buckled.

"I think it's my leg."

Jacob grabbed Bill's arm and placed it over his neck. "Let's get you out of here."

Bill leaned into Jacob's grip and hobbled outside. Once they were far enough away, Sarah helped Bill to the ground.

They looked up at the burning barn as the roof caved in. Orange and yellow ash filled the sky like a firework.

The barn he built with his father was gone. Bill's horse, dead.

First Gabriel, then Felix, and now the barn. Jacob looked over at Bill sitting on the ground. "What happened?" It was the only question he had.

Bill shook his head. "I don't know. I was putting things

away in the tool shed when I caught a glow coming from the barn window. I realized, stupid me, I left the lantern lit.

"So, I went into the barn to check on the horses and turns out the light I noticed… when I opened the door, I caught the stall on fire."

"So you forgot to turn out the light?" Jacob asked.

"That's just it, it was the back stall that was on fire, and it doesn't have a lantern hook. The hook is by the door and the lantern wasn't there."

Jacob sat down. It was too much. "So how did the fire start?"

Bill gave a knowing look. Only one name came into Jacob's mind: Gabriel Grant.

"You don't figure out he'd go that far, do you?"

"Jake, he killed a cow this morning. I don't assume barn fires are beyond him. The lantern's missing and I bet we'll find it in that rear stall."

Jacob let the anger rise in his chest as a vise squeezed against his heart. His chest exploded in pain as blasts of air shot through his nose. Jacob clenched his teeth. Spittle sprayed out with each breath. He stood and staggered a moment.

"Jacob?" Sarah said.

He walked over to the new fence and slammed his fists into the rough wood.

Sarah and Bill remained silent. They could have said something, yet they knew he needed to vent. Jacob didn't care either way.

He raised his leg and kicked against the fence post. Pain rippled through his leg.

Kick. Kick. Kick. Kick.

The post finally gave away and crashed to the ground. He pulled a cross-beam and swung it at another post. WHACK!

It vibrated with each blow. Jacob tossed the beam, and it clattered on the ground. He stared at his cut-up hands, dropped to his knees, and cried.

Sarah rushed forward and wrapped her arms around him. He buried his head into her breast.

The sobbing didn't end. It came in waves. He allowed the emotion to overtake his heart and mind.

Nothing else mattered.

Jacob needed to cry.

CHAPTER FIFTEEN

SARAH DIDN'T sleep well. She ended up tossing and turning while Jacob slept. Their barn was gone. They could rebuild. A horse was dead. They had two more.

She pulled on a robe and slipped out the of the bedroom, doing her best to not wake Jacob. Sarah made her way to the front door and opened it to grab a few logs from the porch. She returned to the stove and tossed the logs in, stoking the fire. Sarah grabbed the egg basket and headed out to the chicken coop. She needed the fresh air and the stillness of the morning to calm her mind.

Sarah stepped onto the porch. The barn smoldered and the sour stench of burned wood filled the air. She didn't move for the longest time and listened as birds sang their morning songs, unaware of the night before. They were lucky, and their praise reached the heavens to a God who would listen to their petitions. Would he listen to hers?

A damp haze hovered just below the tree line and she wasn't sure if it was the remaining smoke or the morning fog that filled the air. Bill had tied the remaining two horses up to a nearby fence post with a long rope that allowed them to lie down for the night. They looked calm but tired, having been in the elements and agitated by the evening before. She walked up to them and placed her hand on Gypsy's smooth back. The horse jumped at her unexpected touch.

"Easy, girl." Sarah's calm demeanor and voice soothed the animal, and the horse closed its eyes. She ran her hand across the neck and down the face. The coarse hair felt smooth as velvet under her fingers. "There, there. You're okay." Gypsy nodded her head in approval of Sarah's touch. She snorted a swirling plume of exhale.

"They had quite the scare last night," Bill said, walking up and placing his own hand on the other animal.

Sarah felt embarrassed at her appearance. She released her hand from the animal and pulled her robe tight against her body.

"Don't stop. They seem to like it."

Sarah smiled. "Gypsy's my favorite. She's the one who carried Virginia and me to Purgatory after the wagon's axle broke." She replaced her hand and covered the horse's muzzle, running her fingers along the edge of her nose. Gypsy's nose popped up and asked for more. Sarah laughed for the first time in a few days.

"Thank you for helping my husband rescue them last night. I know it was a risk, but they're all we have."

Bill nodded. "It's the least I can do. You folks are kind enough to let me have a job running this place. It's become home." He looked at the fallen barn. "I will miss him."

"I'm so sorry about your horse, Bill." Sarah let a frown creep over her face.

"That's how it goes. I'll head into town with Jacob this morning and talk with Freddy at the Livery Stable about securing a new horse. He has a few for sale out at his place." Bill laughed, "I hope he doesn't expect me to pay too much."

"Well, that'd be nice if he had one for you." Sarah looked down at the waiting egg bucket. They would not collect themselves. "I better get the eggs. Jacob'll be hungry when he wakes up."

"How's he doing?"

"He took a while to calm down. I've never seen him so angry before." Sarah let a tear slip out of her eye, wetting her cheek.

Bill placed a friendly hand on her arm. "Neither have I. I know with the death of Leonard and everything that's transpired the last week, Jacob is at a breaking point."

"All he wanted was to preach. That's it. He loves God, but sometimes his emotions take over and he loses clarity. He's more like his father than he realizes." Sarah leaned against the fence. She fiddled with the bucket, this time allowing the tears to rush down her face. Bill said nothing. "I wish I knew how to help him. I love him, that will not change, but I fear his father broke his spirit all those years ago."

Bill smiled and cupped both of Sarah's hands. His hands were warm, and they calmed her mind. "Keep trusting God. He will fight your battles."

"Thank you, Bill. You're a good friend." She looked at her bucket again. "I better go collect those eggs." She wiped a sleeve against her wet cheeks and started walking away before turning back. "Take care of that leg and get rest. You can't run a farm with a sprained leg."

"Yes, Ma'am," Bill said, then hobbled back toward his work shed.

After breakfast and the ride to town, Sarah sat behind her desk. Two more days until her week was over. That would give her time to gather her thoughts and be prepared for the second week of teaching. She set the pencil down, unable to write out the day's lesson as thoughts of yesterday rummaged around her mind.

Thoughts of Jacob filled her vision and the anger she saw him spill out terrified her. He was as stubborn as his father, but gentle, kind, and would give everything so that his loved ones would feel valued and cared for. And she felt cared for and loved. Jacob was her bright and shining star. Even though times were tough, Sarah understood that God had everything under control.

And the past couple days had been better. Even Felix had been better. He was still stubborn and had a nasty little temper, but at least the hitting and kicking had stopped.

Good.

If he were Jacob and Sarah's son, she'd take him out behind the woodshed and teach him a lesson in astronomy.

Virginia sat behind her desk and continued to read her book.

"How're you doing, honey?"

Virginia looked up. "I'm okay. But is Daddy okay? He looked sad last night."

Sarah scooted the chair back. She rounded the desk and knelt next to her daughter. "He'll be okay. Daddy has a lot on his mind."

"I wish he would spend more time with me. I found a really cool creek behind the house. I wanted him to see it. Maybe it will make losing the barn feel better."

Sarah's heart melted like a burning candle. If there was one thing Jacob loved more in life than Sarah, it was Virginia. She was the apple of his eye and that one bright spot that would never go out.

They tried to have another child, but the good Lord kept them from having more. Sarah didn't understand, but if it was God's will, then who's asking for another? "Well, I'm sure you can show him tonight after school. How does that sound?"

A smile split Virginia's face. "Okay! I miss daddy."

Her heart broke. Jacob had become so preoccupied with Gabriel Grant that nothing else registered. "Your Daddy will spend time with you, I promise. He's just busy right now."

"A father who doesn't spend time with his family is a father not worth keeping. At least that's what my old man always said."

Sarah looked up at the sudden intrusion who'd just walked through the door. His black coat hung like a cape and his black hat obscured his face. Gabriel Grant. She saw Felix standing next to him. "Hello, Felix."

"I heard about the barn fire last night. I'm really sorry about that."

It didn't sound like an apology. "What do you want?"

Gabriel removed his hat, revealing a weathered face from years of hard work and a VanDyke that accentuated his cold features. "Go sit down, son." Felix made his way to a desk and sat. "See, that's how you raise a boy. Teach them some manners and they listen." He smiled and seemed to enjoy the quiet nature of his son. He removed from his jacket a folded set of papers. "I tried reasoning with your husband yesterday regarding the cattle your ranch owns." He handed the papers to Sarah.

"As you are, I'm assuming, aware, your family owes me one thousand dollars from a personal loan Jacob's father, Leonard, took from me." Gabriel paced the aisle. "I know you'll do the right thing. Sell the cattle and I'll call it even, and you can keep your little ranch; I have enough land."

Sarah couldn't believe it. The man wouldn't back down. "Why would we owe you something that a deceased man owed? My husband said the debt was clear. Now I believe my husband has made himself clear. We're not selling."

He smiled a crooked, cocky smile. "Spunk! That's what I like about you, Sarah. In fact, my wife has taken a liking to you. I want to see your family well-off. I don't want this to get any more ugly than it already has." He stopped pacing. "Do you know what a warning shot is, Mrs. Creek?"

"Yes." She wasn't liking this.

"That steer and your barn were just that; warning shots. I suspect your husband will be in a better mindset if you present the papers of sale to him." Gabriel secured the hat on his head. "Just sign the bottom and bring them to my office first thing tomorrow." He walked to the door. "Good day, Mrs. Creek." He stopped and flipped a button at Sarah. It clattered against the floor and Felix snickered something Sarah couldn't make out. "And don't forget to vote for me next Tuesday." He tipped his hat and stepped into the sun.

CHAPTER SIXTEEN

"GABRIEL GRANT, you and I need to talk. Get out here… NOW!" Jacob's whole body shook and his throat burned. The moment he found out Gabriel had paid a visit to Sarah at the schoolhouse, he rode straight to town. The nerve and audacity the tycoon had to pay a visit to a man's wife. At the moment, he didn't care who stopped in the street to watch the spectacle unfold. Gabriel Grant had gone too far this time.

The door to Gabriel's office opened. The man's stovepipe hat stood tall on his head. Gabriel's eyes squinted as the sun lit his face. "Preacher, what is all the shouting about?"

Jacob's face flashed hot as he cursed. He slowed his speech, accentuating each syllable. "How dare you approach my wife and threaten her? You're a coward if you need to speak to a man's wife instead of her husband."

Gabriel's smile was anything but polite. Its sinister sneer raised Jacob's hair. "Cussing and a preacher. Now, that's something you don't see every day," Gabriel cackled.

A few onlookers laughed and continued on their way.

"You put a gun to my head the day we rode into town.

You burned down my barn, Bill almost died, and you threatened my wife," he bit off.

Gabriel sighed and leaned against a post that held up the awning. "What's your point, Preacher? I have things I need to attend to, and this squabbling isn't one of those things."

If Jacob had a gun, he'd pull it, cock the hammer back, and let this man know just how serious he was about the matter. His flesh screamed for him to put a bullet in the man just for threatening Sarah. Sarah deserved more respect than that.

Gabriel waltzed down the steps and right up to Jacob. They were nose to nose. He could smell the whiskey and cigar smoke on Gabriel's breath. The man was two inches shorter than Jacob, but at that moment he looked tiny against Jacob's anger. Like an ant to be squished.

"Now, now, Mr. Preacherman. I find it offensive you called me a coward. I'm anything but." He paused for effect, "I run this whole cotton-picker town. Hell, I own most of it. Nobody sneezes without my knowing about it."

Gabriel took a long drag from his half-gone cigar. He held it for effect, then let out a long blue plume of smoke into Jacob's face. "I'd advise you to take me up on my offer, and if you don't," He buried a finger deep into Jacob's chest. "I'm coming for you."

Jacob backed off, then thought better. He moved forward and allowed Gabriel to move off balance. The man staggered back and Jacob pressed forward. He pressed his own finger to Gabriel's chest.

He chewed off the next thought through clenched teeth, "I advise you, Mr. Grant. Come after my family again and there'll be hell to pay. I'll put you in the ground myself."

"Are you threatening me?" Gabriel said it loud enough

that a few people stopped to listen. "Reverend, now, I've done nothing to deserve such disdain from Purgatory's most respected Preacher."

Jacob didn't back down. He knew what Gabriel was trying to do, establish himself the victim. "I'm warning you. Stay away from my family," he bit off again before turning back to his horse. Grabbing the reins, Jacob swung his leg up. Once seated high in his saddle, he stared once more at Gabriel.

This was not the end.

This was war.

He pointed his finger, "Stay away from Sarah!"

CHAPTER SEVENTEEN

J ACOB AND Bill worked hard the next several days cleaning up the fallen barn. Blackened beams, twisted metal, and the skeleton of one dead horse all lay in a heap. Jacob grabbed a beam and heaved it onto a wagon. It would take several more loads into the woods. They didn't need to get rid of all the pieces, just the larger ones they'd try burning again. That'd be the end of the mess.

He rummaged through the debris, looking for anything that the fire didn't destroy. They found a few pieces of tack and an old lantern from his father. Jacob gave them to Virginia to clean up and restore.

The barn was a big loss. Gabriel didn't have to go that far and on top of it all, Jacob felt bad cursing Gabriel out in town. Was that how a preacher should act? He didn't think so, and he knew God didn't appreciate his anger either. But the man rubbed him the wrong way and would not relent. Jacob felt he had no choice. He had to defend the honor of his wife, Sarah. She deserved that much.

Jacob looked at the fallen debris and he suddenly felt sadness and resolve at the same time. In the coming weeks, they'd schedule a barn raising to restore what Gabriel took. It was just figuring out when everyone could come and help. Several farmers offered their hands in building the barn for Jacob, and he was grateful for any help. Maybe a barn raising would bring about the raising of his own heart toward God again.

Purgatory could be a good community. But as the saying goes, one bad apple wrecks the whole bushel.

"One more piece," Jacob finally said, "I don't think the team can pull anything heavier."

"Agreed," Bill said.

Jacob helped Bill hoist another large beam onto the wagon. Its burnt end jutted from the pile and hovered above the ground.

"All set?" Jacob asked.

"Yer good, Boss."

The two men jumped on the wagon.

Virginia ran up, "Can I come too, Daddy? I really want you to see my favorite spot."

Jacob smiled at that. "Tell you what. After your Uncle Bill and I take this load to dump, you can show me anything you want."

Her face split like a canyon. She giggled and ran to the house. "Thank you, Daddy! I'm holding you to it."

Jacob laughed, "Sure love that girl."

"You and Sarah have raised a fine young lady." He scratched his head. "And since when did I become Uncle Bill?"

Jacob punched Bill in the arm. "Since, well…now."

The two men laughed.

Jacob slapped the reins hard on the team and, under the weight, the wagon groaned forward.

They unloaded the burnt wood and made their way back. As they walked, Jacob couldn't shake that Gabriel had been silent for so long.

It'd been 5 days since he cussed Gabriel out in town. Not the wisest move a Preacher could make. Mad; that's what he was. That was Sarah that Gabriel had threatened.

Well, did it matter anymore? Maybe that little chat had calmed the man down. What Jacob couldn't understand: the man had a clear disdain for his family. He figured it wasn't about the money, it was about principle. Being elected Mayor of Purgatory kept Gabriel too preoccupied to bother the Creeks. He wouldn't hold his breath, though; only time would tell what Gabriel had planned.

Jacob's father owed one thousand dollars, that much was clear. It was also clear to Jacob that Gabriel had killed Leonard, based on the last couple days.

The proof was scarce. No evidence and no eyewitnesses. He only had his gut and that gun shoved in his face.

Jacob entered the house and removed his hat.

"Hey now, back outside and you clean up before coming into this house."

Sarah stopped him in his tracks. He looked down at his hands and clothes. They were black as night. Crap. "I'm sorry, my love. I'll go to the toolshed and change."

He glanced around, trying to figure out how to move. No clear path for new clothes.

"Help me out by grabbing some new duds for me."

Sarah shook her head. It was anything for her husband. There were days he tried her patience. She'd ask him to do something around the place and he'd forget. At least that's what she always implied.

Not that it mattered; she loved him no matter what. But the point was, if you want a happy life, you need a happy wife. That's what his late father-in-law had always said.

Sarah returned with the clothes in a neat, folded pile. She kissed his black lips.

Jacob smiled at Sarah's soot-covered lips. "Thank you, dear."

"Anything for my man. Now, go get cleaned up. Your daughter wants to show you her special spot."

He stared at her black lips.

"What?" She said.

Jacob smiled, then giggled, "Nothing."

She wiped her mouth. "Jacob Creek. Go change!"

A splash of water and new clothes later, Jacob looked presentable. There may have been a few streaks of black on his body, but nothing that'd rub off in the house.

He exited the toolshed. "Now, how about showing your old man that special place?"

Virginia whooped and grabbed her cardigan. She had been waiting on the porch. "Come on, Daddy. Let me show you."

She couldn't contain her excitement and beamed from ear to ear as she hopped down the steps and ran up to meet her father.

"I think you will really like this spot. Maybe you could baptize me there."

Jacob knew of a creek that ran through the wooded area behind the barn, though it'd been years since he'd been back there.

His heart melted as he took her hand in his and followed

next to his daughter. She wanted to be baptized. At that moment, everything else faded: the barn, Gabriel Grant, and his father's death.

It was just this moment. Father and daughter.

They headed south as he thought. The brush was cleaned away and in neat piles.

She's been back here a lot, Jacob thought to himself as he moved a branch out of the way.

"How did you clear the path?"

Virginia kept marching forward. "Bill. He helped clear it for me. I tore a dress finding the place."

Jacob was sure Sarah didn't like that one bit. "You tore a dress?"

"It wasn't a big tear. Mommy fixed it real good."

Jacob had to duck several times. The path wasn't cleared for a tall man like him. Virginia had no problems. She sailed through and begged for him to keep up.

They approached an opening as the canopy split to reveal a meadow. The tall grass rippled in the wind and the tree line danced to an unheard melody. Had he forgotten the beauty of his own land? For several weeks, Jacob had gathered his frustration and hatred toward Gabriel Grant. Seeing God's creation faded that frustration into oblivion, even if for a moment.

Virginia beamed with delight and squealed as she bounded through the grass.

Jacob could see the creek cutting its path through the tall grass. It was beautiful. The question being, would it be deep enough for a baptism?

He ran his hand over the tops of seeded heads. The blades ran up to his waist.

Virginia came to a stop at the creek's edge. "Are you coming?"

Jacob smiled. "I'm coming. Just enjoying the view," he said, approaching his daughter.

"I know, isn't it beautiful?" Her face was lit like the fourth of July.

Jacob's heart beat hard against his chest as he watched her twirl and run through the tall grass. Finally, he sat and patted his leg for Virginia to join him. He wrapped his arms around his daughter and smelled her hair, then kissed her cheek.

The day she entered the world was forever etched in his memory. Besides marrying Sarah, Virginia's birthday was the single greatest moment in life. He relished his daughter's affection, and he reciprocated in kind. Nothing else mattered.

Those first moments, holding her tiny life in his arms, the glory of God became manifest. How two people could make such a statement and bring life into the world was beyond him. The fingers, toes, and little button nose were all reminders of that love.

Jacob wrapped his arms around her tighter. "I love you, Virginia."

She snuggled into his embrace. "I love you too, Daddy."

He stared at the rippling water. Tiny waves crashed against the shore. Tiny rocks stuck out like islands altering the water's course. Birds flew overhead, singing a song, and to Jacob's left a woodpecker hammered against a Birch tree. It pecked away at the bark to reveal tiny bugs for dinner.

Jacob let a tear slip down his cheek. He'd been selfish. So consumed with hatred that sitting here made him remember what was important.

Virginia sensed his emotion. She twisted to look at his tear-streaked face. "Daddy, God has everything under his control." She wiped a few tears. "Don't worry about anything. God will take care of the details. You need to trust God, Daddy, and know that no matter what happens, I love you and he does too."

Jacob stifled an audible cry. His throat burned, and he swallowed hard against the emotional lump forming. For ten years of age, at times, Virginia's wisdom exceeded his.

He picked her up and stood. Walking to the edge of the creek, they plunged in. The water came to his waist before setting her into the water. It was deep enough.

He watched her body stiffen at the water's chill before she giggled and spun in a circle.

"Do you want to be baptized?"

Her scream echoed off the trees. Several nearby birds shot into the sky. "Yes!"

"I thought the water would be warm," she said.

"It will be fun."

"Oh," she said, "okay, but I thought…"

"We're here to baptize you, not discuss the water's temperature."

Jacob stepped behind his daughter and held her elbow with his right hand, then placed his left on her back.

"Are you ready?"

"I'm ready."

Jacob tried to stifle another cry and let the second volley of tears fall. They dripped off his chin.

"Virginia, do you profess your faith in the Lord Jesus Christ? Do you believe in the resurrection of Christ? And do you proclaim that he is God and you are his everlasting servant?"

She didn't hesitate. "I do."

"By the power vested into me as a minister of the Gospel,

I baptize you in the name of the Father, the Son, and the Holy Ghost."

Virginia plugged her nose as Jacob lowered her into the water. The water rushed over her face and her hair spread out like angel wings. Her clothes floated and for a moment he saw her smile beneath the rippling creek.

In a splash, she exploded out of the cold water and yelped, "I did it! I'm baptized into faith."

She stopped for a moment and looked at her father. "Does this mean my faith is my own?"

Wise words that joyed his heart. "It does, my daughter. It does." Jacob hugged Virginia tight as they climbed onto the creek's bank. The sun began its downward climb. It was time to go home. "Come on. Let's go get dry. Your mother will be pleased."

She looked up at him. "Daddy, maybe others would like to be baptized?"

The idea struck him deep. A service on Creek Ranch was the right ticket the town needed. A good baptism service. He could use a scenery change.

They walked up the path and Jacob remembered an old boysenberry tree. He looked up and down the grassy plain. There it was, ten yards ahead. "Come on. Let's grab berries and take them to Mother," Jacob said, leading the way this time.

CHAPTER EIGHTEEN

"I AM so privileged to be standing here as your Pastor," Jacob said.

Several people lined the banks of the stream which sat behind the barn on Creek Ranch. Sunlight gleamed against the blue sky as songbirds warbled their praises and children raced in circles, splashing in the water before taking off and giggling downstream.

"Today, we gather at this river to profess our faith." Jacob's hand entered the water and he let the liquid roll off his fingers. He raised his hands and several water droplets escaped into the wind before finding their way back into the water. "This water symbolizes the life God has given you and me. We stand at the spiritual river of life–for didn't our Lord say to 'baptize them in the name of the Father, and of the Son, and of the Holy Ghost?"

Jacob motioned his hand toward Missy Cartwright. She smiled when his hand touched her shoulder and Jacob hesitated before proceeding on to the next person. Missy had not been to church since he returned home to Purgatory. Happy to see her standing there, Jacob wondered if she wished to affirm her faith in Christ.

"Before today, how many have been immersed in the waters of repentance?"

A few raised their hands, while others returned with, "I have, Reverend."

Jacob stepped back into the water, which came up to his waist. "Come, all who desire baptism. Repent, for the kingdom of heaven is at hand. For this was spoken by the prophet Isaiah when he said, *The voice of one crying in the wilderness: prepare the way of the Lord; make his paths straight.*

"The path is straight," Jacob called for a young boy to join him in the water. He was around twelve years old with sandy blonde hair concealing his eyes. The boy smoothed it aside before letting a smile play at his lips.

Jacob asked, "What's your name, son?"

"Timmy," he whispered.

"Okay, Timmy. Are you ready to confess your faith in the Lord?"

"Yes, sir."

Jacob held onto his wrist and back and in a quick motion, he said, "I baptize you in the name of our Lord Jesus Christ," while tipping him into the water.

The boy exploded out of the stream yelling, "Hallelujah!"

The congregation whooped and cheered. A few men lifted off their hats and twirled them in the air.

Timmy's mother ran up to him with a towel, "I'm so proud of you, son."

Jacob walked back to the shore, "Who's next? I see the Lord desires to bless those who honor him in public."

The crowd split and Missy Cartwright walked forward. Several conflicting emotions swirled about in his stomach. For years, he ate her soup and drank her beer in a tavern, known for its prostitution and spirits, and that was her home and life. Jacob had explained the gospel to her many times. Maybe those pep talks accomplished something, because here she stood, ready to enter the water.

He smiled as she joined him in the water. Her dress floated before she forced her it into the water, giggling. Missy's face beamed with delight as the water moved up her waist. She toppled forward. Jacob held her by the wrist to help her stand while placing his hand in the small of her back to keep her upright.

"You, okay?"

She nodded.

They met and her cheeks glowed red. "Hi," she mustered.

"Hi." Jacob rotated Missy and held her close. He caught her right arm and placed a hand on her waist.

"In the name of the Father, Son, and Holy Ghost, I baptize you."

She entered the water, and its ripples rushed over her face. Her eyes were open, staring at him, and she smiled wide.

The action lasted a moment, but Jacob's world stopped spinning for the moment. It was just Missy and Jacob. He pulled her out of the water and her dress hugged her body.

Jacob looked beyond her wet shoulder-length hair to Sarah, who stood next to Virginia on the beach. They smiled as he stared at them. Jacob's heart pounded hard against his ribs. Breath caught in his lungs. He loved Sarah and nothing would ever change that. She'd been with him through thick and thin. Everything in this life he owed to his wife. Jacob pushed the previous moment from his mind and allowed his thoughts to focus instead on his wife, the woman who gave up everything to become a preacher's wife.

He held Missy's hand and helped her to the shore. He cleared his throat, "Would anyone else like to be baptized in the waters of repentance?"

"I would," a gruff voice said, rising above the crowd.

"Come forward and experience the joy of the Lord."

The crowd split once more and revealed Gabriel Grant. He marched up to the water's edge and turned his back to Jacob, "Sorry folks, it'll take but a moment," he turned back toward Jacob.

"I understand you're having a church service. I'll keep this short." He paused for effect. "I tried to find you in town, but someone said you'd be out here having a little shindig."

Jacob balled his fists and stiffened his jaw. He glanced over at Sarah, who appeared to be just as dumbstruck. Bill tried to intervene and Jacob held out his hand, forcing his friend to remain and not speak.

"What do you want, Grant?" he struggled not to let anger slip into his words. He didn't succeed.

"Oh, a little business you and I need to take care of." Gabriel smiled, "We had a deal, Reverend. You were to pay me the remaining money your father owed, and I would forgive everything."

He pointed to the water and then to the boy who stood there dripping wet. "Isn't that what baptism is all about, forgiveness?"

Jacob couldn't argue with that logic, even through its flawed lens. "You said my father's death canceled the debt. I owe you nothing," Jacob bit off. A few gasps from the crowd told him not everyone in town knew what had happened to Leonard. Shame, they deserved to learn that Gabriel killed his father over a debt instead of working it out.

"Now, a man's word is his truth," Gabriel started, "and

your father gave me his word that he would pay the personal loan I gave in due time." He sighed, "Of which I've hardly seen a penny or dime, but who's counting," he laughed.

The tycoon dug a note from his coat, "This here is the receipt I gave your father the day I made the deal to save his farm. So, in all respect, this land is mine."

Gabriel broke Jacob's last straw. He launched from the water, marched up to Gabriel, and dug his finger at the man's chest. "The land is mine, the money is mine, and you are a fool to think I will give you anything." Jacob walked through the crowd before turning back, "I'll say it again, Momma told me the debt was canceled upon my father's death. I owe you nothing."

Jacob continued his climb and grabbed Sarah and Virginia by their hands. "We're done." He turned to the stunned congregation, "My apologies, we'll continue this next Sunday at the church."

Gabriel stood there seething under all his bravado. "I guess your little service is over," Jacob heard him say before entering the woods.

CHAPTER NINETEEN

J ACOB PACED through the home like a caged beast. His heart pounded hard against his rib cage. His world reeled and for a moment, the glint of Gabriel's dead body swung from a noose in his mind's eye. He walked into the bedroom and yanked a case from under the bed. He opened the lid and pulled out a .45 Peacemaker. Its grey metal and mahogany handle felt cold in his grip. He pulled several bullets from a small pouch and dropped them into his hand, a few clattered against the wooden floor. Jacob placed one bullet after another until five of the six chambers were filled. He cocked the hammer back by one click to keep the gun from firing. His eyes bore down at the gun case, which held the smooth tan leather of his holster. Jacob hardly used a gun, except while traveling or out gathering cattle. One never knew who'd be lurking in the shadows. He bent and picked up the holster before fastening it around his waist.

The last time he used a gun to kill something, a cougar tried taking down one of his cows. He pulled his gun, cocked, and fired, killing the animal. It happened so fast, but he saved the cow. Jacob would practice on old cans and bottles, shooting off rounds, but never intending to use the weapon against another human, until now.

Jacob dropped the cold steel into the leather. *Fits like a glove.* Crouching down, Jacob grasped several more bullets and slid them into the belt before saying to himself, "Gabriel's as good as dead."

Jacob stuck his hat to his head, removed his collar, and allowed his shirt to pull open, revealing his chest. Stepping into the living room where Sarah and Virginia sat, he grabbed a long trench coat and slung it over his arms.

Sarah looked up and frowned, then told Virginia to go outside. He recognized she wouldn't approve or understand what he was about to do.

"Jacob, where are you going?"

"I'm bringing an end to this, once and for all."

He watched her eyes glance toward the gun. His heart sank into his gut. This was wrong. God said it was wrong. *Thou shalt not kill…*

The images of killing Gabriel Grant began their slow retreat and a white flag of surrender waved in Sarah's direction.

"Jacob, you know this isn't right. Think about how it would harm your reputation. Think about your family. If you do this—and I'm not saying he shouldn't go to jail for killing your father—your soul, Jacob, it will never be the same if you go through with this. You'll become a hardened man and you'll hang from the gallows. I can't bear that and Judge Talbert will make sure of it."

He paused, needing her to understand. There could be a case for killing Gabriel Grant. Maybe he could label it self-defense—protecting his family from a tyrant.

"I have to do this. We'll never be free. We'll only be fighting and losing against this kind of evil." Jacob walked over to his Bible and lifted it into the air, "Didn't God say he'd fight my battles?" he tossed it onto the table.

"Yes, but not with a Peacemaker."

"Didn't David kill his enemies with a sword?"

She thought for a moment, weighing her words, "David was a man after God's heart. He admitted the battle was the Lord's. But he still had to answer for his sins." Sarah paused and strode over to Jacob. She picked the Bible up and held it to his chest. "This is your Peacemaker. Don't fight Gabriel Grant with violence, you'll lose every time. You're already losing. Maybe it's time to see things from God's perspective."

Jacob's heart gave in. He pulled the gun from his belt, opened the chamber and let the bullets fall to the wooden floor. He let his finger linger on the trigger as the gun twisted around it and let it slid off, clattering to the ground.

His knees pounded hard against the floor. His throat stiffened, and he convulsed and puffed. Bile hit the back of his throat and Jacob dropped his head in surrender.

"I'm finding it difficult to trust God." He looked up at Sarah who knelt next to him. "What do we do? How do we fight this?"

Sarah let Jacob lean into her as she rubbed his head and kissed his cheek. They remained in silence before Sarah broke it, "I don't know. All I know is that God called us here and we will stand in God's grace."

CHAPTER TWENTY

SIX MEN sat around a table in the upper level of Freddy's Livery Stable. The reason for the impromptu meeting: what to do with Gabriel Grant and his threat against the Creek family. Bill approached Freddy about a meeting and the man offered the Livery Stable. Freddy had done a good job clearing the cobwebs and junk off the table. It wasn't much, but they had a place to sit in the dimly-lit room.

For Bill, he'd had enough. The display at Creek Ranch concerned the entire congregation. Several members spoke with both Bill and Momma, asking what they could do to help Jacob and his family escape Gabriel's grip. It wouldn't be right to lose another minister because of Gabriel. The last minister died mysteriously and a good deal worried something might happen to Jacob. Bill always assumed Gabriel was behind most of the strange deaths in Purgatory, but no one could lay a hand on the tycoon. Other than him, it was a peaceful town and most carried on without giving Grant a thought.

He leaned forward, allowing the light to illuminate his face. It was time to begin the meeting. "Boys, we've got a situation. Gabriel Grant has gone far enough. He has threatened our good Reverend and his family, and now he threatens to shut down our church. We can't let that happen."

The chorus of agreement filled the room.

"Jacob and his family have been good friends of ours—many of you appreciate Mrs. Creek, you've had her cooking at the Lodge. This is her land, her boy, and her granddaughter we're talking about."

"How do you propose we stop him from taking the Church?" Ray, one miner who attended the church, asked.

Bill pressed his fingers together and leaned forward, "We need to raise money… help Jacob out by getting rid of his debt."

The noise of shuffling feet turned the heads of several men. Each man stiffened as someone climbed the steps. Freddy reached for the lantern and Bill stopped him. The clicking of a hammer echoed off the blackened beams.

Joe raised his gun, ready to fire. Bill saw the cocked hammer and waved him to disarm the weapon.

"I'd advise you to put your gun down, son."

A woman's voice.

Joe disarmed and holstered.

That's when Bill saw Momma Joanna Creek. A wave of relief washed over him like bathwater. He figured it was Momma, but with Gabriel on the prowl, one could never be too cautious. He stood and helped her up the remaining steps. Momma's hair was up in a bun with a pair of chopsticks holding it in place. Her long blue cotton dress hugged her wide hips and brushed the dusty floor.

"Momma, please have a seat," Freddy scouted a barrel and rolled it over, "I'm sorry Ma'am, I have nothing fancy for a lady."

Joanna smiled and lifted her dress so she could sit. Nothing fancy about her. She was as plain as they came, but the nicest person in town. Everyone knew Momma Creek. She was well respected and loved by the miners. Well respected and loved by most in town. Bill was glad she showed up. He wanted to tell her how he felt. They'd been friends for years, but after Leonard's death, he'd looked after her, made sure she was okay, and then fell in love.

Watching her next to him on that barrel tugged his heart and the fear washing over him evaporated. Bill didn't want to see her hurt and didn't want to see her land taken away. The love filling his heart this moment ebbed and begged to flow over the dam of his heart.

"Did you realize she was coming?" Joe asked.

Bill smiled and patted her hand. "I did. I invited her after today's events. It horrified her, what Gabriel did to her son."

Bill felt a sigh of relief wash over the group. Everyone was horrified they might not have a Reverend much longer. Not if Gabriel got his way.

Momma straightened her dress, smoothing it at the legs. "How do we get Gabriel Grant off the back of my son? He took my husband's life and now threatens to take everything Jacob's worked hard for." She leaned forward, allowing the light to illuminate her face. "My husband was not a nice man and many of you drank with him at Missy's." A few started their protest. "Don't say otherwise," she scolded before continuing, "Leonard's mouth got him into trouble, and my son is paying for my late husband's drunkenness and stupidity."

Bill knew more than most, but a thought occurred to him, "Is that why Jacob left town… all those years ago?"

She nodded and wiped a tear peeking at the corner of her eyes. "I love my son, but Jacob…well, he's built like his father…stubborn. If he gets an idea into his head, it's hard to shake it.

"Years ago, before marrying Sarah, Jacob had pulled out my Bible and read it. He fell in love with the words and in a moment of sobriety, Leonard encouraged him to go to seminary and become a minister."

Bill had never known. To him, Jacob had left the ranch in his hands then left with Sarah to escape his father's legacy in Purgatory. The town lives up to its name: once you arrive, you're here, never to leave again. Welcome to Purgatory.

Bill leaned forward and placed his palms on the table. He examined the wood's grain before speaking, "I asked you here because we're wanting to help Jacob and his family out. Outside of Gabriel Grant, there's not a single family who can afford to pay Gabriel the monies owed by your late husband. Everyone is in debt because Gabriel likes to keep a strict line of who has money and who doesn't. And those who have it, Gabriel figures out how to buy them and dispose of them in quick fashion."

Momma pulled the chopsticks from her bun and let graying hair fall into her hands. She pulled out several rolls of cash. She placed the money in her lap and grabbed the chopsticks. Rolling them back into her hair, it looked as if she never touched the bun.

She picked up the money and tossed it onto the table near the lantern. "Boys, this is three hundred dollars. It's all I have for cash that's not stored up in cattle on the ranch."

Bill pulled the money toward him, "Momma…"

"Now, I don't want you to feel bad. This is my husband's mess, and I'm cleaning it up. It's not much, but if we can gather more cash from sympathizers in town, we may have enough to satisfy Mr. Grant," she turned to Bill, "Do you think it'll work?"

"My guess it'll be church members who'll fit the bill," Joe said.

Alex, sitting to Momma's left, spoke. "I sold a dozen cattle. After paying the bank their share on a loan and my men for the drive, I have two hundred I can give you, but that will leave me with little."

Bill smiled. That brought it to five hundred dollars. That was more than they had before. "Thank you, Alex."

"I have fifty," Joe said. "I know it's not much, but it's all I have."

"Every bit helps," Momma beamed.

Freddy left the table. Bill heard him rummaging around below. When he returned he had a small bag in the left hand. He tossed the bag onto the pile of cash. Bill reached over and opened the bag. He pulled out a small handful of gold.

Freddy had gold? "Where'd you get this?"

"Customer paid me. Needed me to fix his pick and axe. He bent it in the mines. Then said he needed a new saddle. Said it's worth around a hundred dollars." Freddy scratched his head. "I don't know noth'n about gold. Guess you'd have to take it to the banker."

"Thank you. That brings us to six hundred and fifty dollars."

The rest of the group chimed in and brought the final total to seven hundred. It was more than they had coming into the meeting and Bill wondered if that would settle the debt.

"Momma," he said turning to her. "Do you think we could sell a few cattle and make up the rest?"

"I'm not selling any cattle. There are no buyers," her eyes narrowed and her voice lowered, "and I'm not giving a single head of cattle to Gabriel Grant. That's what he wants, and he's not getting one hair." She leaned back, satisfied with her answer, and crossed her arms. "We have a good start; it should shut the man up for a while."

"And when he comes back for more?" Bill asked.

"Then we'll see where we can squeeze money, even take a loan from the bank if we have to."

"But Gabriel owns the bank," Freddy piped up.

"Then we'll work something out, but I'm not selling a single cow to that man."

Momma Creek got up and walked to the stairs, "This should have never happened. Gabriel originally cleared the debt, and when he learned of Jacob's arrival in town, he recanted his original offer."

"I'm sorry, Momma. I had no clue," Bill said.

She gave a curt nod. "Thank you, gentlemen, for your help." She turned to Bill, "Please give it all to Jacob. They can't suffer any more."

Bill watched her walk down the steps until she disappeared and the door closed. He rounded the table, "Okay, boys. I'll ride back tonight to Creek Ranch and give the cash to Jacob." He gathered the money and placed it into the gold bag, "It's a start. Thank you."

Bill prayed and adjourned the meeting.

God, let this work.

CHAPTER TWENTY-ONE

WHEN JACOB learned that his church had raised seven hundred dollars to help his family, he melted in the chair. Running fingers through his hair, he sat dumbfounded. Why anyone would part with that much money was beyond his mind's comprehension. Bill arrived late into the evening to give Jacob the news. He explained he met with several men from the congregation. Everyone chipped in. Never in his life did he give of himself as these men gave to him. Their generosity was more than he could take.

He thumbed the gold and watched it dance on the table. Gold. Someone gave up their gold. Jacob knew no one who would do that. He put the cash and gold back into the pouch and tied it shut. He found the saddle bag leaning against the doorpost and Jacob secured the money pouch into its abyss. It was time to head into town and have a chat with Gabriel Grant.

Jacob wasn't sure if the amount would satisfy Gabriel's money lust. Maybe this would buy enough time to gather the final three hundred dollars. He leaned against the door, holding the bag, and for the first time, Jacob felt good. The ships were turning, and the stars aligned. He knew this was where God had called him. He knew this congregation of believers were here for such a time as this.

God answers prayers.

It was a thought; not that he didn't believe God couldn't answer prayers, but he couldn't believe this was happening. He pulled the door open, kissed Sarah, and walked to the makeshift shed they had built to house the horses until they could rebuild the barn.

Jacob saddled his horse as Bill walked up behind him. He turned to look at his friend and then shifted his gaze to the blackened mess of a barn. Did Gabriel have to go that far? Some men are evil and nothing will change that. No amount of pleading or begging would change Gabriel's attitude toward the Creek family. Some men like to buy and sell, others like to watch the world burn. Gabriel Grant did both.

Jacob fastened the bag to the back before acknowledging Bill. "I can't thank you enough, Bill."

Bill waved it off, "It's no big deal. We're all happy to help. And besides, you're our Reverend. Where would we be without you?"

Jacob laughed and patted the bag. "Without a Pastor."

The two men nodded at each other as Jacob mounted the horse, "You're a good man, always treated me with respect and dignity, and really, you're more of a father than my old man was. He tried his best, but you… Bill, you took me in as your own after my father all but abandoned us to the bottle."

Jacob looked out over the farm and his heart warmed at the sight of the family property. "You've done well around here and I'm thankful. This place is as much your home as it is ours."

Bill wiped his nose, then spit tobacco. "Jacob, it's my pleasure to serve you and your family. Momma's been good to me."

That was the other thing Jacob didn't get: for years, Bill and Momma had remained kindred spirits. They might as well tie the knot. Jacob would like to see Momma married again. She didn't get the chance at happiness with his father. Sure, they had fallen in love years ago, but the consistent drinking and failure to be the father a son needed had forced Momma to raise Jacob. Bill would be good for Momma, and she would be good for him.

Bill must have picked up on Jacob's thoughts. "Jacob, stop thinking about it. Your Momma and I are fine with the platonic relationship we have."

He laughed at his friend. After all this time, Jacob knew Bill lied about his feelings for Momma. "All right, Bill. Time to pay the piper." Jacob pulled the reins and circled down the path. He'd be in Purgatory soon enough.

"I'll be praying for you, Jacob. Godspeed."

Jacob waved and called back, "Move the cattle to the East pasture, it's time they get a new view."

Bill waved his hat, "Yes, sir."

He dug his heel into the ribs of the powerful animal and took off in a full gallop toward hope. When he arrived in town, the place buzzed with activity. People milled around the General Store, getting their weekly goods. The train's whistle reverberated through the streets. Another day and new arrivals would begin their search for gold. How long had it been since coming to town on a Monday? The Mayor's office was on the other side of town. Jacob slowed his horse and trotted into town.

Several passersby pulled their hats off and waved.

"Reverend," a man said.

"Beautiful day," another said.

Jacob decided that it was a good town, filled with good people. But the one bad apple seemed to ruin the view. He placed his hand against the saddle bag with the seven hundred dollars and some gold. This would be his salvation. It still bothered him that Gabriel wanted the money when Momma told him years ago that Gabriel no longer demanded payment after Leonard died. Why the change? It was something he'd have to bring up to Momma.

As he passed Missy's, a scripture came to mind. *All things work together for the good of those who love God.* Jacob hoped the Good Lord was right on this one. Life was hard; not as hard as those in the book of Acts, but hard enough to feel the strain of life. After an hour's ride, Jacob trotted up to the Lodge. There Momma sat, drinking her morning tea.

He dismounted and tied off the horse. "Momma."

"Don't even say it. I told Bill it was all I had." She set the cup down and stood to give her son a hug and kiss.

He paused from her embrace. How much did she give Bill? "Momma, you didn't give Bill your money…did you?"

"I said, don't even say it. It was your father's mess, and mine to clean up." She straightened her apron. "And besides, I couldn't let that brute of a man hurt my Jacob or Sarah." She smiled, "ooh, and I just love that Virginia of yours."

Jacob knew better than argue with his Momma. So all he could say was, "Thank you, Momma, and I love you too."

"Now, give your Momma a kiss and go make things right between you and Mr. Grant."

He unbuckled the saddle bag and slid it to his shoulders. "Momma, there is one thing I need to talk to you about."

"That can wait. Off you go."

Jacob nodded. Gabriel's office sat across the street. After pulling the bag of money out, he kissed it and shoved it deep into his right pocket.

God, I need you now, more than ever.

His boots crunched under the street's gravel. He noticed that people watched his slow stride toward Gabriel Grant's office. The man stood outside, smoking another one of his expensive cigars. The puffing smoke swirled in the air before disappearing in a blue cloud.

Jacob kept his eyes on the man and for the first time, he felt his size. Most men averaged five feet, nine inches. Jacob, he was six feet, two inches. It wasn't hard to make men feel small. Now, as he approached Gabriel Grant, the man seemed smaller as Jacob stretched his back.

"Mr. Preacherman," Gabriel said. He wore his standard black coat around a white shirt. A black tie accentuated his neck and his top hat stood tall like a stovepipe, with cigar smoke to match.

"Mr. Grant. Can we step inside to talk?"

Gabriel tossed the cigar onto the street and motioned to the door, "By all means."

Jacob followed behind and closed the door. The office was small, but that was to be expected. A desk, chair, and stove all arranged in the otherwise tiny room. Nothing elaborate. Everything simple. He watched Gabriel sit down and finger the curls of his VanDyke.

He took a small wooden chair in front of the desk. The Mayor's office seemed insignificant compared to Gabriel's home office. No wonder he probably worked from home. Jacob pulled the bag from his pocket and tossed it onto the desk. Its smooth surface caused the bag to slide to Gabriel.

The man smiled and twisted the hair by his lips again. Jacob felt sick to sit in silence as Gabriel gloated with giddy smiles.

"This is seven hundred dollars, with some gold. They told me that's the amount it all comes to."

Gabriel snickered then leaned back thumbing the paper money. He pulled bill after bill until satisfied there was seven hundred dollars. Gabriel pulled open the bag and dumped the gold onto the table. Its yellow, twisted fragments danced as they fell from the tiny bag.

"Does this please you? It's not the full amount, but it's more than you had with me coming into town a few weeks ago."

Gabriel pulled the chair forward and rested his elbows on the desk. He gathered the gold and cash and stuffed them back into the pouch. He pushed back from the desk and took the bag to a strong box hidden behind a picture. Once it was secure, he sat down and grabbed another cigar. Pulling two from the box, he offered one to Jacob.

"No, thank you." Frustrated that Gabriel wasn't answering, he tried again, "Does this please you?"

The man cut off an end and lit the cigar. He pulled a long, smooth drag in and swirled it in his mouth before exhaling, "Yes, yes. That's fine. We'll work something else out to get paid for the rest of the money."

All that bravado. All those threats. Gabriel was letting things rest in peace? Maybe the man had a heart. Jacob's own skipped a beat and a bead of sweat slid down his face. "That's it. No snarky comment? No demanding final payment and no apology for hurting my family and killing Bill's horse?"

Jacob saw Gabriel's eyebrow raise at the dead horse, but as quickly his lips received the cigar for another round of tobacco. "I'm a man of my word," he stood, moved to the door, and opened it for Jacob, " and we'll discuss the final payment later."

Gabriel extended his hand and Jacob accepted this time. "Thank you, Mr. Creek. We'll talk later. Maybe I can put a good word for you in with the bank for the remaining three hundred dollars. You must pay it back, but this time it'll be more manageable."

Jacob nodded, "Thank you, Gabriel. That means a lot."

Gabriel patted him on the back, "See, I'm not the monster you think I am." He puffed more smoke, "I can be reasonable."

Jacob's boots clacked down the steps before crunching on gravel. Then a thought swept over him. He turned as Gabriel leaned against the post once more, "Can I ask you a question, Mr. Grant?"

Gabriel twiddled his fingers with a small wave for Jacob continue.

"After my father's funeral, did you tell Momma my father's death paid his debt? And if so, why the change of heart?"

Gabriel stepped onto the gravel. He pulled another long drag of smoke into his mouth before exhaling. He smiled and tapped the cigar's end. Grey ash fell onto Jacob's boots. "I wasn't about to have a woman pay a man's debt. But when I learned you were coming back home…well, that's a different story." He placed his hand on Jacob's shoulder, "As I said, I'm not the monster you think I am."

Gabriel crossed the street, tipped his hat in Momma's

direction, and kept walking. It was over. The debt paid. Maybe not in full, but Gabriel Grant looked satisfied. Jacob glanced back again at Gabriel, and the thought that Momma had lied to him toppled his heart to the ground. She knew full well that Gabriel was coming and had said nothing. He crossed the street and looked at Momma.

"Why?"

"Jacob…It was for your own good. I was handling it."

Anger rose inside, igniting a fuse to explode like dynamite. "By making a deal with the devil? You can't trust him. You assumed everything was fine and now he wants full payment! He killed father, burned down my barn, and God knows how far he'll go now that he has over half his money."

"I was paying him back. But when the money ran out, I stopped. The well was dry. The mines were not producing like they used to, and the boys couldn't pay me what I needed to pay back your father's debt."

Jacob ran his fingers through his hair. He squeezed his fists, "How much?"

"How much what?"

"How much did Leonard really take from Gabriel?" She hesitated and walked inside, shutting the door behind her.

Jacob clomped up the stairs and threw the door open. "Momma?"

She turned to face her son. He knew he shouldn't blow up at her, but the anger forced by everything else boiled his blood. The steam needed releasing.

"Your father took two thousand dollars."

Jacob paced and ran fingers through his thick brown hair.

"It has taken six years to pay back just a portion. Now, I've helped pay down a sizable chunk."

"You're saying I owe Gabriel more than the three hundred dollars?"

She plopped into a chair by the table. "It's possible, maybe a few hundred more."

Jacob opened the door, "I love you, but I need air. I need to think." He slammed it on his way out.

CHAPTER TWENTY-TWO

THE BATTLE was over. A wave of relief washed the fear of uncertainty away. Jacob sat at the dinner table and saw Sarah set down a plate of his favorite food, fried chicken, on the table. Early in their marriage, Sarah had asked Momma for her recipe. The greasy aroma wafted over him like the new day's sun. They had won. Momma and Sarah finished lining the table with potatoes, spinach salad, and carrots.

Bill arrived moments later. He removed his hat and tossed his boots near the door. For the first time, Jacob noted how much the man had aged. Ranch life was hard. The crow's feet touching his eyes were a telltale sign of how hard Bill worked to keep the place going. He stretched and made his way to the table, then sat with a thud.

"There's a lot of work to do to build the new barn." He filled a glass with water from a nearby pitcher and took a long drink before setting the empty glass down, "Man, that's good stuff."

He turned to Jacob, "I had talked with Joe and Freddy.

They're working on gathering a few other men to help rebuild your barn. It'll take a few days, but we'll have a functioning barn in no time."

Jacob appreciated all Bill and the others had done for his family. They had saved his bacon by gathering the funds to get Gabriel off his back. Tomorrow, he'd head into the bank to secure a loan for the remaining three hundred dollars. He'd try for a larger loan to buy lumber and nails to build the barn.

"That sounds good. We'll find out when they can come on down to do a barn raising." Jacob considered for a moment., "I'll announce it this Sunday and see if we can't make it a congregational event. Should wash the taste of Gabriel out of their mouths."

Momma sat down and pulled her chair close to the table. She smoothed her dress and asked Virginia and Sarah to sit. "Enough about Mr. Grant. We have a lot to be thankful for and don't need him clouding up the mood. The good Lord has blessed our family and has provided in our most desperate time of need." She folded her hands, "I expect it's the right time we ask for grace for his bountiful blessings."

"Yes, Ma'am."

As Momma prayed, Jacob smiled a genuine smile for the first time in weeks. Time would heal the wounds. The reason everything happened now was because of Leonard, and he shouldn't blame Momma for doing what she felt best, even if it was flawed. If Leonard hadn't taken that handout or been a drunk, this meal wouldn't be so bittersweet.

They won the battle, but did they win the war? He still had over three hundred dollars to pay Gabriel Grant. If the bank could give him what he needed, he'd owe the bank, not Gabriel. Even though the Mayor owned the Savings and

Loan, how close did he examine the books or did he leave it up to the banker?

After the prayer, Jacob scooped a heaping pile of potatoes and a large chicken breast onto his plate. For now, he'd enjoy the meal his Momma and wife prepared. He turned to Sarah and mouthed, *I love you*. A wave of emotion wrapped its arms around him and squeezed. He understood it wasn't victory, but the battle—a little bruised and bloodied—had been victorious. It's why he said *I love you*. It's why she's always been by his side; he never gave up.

Sarah nodded and smiled in return. Her foot touched his and gooseflesh ripped across his arms. He felt his body temperature rise and knew what that touch meant. Letting a smile play his lips, he winked at her. But that would have to wait until he returned from taking Momma home. It was an hour's ride into town, so he'd be back before Sarah retired to bed. He hoped he wouldn't miss the window of opportunity with his wife.

After dinner, Jacob took Momma back to town. Their ride was silent and Jacob watched the stars begin their sparkle in the night sky. Cool air chilled his bones, so he reached, pulled a blanket from behind them, and covered Momma.

The last six years had been hard on her. He'd watched Momma lose her husband. He'd helped her move to town and deal with changing the town's perception of the Creek family. Most people loved her, some didn't care, and others remembered who Leonard was and pitied her. Jacob felt bad for Momma; she deserved a better life. She deserved someone to love her. It wasn't her fault. He blamed Leonard for her sorrow. Yet, reflecting back to previous conversations, Bill had been good for Momma. They weren't romantic, but Jacob wondered if that would change with time.

"You're awfully quiet tonight, Jake." She always called him that. She pulled the blanket closer.

"You cold, I have another one in back?"

"I'll be okay, and you're avoiding the question."

Jacob sighed. The past twenty-four hours had proven to be taxing. He was glad for the money, but regretted blowing up at his Mother. She deserved better, and he felt even worse that she had used her money to pay for her late husband's mistake. She earned every penny, and didn't deserve it going to a man who needed none–the man who had killed her husband. He knew Leonard deserved better in life than to be murdered over a debt. But that's how it was in Wyoming or any of the U.S. Territories. Far fewer grievances got people killed.

"I guess…I wish you would've talked to me before using your money." He pined the next thought, "You deserved better than Leonard."

"It's Dad, to you," she chided. "And I have had a good life, Jake. The Lord's been kind to me and I've seen my share of victories over the years." Her head drooped, "I wish you had had a better father. You didn't deserve the way he treated you. Lord knows, I scolded him for the yelling, hitting, and abuse."

"He never laid a hand on me, other than a good tanning, you realize that…right? His words were brutal and cut me deep. I still deal with those thoughts of inadequacy daily."

She wiped a few tears. He couldn't see them, but could sense the hurt radiating from her.

"Momma, God is good, and I know I've been a brood. I get that. Sometimes I think…no, I feel as if I'm becoming more like him. I don't plan on starting up heavy drinking anytime soon, but the same anger he had boils in my blood. It comes out in waves, then crashes over the beach of my soul." It was Jacob's turn to drop his head, "I've been so angry at

Gabriel that I couldn't see. I'm afraid of losing Sarah because of that anger."

Momma's head popped up, "Jacob Elliot Creek, that woman is the best thing God has given you. You're not losing her. She's worried about you, yes, but you're not losing her." Momma tightened up the blanket, "Time will give you everything you need. You need to trust in God, he'll pull you through. And that anger of yours, you may have gotten that from your father, heck, it's how you identify, but one thing's for certain: you have God to guide your choices. Jacob Creek, trust in him."

She was right. Course, Momma was always right. He'd been a brood, consumed with anger for a man who killed a man Jacob despised. Seems logical, doesn't it? The tide had to turn. If Gabriel Grant was determined on getting the money, selling a few cattle would do the trick. He would get the full three hundred dollars and more than enough to rebuild their barn. First, he would need a loan from the bank. It would require selling most of their cattle. Momma wouldn't like it, but Jacob saw he had no other choice.

Jacob needed time. The past few weeks had been tough, and neither man had shown restraint on their anger. Maybe that was why it'd been so tough. Jacob had never worked with Gabriel like a man. He'd allowed the anger to build until that was all he worried about. Even preaching had been hard. How do you teach God's people while consumed with the sin you condemn as a minister?

He sighed as the team of horses pulled near the Mining Lodge. Several men lingered around the front porch and tipped their hats at Momma. Jacob could see the love she had for them and the love they had for her. These dirty men were her children. Momma waved back and smiled.

She put her hand on his cheek and told him everything would be all right. Her last words, before heading to fix them some grub of their own, were: God's got this, and I love you.

Jacob smiled at that and slapped the reins to head home. The wagon lurched forward and began its descent into town. He looked over his left shoulder at Gabriel's office and sighed again. Tomorrow, he'd have to eat his pride and figure out how to pay the rest of the money.

But that was enough judgment concerning the mining tycoon. Sarah was waiting for him. Jacob reflected back to her leg rubbing against his at dinner and the wink and the mouthed 'I love you.' Warm heat radiated down his body and he smiled at the image of making love to his wife when he returned. Too bad the horses could only go so fast.

Jacob laughed and slapped the reins again. The town behind him, his past leaving him, and Sarah and his future ahead of him. Jacob felt good for the first time in weeks.

LAND GRAB

TRUST IN THE Lord with all thine heart; and lean not unto *thine own* understanding. In all thy ways *acknowledge him*, and he shall direct thy paths.

— *KING SOLOMON*

CHAPTER TWENTY-THREE

LIGHT DANCED across Jacob's closed eyes. He squinted and opened them, allowing the sun's rays to illuminate his world. Gazing through clouded vision, he noticed the bed was empty and Sarah was missing. Sitting up, he pulled on a pair of pants and strapped suspenders up over his shoulders. He'd put a shirt on later. Peeling back the curtain, he saw the house was empty, but smelled the freshly brewed coffee.

Jacob smiled and shuffled across the floor to grab a cup of Sarah's coffee. An empty coffee can sat on the counter. He should get more from the Mercantile later today, he thought as he poured a cup. The thought passed as the warm liquid jostled about the inside of the cup. He breathed deep before taking a sip. The brew slid down his throat and warmed his stomach, which growled upon the coffee's intrusion.

He pulled a chair to the table and sat, warming his hands. The month prior, his friends and family had filled the table and enjoyed the blessings of God. Gabriel Grant was now decent and respectful. Shocking, after everything he did to their family–burning down the barn, killing a cow, and threatening Sarah. After several men gave their money to help Jacob's family out, Jacob could get a loan from the bank. The loan would do two things for Jacob: pay off what was left to Gabriel and rebuild the barn.

The road would be long, but the plan was to sell off cattle to pay back the bank's loan. He had found a rancher in Cedar Grove who would buy what was left of Jacob's cattle. The sale of just two hundred fifty cattle would set them up to re-establish Creek Ranch. But being out from under Gabriel's thumb felt good and caused Jacob to relax. He still owed money to a bank, but that was manageable. They wouldn't burn down your barn or shoot your livestock.

Gabriel demanding the money only caused both men frustration and agony. The newly elected Mayor wanted his cash, and Jacob wanted to be left alone. Seemed fitting and respectable on both their parts.

Jacob swallowed the last of the coffee as the door opened. Sarah's silhouette stood in the doorway. She lingered there a moment and Jacob fell in love all over again. Sarah held a basket of eggs and walked into the house. Virginia followed close behind with a few canned onions and tomatoes from the cellar.

"Hi, Daddy," she said, waltzing past him to the other side of the table.

"Eh-hem."

"Oh…sorry, Daddy," Virginia tossed the cans on the table then bounced back and kissed Jacob's cheek.

"Good morning to you too," He scooted back the chair, stood, and grabbed Virginia. She squealed with delight as he swung her around. Her off-white dress floated like a flag before he set her back down. "You're getting so heavy."

"I am ten years old today, you know."

How could he forget? Today was Virginia's birthday. Jacob smiled to himself as he sat back down and picked up his cup. Bringing it to his lips, he felt the last few cold drops hit his tongue. Disappointment washed over him and he set the cup down with a thud. "Virginia, could you bring your old man a new cup of coffee?"

She pursed her lips, giggled, then took the cup and poured another round for her father. "Here you go," she said, bringing it back.

"Good, girl. Now, go help your mother fix breakfast. I'm off to see what Bill's doing."

Sarah turned from the stove, "He's out behind the barn putting something together."

Jacob got up and meandered outside to find Bill. Besides Momma, Bill had been a rock and a good shoulder to lean on these past few months. He had traded one father, who neglected him, for another who loved him as his own. Life's full of lemons, but it's what you do with those lemons that makes all the difference. Bill had only been a work hand and had taken a liking to the boy. He often found Jacob near the creek behind the barn tossing rocks. That's when Jacob realized Bill was a good man, and besides Momma, that was how he had learned about God and his goodness.

He saw Bill working in the new barn. It went up the prior month and had required a lot of work to make it functional. They'd worked hard the past few weeks, getting the siding up and the roof covered. Bill grabbed several boards and moved out of sight. As Jacob approached, he heard the consistent heartbeat of a hammer and nails.

This barn was larger and had four horse stalls, instead of the three the other barn housed. They converted the tool shed into a new garden house and moved everything to the barn. They quipped the barn with a tack room, saddle stations, and a large workbench. The new barn far exceeded the value and expanse of the old one. Jacob had to take a little more out in loans to finish the barn. Now, he was in for at least two thousand dollars at the Savings and Loan. Jacob hated it, but what's a man to do without a functional barn? At least he and Bill secured a deal to sell their cattle to a rancher in Cedar Grove. He'd pay back the loan, pay his men, and be out from under Gabriel's financial grip.

"How's it going?" Jacob asked.

Bill stopped nailing and wiped his brow. "It's coming. I'll have the fourth stall finished by end of the day." He pulled a bent nail and tossed it aside. "How do you want the new garden house to look?"

Jacob hadn't thought much about the garden house. It'd be nice to put on a back door to it for easy access to the garden. Have everything self-contained. Seemed like a good idea, and he knew Sarah would enjoy having a new fenced-in garden. He walked Bill to the converted toolshed and explained his idea. It might work. They both figured it'd keep out the deer, but they'd still have the rabbits to deal with.

The way Bill thought through everything—the detailed plans, moving the tool shed to the barn, and adding a fourth horse stall—made Jacob admire the man. Even though he gave credit to his father for seminary, in one of those few lucid moments, it was Bill who had raised him to fall in love with the Bible. Bill taught him what it meant to love God and his people. Course, he didn't enjoy loving God's Word as of late. Gabriel made that difficult. How do you show God's love to a man who murdered your father and burned down your property? He didn't have the answer and no one else seemed to either. For now, the battle was over and the new battle of paying off his own debt began.

After finishing up with Bill, Jacob rode to town to see if he could find something for Virginia's birthday. He had made a rocking chair but the fire had taken care of that gift. Now, he wanted to see what else he could find for his daughter.

When did she turn ten? Ten! Jacob remembered the day she was born. Holding her in his lap the first time, rocking her as she slept, made him feel closer to God than anything else in life. Now to find a gift fit for a princess. Jacob tied his horse and walked into the store.

"What brings you to town, Reverend?" Joe said.

He took off his hat, "I need a gift for Virginia. It's her tenth birthday."

"Ten years old already? She sure gets along with my little one quite well," Joe smiled and Jacob saw the man's wheels turning. Snapping his fingers, he said, "I have just the thing. Wait right there." He headed to the back of the store. "It came in on the train yesterday. I'd be remiss, if I were you, it's perfect for Virginia." He walked back to Jacob holding a beautiful doll. The doll's white features and rose-colored cheeks stood out against the beautiful blue dress. Her curled hair was dark brown and tied in the back with a matching ribbon.

"Wow!" Jacob took the doll. It looked expensive. He only had ten dollars. "How much is this going to cost me?" he hated even asking.

Joe looked it over again. "I'll give it to you for…five dollars."

So much for getting anything else Sarah needed. She had

asked for flour and cornstarch. He might have enough for those items, but not nails or coffee. Those would have to wait. Joe saw Jacob's frustration and squeezed the bridge of his nose. "Tell you what, Reverend, I'll give it to you for four dollars. I can't go any lower, I paid three for it."

Jacob pulled out the cash. "Deal. I also need flour, cornstarch, and coffee."

Neither man had heard Gabriel Grant walk in. "I like it when men make good deals." He stared at the doll, "Pretty. Guessing it's for that girl of yours."

Jacob nodded.

"Well, how's the paying of that loan coming?" He didn't give him a chance to respond, "I stopped over at the Savings and Loan and they say you've asked for more money to finish the barn? Now, I could be wrong, but isn't that a little reckless?"

"I need a barn, Gabriel. It's the main functioning building on my property. It will help keep things running so I can make money to pay back the bank. Spend to earn. You of all people should know that." Frustrated, Jacob handed the money to Joe before continuing, "I'm getting this doll for Virginia. It's her birthday." He shoved his change deep into his pockets, "Now, if you'll excuse me I have to head home."

Gabriel moved in front of the door. "I'm sorry, didn't mean to offend you. I came in to gather a few goods before heading home."

Jacob's heart pounded deep. He extended his hand. "I'm working on getting the money paid. It's the bank I owe, not you."

"Understood, Preacher. Take the time you need; that's what a loan's for." Gabriel accepted the outstretched hand. "Oh, and I wanted to let you know that I had a little stop over at the bank to finalize my purchase of it, so you now owe me the rest of the loan."

Jacob bit his tongue. He'd deal with this later. "Good day, Joe." Jacob walked out of the store and loaded the goods into the wagon. Without another word, he slapped the reins and headed home.

CHAPTER TWENTY-FOUR

G ABRIEL GRANT waited until the Preacher left. It took every ounce of self-control not to force the man's hand; he was trying the nice card and with the right amount of pressure, Jacob Creek had come up with the monies owed. Well, seven hundred dollars' worth. Taking the Preacher to get a loan forced him to swallow his pride. His wife, Moira, told him as much. Gabriel hated that she took a liking to Sarah, but the whole nice shtick wasn't working, and buying the Savings and Loan might put just the right amount of pressure on Jacob to finish his father's payment and now his own. The barn fire melted away some of that righteous indignation and forced him to ante up. The Preacher now owed the bank, a bank that Gabriel now owned.

He stared around the dump of a shop and wondered how Joe kept the place open. In debt to his eyeballs, Joe tried everything to stay afloat. Two years ago, Joe came groveling to Gabriel, asking for a little help. Now, he was late on all payments and had tried leaving town a year prior. He owned Joe and everything he had, so, to help the poor man out,

Gabriel had bought the store and gave Joe the money he needed to restore the place. Judging the way the shelves looked, he wondered what happened to the money. Goods and services came before shop repairs, but a little paint might help business. Gabriel hated the place. It stank of stale wood and urine from the cat Joe kept.

He turned to Joe, who stood there like an idiot. "How much did he spend today?"

Joe counted the money on the counter. "Ten. But last week he spent at least forty dollars on goods."

If the Preacher spent fifty dollars in the last week, it's money he could have used to pay back part of the loan. The thought of using the money on anything else seemed stupid and petty. Why would Jacob spend money he didn't have? Gabriel couldn't understand how some people thought it was okay to spend without knowing the horrible consequences of being a slave to the lender. He'd learned that the hard way, before making his money in the mines.

Gabriel didn't come from a rich family. He inherited nothing from his old man. In fact, his father died dirt poor, a pauper by all standards. Rest his soul. Gabriel had worked hard for his money. He bought and sold property all throughout the territory of Wyoming. He purchased the mines and found gold and silver. They also found a little platinum, but that's not where he came into his money. It was the logging industry combined with the mines. The more lumber that was needed, the more buildings could be bought. So, he invested in a logging company, bought it, and owned it. It was his most lucrative company.

The tiny Mercantile didn't amount to a solid cash flow enterprise. Joe owed him and owed him big. Cursing under his breath, Gabriel pulled a cigar from his left coat pocket and snipped off the rolled end. He grabbed a match from a box on the counter to light his cigar and puffed a few rounds of smoke before blowing it into the air, watching the blue plume dance about and haze the air. The smoke smelled better than the dingy space. He turned to Joe, who sat there, quiet.

"Oh, come on. You can't tell me you actually care what happens to the Preacher?"

Joe contemplated his next words. He pulled a towel from his shoulder and wiped the burnt tobacco from the counter onto the floor. "He's a good man, trying to do what's right. I even helped him out. And besides, you're not helping by killing cattle and burning down his barn."

Joe had a way with words and Gabriel hated the remark. He spoke his mind; guess that was better than squabbling about. "Listen, Joe. You owe me. Now, where is he getting the money to pay back this loan?"

Joe remained quiet and continued to clean.

"Joe?"

The shop owner set down the broom and leaned against the counter. "I shouldn't."

"Do I have to remind you, you're under my employ? Now tell me, where's Jacob getting the money to pay me back?"

Joe acquiesced, "All I know, in talking with Bill the other day, they're planning a cattle drive. A big one. Some rancher in Cedar Grove bought a couple hundred head of cattle. They're leaving the day after tomorrow."

Gabriel scratched his chin and whistled some Dixie. That would be a lot of money. "Do you know who's buying?"

Joe said all Bill mentioned was that it was a good deal and would leave them debt free from the bank so that Jacob could pay back all the money people had given to help him out.

That rocked Gabriel to the core. Give the man a dollar and he thinks he can pay everyone.

"Who's he selling cattle to?"

Joe shook his head, "I don't know. Bill never told me."

He looked Joe's shop over. Joe had more debt than the other store owners. The building was worse for wear and the wooden shelves needed replacing. Gabriel stomped on the floor. Yep, even the floorboards needed a reset. Idiot should have used the money to fix up the dump. That's when an idea struck him like gold. "Joe, tell you what. You know that building on the other side of town I'm erecting?"

Joe nodded.

"I'll forgive all your debt and give you a new store if you find out where and to whom they're selling. I want that cattle and I'll pay double to the rancher for his land. Just need someone to push the right buttons to get the information I need."

Joe thought about it and Gabriel knew the man wanted out from under the debt. Was it worth selling one's soul to Gabriel Grant? Gabriel sure thought so. Heck, he owned the town anyway. "Under one condition," Joe said.

"Name it," Gabriel smiled. He always got what he wanted, and Joe was a good lap dog.

"I want out from this store, altogether. I hate working this place and miss being just a rancher. Name me the new foreman of the ranch when you buy it. I'll move to Cedar Grove and run the place. Lord knows you can't run two ranches without the help."

Gabriel didn't see that coming, but what could it hurt? Joe was loyal. "I'll make you the foreman, it'll be your ranch to run and you'll be the one to buy the cattle from the Preacher." Now he didn't have to give up a good building to a Mercantile shop. This one, he'd burn to the ground after tying up the stupid cat.

Joe objected.

"That's the deal. Take it or leave it. If you don't… well, I'd hate to find out what happens next," Gabriel offered his hand.

Joe accepted.

"Congratulations. Once you find out who, I'll draw up a bank note to purchase the land."

"I'll get back to you as soon as I can."

Gabriel Grant smiled and left Joe alone with his thoughts.

CHAPTER TWENTY-FIVE

JACOB SLID his Henry Repeating rifle into the brown leather scabbard affixed to Gypsy's side. Out of all his guns, the Henry .45 long colt was his favorite. Jacob and Bill had toiled the past seven days getting ready for the drive to Cedar Grove. When he received a telegram of someone interested in gaining more cattle, Jacob knew God had answered his prayers. Gabriel Grant held a gun to his head, killed a cow, and burned down a barn. Not to mention the numerous threats against Sarah and that confrontation down by the creek. Gabriel Grant was like the businessmen in Salt Lake City. Men with money and power, who'd stop at nothing until paid in full.

Grateful for the men who stepped forward to help take the cattle to Cedar Grove, Jacob knew things should start turning around. Yesterday, Joe said he wanted to join up. He closed his shop and traded his usual apron for a trench coat and hat. There were a few others who joined up and for each man, Jacob had little worries about the upcoming drive. After talking it over with Bill, he needed him up front running point next to him.

It took a few hours to round up the herd. They only needed two hundred fifty cattle. The Creek family had three hundred head and the rancher only asked for the majority. He'd pay around three dollars a hundred-pound. Not bad, but Jacob wanted more. They finally settled around four dollars per hundred-pound. It would be enough to satisfy the second loan to get Gabriel off his mind.

Bill finished loading his saddle bags. He took time to get used to the new horse. Bill patted the new animal and mounted. He pulled on the reins and pulled up next to Jacob. "All set, Boss?"

Jacob hadn't mounted his yet, still having to say goodbye to Sarah and Virginia. "Soon. Is Freddy ready to go? And how's his cooking? I never could bring myself to ask."

Bill shook his head, "It's bad but at least his coffee's good."

"Okay, at least we have coffee," Jacob laughed. He walked over to Sarah, who stood on the porch. The wind blew her hair, and he took her cheek into his hand.

They kissed as she blushed. "Mr. Creek. I believe the men are looking on."

Jacob smiled, "I know," and kissed her again.

The men whooped and hollered.

Jacob shot back, "Can't a man kiss his wife goodbye?"

Sarah turned back to him, "Ignore them. It's just us." She reached down and placed Jacob's Bible into his hand, "Take this and think of us."

"I will. I'll be back in two weeks." He pulled her aside, out of ear shot, "The guy I'm taking the cattle to, he's a lawyer and thinks I may have a case against Gabriel Grant for damaging our property and killing our horse. But I will also bring up that Gabriel killed my father. If we can find evidence, we can put him away."

Sarah's face paled, and she lowered her voice, "So, all of this…this drive…it's all about getting back at Gabriel?"

It was a valid question, but there was more. "If we can't put him away, I'll satisfy the second loan, since he bought the bank. We'll have money and I can continue God's work here in Purgatory."

He could see Sarah wrestling with it, but she also understood there might not be another way around Gabriel Grant. "I'll be okay. The Lord will guide us. I know I've been angry and sometimes I feel I'm turning into my father."

She kissed his cheek, "Never think you're not a good man, Jacob Creek. The people love you, I love you, and God loves you. That's all you need in this life. Trust that God will fight your battle for you, because if you try to do this on your own, without God's help, you'll fail and it will hurt the people who love you."

She pulled his chin close to her lips, and they kissed.

"C'mon, Jacob, the cattle won't drive themselves," Joe said.

"Be safe," Sarah finally said.

"I will," Jacob's boots tossed dust into the air as he mounted his horse. He gave one last lingering look at his wife and daughter, "I love you both. Virginia, listen to your mother and to Momma."

"Yes, sir."

Turning to Bill, he asked, "Are you ready?"

"Okay, boys! Let's move 'em out!" Bill cracked a whip and Jacob took the lead. The cattle, the other men, and the Chuck Wagon started the journey to Cedar Grove. Dust filled the air as the cattle moved forward through the ranch and into the pasture. Their journey had just begun.

Jacob prayed as they rode, thanking the Lord for providing a buyer. He turned back and watched the ranch below. Sarah waved, and he shot back a smile and a returning wave.

CHAPTER TWENTY-SIX

J UDGE RAYMOND Talbert leaned back in his wooden chair, crossed his fat fingers, and exhaled. A low gargle from his bulging jowls reverberated through the tiny office behind the courthouse. The room had a small bookshelf with legal books, a desk that appeared tiny to the large man, and a chair in front to accommodate one guest. Gabriel never sat. The Judge was the closest friend Gabriel had, and it was more a friendship of necessity. Talbert got what he wanted and Gabriel bought land. It was a quid pro quo for the two men.

"So, what brings you in today, Grant? I've got work to do and you're interrupting me," Talbert settled his fat before opening a bottle of scotch.

The man's stench filled the air with a breath-choking, rotten cabbage smell that caused him to cover his nose. He coughed and waited for Talbert to finish pouring a drink. He offered one but Gabriel declined.

"Suit yourself."

Gabriel wanted to procure another piece of land. The

only one to make that happen was the Judge. The disdain he had for the Preacher had reached a tipping point. It's not that he was a bad man; he wanted his money. He needed to get rid of the Creek family. Sure, it'd been a month since helping the Preacher secure a loan from the bank, an establishment he owned, but if he could take the church and school land, while stopping the cattle sale in Cedar Grove, he'd own Jacob.

The Good Book said the man who hid his Master's money was called a wicked and lazy servant. Someone fit for hell. The Preacher's father was no different and time had run its course with Gabriel's bullet. Gabriel remembered the night well.

He found Leonard in the tavern drunk as a skunk. Leonard rambled on and on about how Gabriel Grant was power-hungry and didn't care who got hurt on his road to riches. Gabriel stood at the door, hearing every word.

"Power-hungry? Is that what people are calling me today? Wow," He laughed.

Leonard tossed a shot down his throat and scooted back before wobbling up to Gabriel. He stuck his finger in Gabriel's nose, "Listen, I'll pay you, when I'm ready to pay you," his words slurred.

"You're drunk, Leonard. I think we'll have this conversation when you're a little... more sober," he shoved Leonard back.

Leonard staggered back before pulling a gun from his belt. He cocked the weapon. "You think you're ssso sma...sma... smart. You think you can run this town and claim to be a g...god? Well, I have news for you. You're not! God that is... You're just a power-hungry, no-good, thief who thinks you can demand, demand, and demand from the little people." His words continued their slur. His tongue filled with insults and curses.

"Put the gun away, Leonard."

He waved it in Gabriel's face again, "Why? Afraid a… ma… man like m…me would kill ya?"

Gabriel grabbed Leonard's shirt and drug him through the Tavern and tossed him outside onto the boardwalk. He rolled, tumbled, then staggered to his feet. Gabriel ducked out of the way as his gun fired. The sign splintered above his head and showered down chucks of wood. Gabriel pulled his gun, pulled back the hammer, and shot into the air. "You're drunk, Leonard. We'll discuss this tomorrow, but I expect you to arrive with some cash to pay what's owed. It's been one year since loaning you the cash. I think I've waiting long enough."

Leonard shot off another round. Gabriel rolled out of the way as the bullet whizzed by his head and thumped into the wooden post. He cocked his gun again and fired, this time striking Leonard in the shoulder.

Picking himself up, he walked over to Leonard and kicked the gun away.

Leonard wailed against the pain.

Gabriel looked over his shoulder as a crowd began its slow build around the Tavern's front. He pointed his finger as Leonard gripped his wound. "I've been patient and cordial by loaning you two thousand dollars. You mock me, shoot at me, and then say I'm just a power-hungry, greedy sonofagun," He cursed and then aimed his gun at Leonard. "Get up," he kicked the man, "Get up!"

Leonard rose, clutching his left shoulder.

Gabriel kicked Leonard's gun to his feet, "Pick it up."

Then man obliged, dusted off his gun, and holstered it. Gabriel walked several paces away. "You think you're such a man, shoot me and I'll forgive your debt. Kill me, you're free. Miss, and it'll go bad for you. Poor Momma will be without a husband and that son of yours won't miss you the next time he comes into town looking for his drunk, no-good, abusive father." Gabriel spun on his heel, looking Leonard square in the eyes, "Now, shoot me!"

Leonard growled, pulled his gun, and tossed it to the ground, "I'm not going to shoot you, Gabriel. Just leave my family alone."

Gabriel stood there for just a moment; then in a flash, he fired. The bullet made a sickening sound as it struck Leonard's head. His skull cracked open, erupting spatter into the air. The man didn't move at first, then toppled forward, dead.

The following days, the Judge came to Gabriel's rescue and helped him convict and hang another man for Leonard's death. He'd spent six years putting it behind him, but when Jacob Creek arrived, all those emotions came rushing back like April storms. Then the stupid people of Purgatory gave Jacob their money. Nice gesture.

Gabriel figured the only way he could get rid of Jacob and his pesky family was to take everything away, starting with the cattle–Joe's taking care of that–then the church and school. The land they occupied would make a nice place for a brand new hotel and saloon.

"Gabriel, I'm a busy man, you going to tell me why you're here?" the Judge said again, pulling Gabriel from the memories.

"I want the land the church and school occupy."

"Didn't think you a religious man, Grant."

Gabriel scoffed at that, "Listen, I want the land. It goes to waste sitting there, used once a week, and the congregation is small. The town is growing and we don't have a suitable hotel. I want one built."

"And you think I will go along with this because…?" The man poured another drink. "I don't care, but why the church? There's plenty of other land in Purgatory. Not as much paperwork to put together."

"I want Jacob Creek gone."

"Listen, the Lord knows you could give the town some of that cash of yours. I'll draw up the papers and it'll be yours. Make sure you let the man know you're buying the land," he tossed back the drink and coughed.

Gabriel smiled, "I'll take that drink of yours now."

The Judge poured another glass and handed the scotch to him. He threw the golden liquid down his hatch and allowed the burn to warm his chest. With that, he placed the glass down and left the courthouse. It was time for Jacob Creek to leave.

CHAPTER TWENTY-SEVEN

THE SUN began its slow decline, igniting the horizon in shades of purple, red, and orange. Jacob felt it was time to break for camp. The last time he had gone on a cattle drive was with his father fifteen years earlier. One thing he never forgot was how hard the travel could be and how it could wear on a man. Jacob felt immense gratitude for each man who had stepped up to help his family. He knew it wasn't an easy decision on most of their families, but they understood and hated Gabriel Grant just as much.

They settled on just four dollars a hundred-pound. In theory, he'd pull in enough to pay each hand their fair share of the proceeds and settle with the bank. Truth to tell, it could put Creek Ranch on the map as a serious contender to the other small ranchers in the lower Wyoming Territory, if he had enough left over to purchase a few more cattle.

Freddy opened his wagon to prepare the evening meal. It wasn't pleasant work to feed six hungry men, but that didn't stop the wiry man from trying to appease the growing appetites. The average meal consisted of canned meat, beans, and potatoes from each man's farm. Jacob watched as he opened cans and dumped them into a large cast-iron pot. It hung from a hook Freddy had shoved into the ground and then dangled the pot over a waiting fire.

Jacob needed someone to do a head count on the cattle; shame if any went missing from Purgatory to Cedar Grove. He called Joe over to take two other men and do the count before dinner and before the sun disappeared.

The dinner bell rang after the sun set behind the mountains. The air chilled as its warmth faded with the light. They still had a three-day journey ahead. He couldn't wait to meet this lawyer-turned-rancher. The prospect intrigued him, that there could be a case to bring before a judge of Gabriel Grant's illegal activities. Jacob wasn't sure if Sarah was in favor of this, but understood something had to be done. Jacob didn't understand the extent of the law, but knew enough to at least warrant a conversation. He'd not only make his money to pay the bank, but could gain legal counsel to pursue further investigation into Gabriel Grant and his business.

Jacob finished his meal and leaned against a nearby rock. He pulled his gun from the holster and rotated the chamber. Each click reminded him he should practice a few rounds to brush up on his aim. Too late now; it'd scare off the cattle. He holstered the weapon and let out a sigh before closing his eyes.

"Boss."

Jacob snapped his eyes open. Bill stood over him. "Yeah," he said, trying to focus.

"The cattle count is complete. Two-hundred fifty head."

"Great. Tell Joe he's our Night Herder."

"Joe's not here."

Jacob sat up, "What do you mean? I thought you said they were back."

"They are. He disappeared during the count, said something about one of the young cows gone missing."

"Didn't you say…"

"Yep. They're all accounted for."

Jacob stood up and grabbed his hat. He secured it to his head and wiped the dust from his chaps, "Where'd he go?"

"Frank said Joe went east, toward Cedar Grove."

Jacob called for his horse. Once it was ready, he grabbed the horn and pulled himself into the saddle, "Tell the others to press on in the morning. I'll meet you."

"Jake, where are you going?"

"I'm going after him. He knows the cattle's accounted for and my gut tells me he's up to something, and I don't like it, not one bit." Jacob steadied his horse and circled it, "The other day…Virginia's birthday…I went to his store, Grant showed up and Joe became unusually quiet. I left and Grant stayed."

"You think Gabriel has something to do with this? Let me go with you."

"I don't know, probably. But I need you to stay. You're the only one I trust, Bill."

Jacob kicked his horse and shot into the night. He prayed a quick prayer that he'd find Joe in the dark and talk sense into the man. No doubt in his mind that Gabriel Grant had threatened the man. But what could he be doing? Why leave the group and why keep heading to Cedar Grove instead of heading back to Purgatory? It made little sense to Jacob. He rode for the next hour and saw nothing. The trail went cold and Jacob's horse grew tired with each passing mile. He'd have to pick up the trail in the morning; maybe they'd catch up with Joe in Cedar Grove. When he did, they'd have a chat on his sudden disappearance.

CHAPTER TWENTY-EIGHT

JOE PACKARD sipped on some whiskey in the Saloon. He'd arrived in Cedar Grove the night before to get a feel for the town before purchasing the ranch promised to him by Gabriel. He cracked a pocket inside his vest and fiddled with the banknote in the amount he'd offer to buy the land. If the rancher, Clyde Heller, refused to sell, Joe was to take it by force. As he drained the glass into his mouth, regret washed over him.

He felt like Judas. Those Bible lessons danced across his memory and he remembered things didn't go well for Judas Iscariot.

All Joe thought about was the well-being of his family. He had worked hard to achieve what he had in life, and if that meant taking from one man to supply the needs of his wife and child, so be it.

He ate a few peanuts, asked for another drink, then chased them down with the liquid. It burned as it hit the back of his throat. Feeling better and a little wobbly, he let the bartender know he was waiting for Clyde Heller, then pulled up from the counter and lumbered over to a vacant table.

The place was busy. Men moved about, got drunk, and placed their bets for an evening poker game. Several prostitutes roamed around, seeking for an easy man to seduce into their beds upstairs. Joe's eyes lingered on a cute redhead sitting near the bar's corner. She noticed and smiled. He averted his eyes, pretending not to stare as she walked towards him. She wore a red, black, and white laced corset dress.

"Hi there, Darling," she said.

Joe swallowed hard, "Hi," he squeezed out of his dry throat.

"Saw you looking at me. Like what you see?" she moved away and exposed her bare leg before sliding onto his knee.

Joe's ears burned hot, and he wanted another drink. He reached for his whiskey, then watched as she poured the drink for him. She lifted the tiny glass to his lips and begged him to take a sip, which he did. Joe licked his lips and tried to smile.

"Now, Mister, I believe I asked you a question. Do you like what you see?"

Joe nodded, then wrapped his hands around her back. He swallowed hard again. He needed another drink and fumbled for the glass. She knocked it away, pushed him against his chair, and kissed him deeply. When she pulled away, Joe smiled and his mission vaporized.

"What's your name?"

She giggled and said, "Betty."

"Hi, Betty. I'm Joe."

She blushed, "Hi, Joe." Betty pulled him to his feet, and she giggled while leading him to the stairs.

"Joe Packard?" The new voice stopped Joe and pulled him

back to why he was in the Saloon to begin with as he realized the stubby man standing before him was Clyde Heller.

"I'm guessing you're Clyde," Joe said.

"I notice you've met Betty," Clyde smiled. "She's one of my favorites. Though I guess a God-fearing man like myself will burn for having her." He growled and waved at Betty, "Hi, Betty." He growled at her again.

Betty smiled and began her climb, begging Joe to follow, "You coming? Ignore Clyde, he likes all the women here."

Joe remembered the banknote stuffed in his shirt pocket, "Sorry, Betty. I have business to discuss with Mr. Heller."

"Have it your way." She whistled and several men stopped, "Anyone want to give a girl a good time?" as several men jumped at the chance. She picked her chosen fellow and they disappeared into one of the upper rooms.

Joe shrugged his shoulders and Clyde let out a belly laugh, "That's Betty."

Joe had enough of the chitchat and wanted to get to business right away. The two men found a nearby table and sat down, each with a beer. Clyde was a short, stubby man. Not fat by any means, he seemed dis-proportioned to the average man. Joe's guess was that he was one of those midgets he read in a dime novel once. The man's fingers were small and pudgy but he was clean cut, shaved, except for a small soul patch, and good-looking for a small person.

"So, John says you came to town looking for me. He pointed you out when I walked in." Clyde took a long swig from his mug, "What brings you to Cedar Grove, Mr. Packard?"

"John?"

"The barkeep."

"I see," he cleared his throat. "Mr. Heller, I'm here on official business from Purgatory."

Joe knew he'd have to play it easy before breaking the news that Gabriel Grant was buying the tiny man's land. He poured some beer down his throat. Joe figured the man to be easy going, just by his interaction and joking around with Betty.

The little man sat back, thinking it through, "So, my question still stands; why are you here? I've got a game to attend to and they don't like to wait."

Joe cleared his throat again, "Mr. Heller, I work for Gabriel Grant and he's very much interested in your ranch," so much for easing into the topic.

Clyde didn't budge, laugh, or even snort. He sat there nodding his head and thumbing his mug. He motioned with his fat fingers for Joe to continue.

"I have a banknote saying we'll pay you a premium for your land and cattle." He unfolded the note and slid it across the table, "We'll pay you two dollars an acre and five dollars a hundredweight for your cattle. Now, how many cattle do you own, Mr. Heller?"

Clyde Heller leaned back against the chair and played with his soul patch before standing. "You have just two minutes to pack up your things and get out of town, Mr. Packard, before I throw you out myself. My cattle, my land, and my home are not for sale and Gabriel Grant can kiss my little white butt." He pushed off the chair and landed with a thud on his feet. He waddled over to a nearby table and pulled up into the chair. Clyde pulled out a wad of cash to buy into the next hand.

CHAPTER TWENTY-NINE

J OE SAT in the back of the Saloon and watched Clyde Heller play several hands of poker. He chided himself for jumping right into his sales pitch. There had to be a way to convince the little man to give up his land and cattle to Gabriel Grant. It wasn't Jacob who'd kill him, no, that would be Gabriel Grant. In Grant's world, failure wasn't an option.

He had to try something. He walked up to Clyde and said, "Mr. Heller, just hear me out."

The little man sat there, contemplating his next hand. Joe saw he had a decent hand, doubled down, and won. Impressed, Joe had an idea that just might work. If the man liked to gamble, maybe he'd gamble with his land?

Joe leaned forward and said, "Let me play you in a game of chance. If I win the next game, I get your land and cattle and pay you a total sum of seventy-five thousand dollars. If I lose, you get to keep it all and I'll leave town, never to return."

Clyde looked up from his hand. He drummed the table, then asked the men to leave. "Pay me seventy-five thousand dollars if I win and we'll play your little game. I want a guarantee you'll pay and that I will not owe Gabriel Grant any of my land."

Joe stuck out his hand, "Deal." He sat and handed the cards to the nearest cowboy. The game had to be fair and square. No cheating, just straight-up chance. "We'll play the best of three games," and Joe slid the banknote across the table as payment. If this didn't work, he was a dead man.

"Stop talking and deal," Clyde bellowed.

They were handed two cards: one face up and one face down. Joe had a Jack of spades and a ten of diamonds. He looked across at Clyde's face-up card. He had a six of hearts. The dealer placed the first of five cards in the center of the table, a seven of spades.

Clyde called for the next four cards to speed up the game since all bets were made. The ranch and cattle and seventy-five thousand dollars were the placed bets.

The dealer laid the next four cards down and produced a four of spades, an ace of diamonds, a five of hearts, and a King of clubs.

Joe's heart sank. He went bust on game one. Clyde laid out his unturned card, the eight of hearts. A beautiful flush. He cursed and saw a smile crawl across the rancher's face.

The next hand didn't go according to Clyde's plans. Joe produced a pair of Kings and a pair of threes. Each man won a game and you could cut the tension with a knife. The saloon grew quiet. The pianist abandoned his post to watch, and the ladies mingled, but Joe hardly noticed.

Joe sipped another round of whiskey. He wiped his moist hands on his slacks. Clyde called for the third round of cards to be dropped on the table. When Joe received his, he glanced down at the upturned ten of hearts, then peeked at the face-down card and smiled at an Ace of hearts. Joe asked for the dealer to flip the remaining cards. Beads of sweat poured down his face as Clyde thumbed the two cards in front of him. At least one looked to be a two of spades. Joe had this in the bag.

The dealer flipped five cards into the center of the table. The first one landed. A King of hearts. The second card landed. A Queen of hearts. He felt excitement course through his bones.

Joe snuck a glance at the short midget and smiled. A single bead of sweat formed and slid down the man's face.

The third card flipped. A three of spades. The little man smiled and giggled to himself. If Joe was right, the man was gunning for a royal flush. The dealer hesitated, then flipped the fourth card. A five of spades hit the table and Clyde laughed.

For the first time since starting the game, Joe felt sick to his stomach. It churned, and the spirits begged to vomit all over the table. He couldn't lose. He had to win. The room spun and a dark cloud rolled into his vision. He breathed heavily and fought to keep upright.

One more card, please don't screw this up. Chancing everything, his life, his family, and his livelihood all rested in the balance of one card. A tiny piece of paper filled with color, shapes, and numbers would be the deciding factor if he lived or died.

Clyde looked shaken. Each man stood at the edge of winning or losing. One had everything to gain, the other would land on his feet in due time. Clyde would be fine; Joe, not so much.

The dealer's face was ashen as he stared at the card he was about to lay. His shoulders dropped and his eyes pleaded a deep apology. The card floated and landed face down.

Clyde reached and flipped it over. The man sat back sighed and flicked the card to Joe.

Joe reached over and picked up the small, insignificant, yet coveted piece of paper. He flipped it over and he felt the color run off his face. He couldn't believe it, yet there it was: a beautiful, red, Jack of hearts. Joe pocketed the winning hand and gave the banknote to Clyde, "I'm deeply sorry it had to come about this way. Just know you'll be seventy-five thousand dollars richer and you can do whatever you want with your life."

Clyde slid off his chair, grabbed his hat and said, "I'll go to the bank tomorrow and draft the papers. Congratulations, you now are the proud owner of my land."

He hobbled up to Joe and poked a finger into his belt, "Just remember, Gabriel Grant owns you. Never forget that. You can try to escape his grip, but he will consume you, your soul, family, and life. Get out while I still consider you a man."

With that, Clyde Heller strode through the door and down the street to who-knows-where.

CHAPTER THIRTY

J ACOB CRESTED the hill overlooking Cedar Grove. The town seemed average, not the bustling city of Cheyenne, but a respectable, railway town stuck thirty miles from Cheyenne—the town where Clyde Heller practiced law. Jacob grew tired of the journey from Purgatory to Cedar Grove, and keeping men happy while promising to pay them their wage weighed down on his shoulders. The sale would happen even though some monies paid to Heller Ranch in cattle would be for services rendered, Jacob calculated enough cash to make sure each man got paid. The only problem he encountered was Joe Packard's sudden disappearance. Last night he had taken off, claimed a cow fell behind. Joe had headed toward Cedar Grove.

Some men questioned why they weren't waiting for Jacob. Clyde's ranch sat north of Cedar Grove and Jacob knew Bill would take the cattle for processing out at Heller Ranch. After giving Bill instructions, he sent the men, cattle, and wagon north. Jacob, however, had business to discuss with Clyde Heller at the hotel in town.

Two weeks ago, when Jacob met Clyde, who was on business in Purgatory, he had learned of Clyde's profession as a lawyer from the Cheyenne area. He was experienced at dealing with big ranchers with lots of power and money, and Gabriel Grant was no exception. Wyoming had 8 millionaires, and Grant belonged to that privileged group of businessmen. Clyde informed Jacob that Grant was dirty. Not just 'I'm dirty and filthy rich,' he had blood on his hands.

Jacob cared for only one man's blood, Leonard Creek's.

The sun beat down on Jacob as he descended into town. Sweat poured off his face as he dismounted in front of the hotel. It sat next to the Saloon, and sandwiched on the other side with the General Store sat the hotel. He wondered how many people use the hotel. The differences between Cedar Grove and Purgatory were striking. The town of Purgatory was a bustling mining town filled with ranchers, few businessmen, and those who are looking for a quick way to get rich out at Purgatory Gulch Mines. Much of Wyoming was untouched by the Civil War a few years back and most came to escape the war. Jacob's family had used their cattle to supply meat for both North and South, but it left them lacking funds to replenish their livestock. His father begged for a loan from Gabriel Grant. It got him killed.

Jacob walked into the hotel. A desk sat against the wall opposite the door, and the clerk looked up, but said nothing. A short stature of a man sat in one of the two green clad chairs to his left. The man looked up from the paper he read, folded it, then hopped to the ground and waddled over to Jacob.

"Jacob Creek," he popped out his little hand, which attached to a short dis-proportioned arm, "Clyde Heller."

Jacob shook his hand, then regretted thinking he took the

hand of a ten-year-old boy. "It's good to see you again, Clyde," Jacob said.

Clyde approached the hotel clerk, "We're using the back room to talk. No one may bother us."

"Sounds good, Mr. Heller."

They walked up the stairs to the right and made their way to a room near the end of the hallway. Clyde opened the door and there sat a desk, two chairs, two bookshelves, and piles of junk and empty bottles. He knocked several papers to the floor from one chair and told Jacob to sit down, then proceeded to the desk chair and pulled himself up, adjusting his seat.

"Thank you for seeing me, Mr. Heller," Jacob said.

"Mr. Creek, please call me Clyde."

"Clyde, the reason I'm here: I have real concerns with Gabriel Grant and you mentioned back in Purgatory you're building a case against him."

Clyde folded his tiny hands and leaned forward on the desk, "Gabriel Grant is being investigated by the United States Marshal's office. And it's not just him." He shoved papers around until he found a stack. Clyde opened the stack and pulled out several briefs and explained they regarded not only Gabriel Grant but also that of Judge Talbert.

Jacob leaned back in his chair. No wonder Gabriel gets away with so much, he has a judge in his back pocket.

"So, how do we fight them?"

"We don't. Not unless you desire an early funeral. We keep building our case and bring it before a federal judge. There's one that lives in Cheyenne. Real nice guy, worked with him on several cases."

"How do I get Gabriel off my back?" Jacob didn't feel he had years to wait for a case to build, and too many things get swept out the door because it's Wyoming.

"Listen, I know he's banging down your door, demanding money and all… heck, paid me a visit by one of his cronies the other day."

That pulled Jacob deeper into the moment, "How did he know about you?"

"The man offered to swindle my ranch out from under me," Clyde's eyes darted upward as if remembering something important. "It was a terrible hand of poker. The guy knew how to play."

"He didn't…did he?" Jacob just sent Bill and the crew to Heller Ranch. Would Gabriel Grant be meeting with Bill? Did the tycoon want money so bad he'd steal the cattle from under him by buying out another man's ranch? That alone would leave him penniless. This drive was all he had left. And what about Bill's safety?

Clyde laughed and leaned back, "No. I bet the poor soul is half-way to Cheyenne now. It's a piece of land I bought intending to build something on it. There's no water, not much vegetation–though the potential is great–and Gabriel will have a heyday. The land isn't worth much, not like here in Cedar Grove or Purgatory. Told him that my ranch sat between Cedar Grove and Cheyenne. That's where he's headed, I suppose," Clyde laughed so hard he snorted.

Jacob stifled his laugh. Somehow it felt like sweet revenge. The man took so much from so many people that getting a worthless piece of land seemed like a victory for his family. "And if he comes after me?"

"He won't. I'm the one who tricked the poor idiot into playing for the land. Never said it was in Cedar Grove. Besides, I got seventy-five thousand dollars for a chunk of land that's worth half that amount."

"Unbelievable," he scratched his head, "and if you lost?"

Clyde stood and walked to the door. He turned with a smile, "The same."

Jacob laughed at that one.

"In all seriousness, there's a U. S. Marshal who the Governor commissioned to use whatever means necessary to investigate Gabriel Grant. Remember, Grant has blood on his hands and if we can find just a few witnesses to come forward and say he shot and killed your father, we'll have a case to put him away."

"I appreciate everything you're doing. My family is grateful."

Clyde opened the door, and they walked down the stairs and pushed through the door into the hot noon sun, "Don't mention it." He stuck out his stubby hand again, "Listen, let's head to the ranch and get grub."

There was one question Jacob hadn't asked yet, "Who'd you sell the land to?"

"Some guy named Joe Packard. He contacted me two weeks ago and said he had a legal question. Stupid swindler."

That explained everything. Joe took off and came here to talk Clyde out of his ranch. That's why he'd abruptly closed up shop and begged Jacob to let him come on the drive. Jacob was thankful for Joe, as the man had prior experience on a ranch, but never expected the man, who seemed a humble family man, to trick him and do something as stupid as being Gabriel Grant's pawn. Joe had better not return to Purgatory; otherwise, he'd have to answer to Jacob for his lies.

"Let's go get some grub."

CHAPTER THIRTY-ONE

SEVERAL HOURS later, they sat down for dinner after counting the cattle. Branding would take place at a later date and Jacob didn't need to be around. The conversation earlier at the hotel bothered him. He trusted Clyde Heller, but he also worried for Joe's safety. When Gabriel would learn of Joe's failure, he'd probably kill him. The dilemma of catching up with Joe, talking some sense into him, and convincing him that Gabriel was just using him as a pawn for his own gain was Jacob's battle.

The dinner table sat in a large room filled with ornate carved wooden items from around the world. Sitting next to the fireplace sat a spice cabinet from India. Spices were expensive and the only way to get some from India: you'd have to visit yourself. Clyde had money, and it didn't come from practicing law. A house maid set a plate of roast beef and hearty serving of beets and tiny red potatoes before them. Jacob unfolded the napkin and wrapped it over his legs. The idea seemed proper since he and the boys sat in a fancy dining room. He cut into the beef and savored the warm juices as they filled his mouth. He told Freddy he needed to take some lessons from the staff.

"Not very nice, boss," Freddy said.

AFTER DINNER, Jacob and Clyde retired to a smoking lounge to discuss the legal matter at hand regarding Gabriel Grant. The room was large enough for two lounge chairs to the left, a letter desk near the window across the door, and a lit fireplace to the right. The walls were lined with bamboo sitting over a metal wall.

"I'll shut the door," Clyde said. "Don't want your boys to know why you're here in Cedar Grove."

"I appreciate that," Jacob said.

He handed Jacob a cigar, and he declined resorting to the tea he brought from the dining room. Clyde sat down at his desk and pulled out several sheets of blank paper, followed by a bank note. It was time to begin business.

"I know we already agreed on the fee of half your cattle for my legal services and I'll pay you for the other half. Now, going market rate is around five dollars per hundred-weight." He paused, "I'm guessing you already know their weight?"

"I do. The average weight of each cow is around a thousand pounds."

"Great. The going rate at the moment is around three to four dollars per hundred-weight. I'll pay you four dollars for your troubles. This ought to help you dig out from under Gabriel's thumb. That will give you, after my take, around…" Clyde did a quick calculation, "seven thousand dollars." He signed the check and handed the money to Jacob, "It's a pleasure doing business with you."

Jacob stared at the number written. He'd never seen that much cash in one bank note in his life. It wouldn't just cover the cost of the barn by paying back the bank Gabriel owned—Jacob figured it'd pay the men for their time and leave him with at least twenty-five hundred left over. Each man would get their share of two hundred dollars for their time except Bill, he'd get five hundred. Maybe he could purchase some young bovine to replace some herd?

Happy with that prospect, the next question lingered in his mind like a crow waiting for his next meal—what do to with Joe Packard? Joe betrayed him. Jacob didn't know how to handle the situation, a situation he never saw coming. If Jacob behaved like Gabriel Grant, he'd send a posse after the man, demand final payment, then hang him for betrayal. Because of Clyde's craftiness, a noose just might be Joe's final curtain. He didn't blame Clyde, he should protect his assets, but one thing seemed certain: Gabriel wouldn't like unprofitable land.

"So, you got seventy-five thousand dollars for that worthless piece of land?"

Clyde laughed as he lit a cigar, "I sure did, and I don't feel bad one bit."

Jacob let out a whistle before taking a sip of his tea.

"Course the man had it coming. One of my hired hands informed me that Gabriel was about to make a move, so I countered and because Joe isn't the sharpest tool, I tricked him in a game of poker. Didn't matter if I won or lost, I got money."

"You were hoping you'd lose."

"The land is worth around a dollar seventy-five, so yes, made a lot of money on that land. Joe thought he made out, and he lost big time."

"What if Gabriel kills him?"

"We won't let that happen."

"We...?"

Clyde placed the cigar in a glass tray, leaned forward, then lowered his voice. He explained that a Federal Marshal named Tan Bennington approached him six months ago looking for information on Gabriel Grant and that U. S. Marshals were dead set on apprehending the tycoon. Rumors circulated six years prior, after the death of a one Leonard Creek, Jacob's father. The judge in Purgatory manipulated the Wyoming law code to keep Gabriel out of court and a trial for manslaughter. They even hanged another man for the crime Gabriel committed. When Clyde caught wind of Gabriel's plan to sneak the land out from under him, he contacted Tan Bennington from the U. S. Marshal's office in Cheyenne and informed him he'd been in contact with Leonard's son, Jacob, to purchase cattle for access to Gabriel Grant.

Jacob set his tea down and leaned on his elbows, "Are you asking me to spy on him?"

"Not at all. I need access to him. He'll come looking for me, wondering what happened and why he doesn't own my land. It'll frustrate the man to no end and then Marshal Bennington will travel to Purgatory to assist Sheriff Sam Ballot in a prisoner transfer back to Cheyenne to stand trial for murder. That will give us an excuse to sniff around town to gather evidence and information for the Marshal to issue an arrest of Mr. Grant."

Jacob had heard of the prisoner, Phil Tingleston. He murdered his wife and son while they slept, then went to the tavern for a drink and opened fire, killing his other son who played cards at a nearby table. The whole thing shook the town, and had all taken place before Jacob and Sarah moved to Purgatory. He's been sitting in the jail cell for two months awaiting trial.

"Is Phil connected to Gabriel?" Jacob asked.

"Not that I'm aware of, but that doesn't mean the two haven't done business. Who knows? All I know, Gabriel is as slippery as they come. He dodges one bullet, then uses the law as protection and keeps a sheriff and a local judge in his back pocket for safe keeping. But with the Marshal coming, Ballot doesn't have much choice but to comply with Federal law."

Clyde informed Jacob he'd return to Purgatory with him after they'd met up with Marshal Tan Bennington to discuss further action and see if they could find probable cause to arrest Gabriel Grant for circumventing the law for his own gain.

"When do you plan on heading back?" Clyde asked.

"We're leaving at first light, but I need to talk with the Marshal first. And what do we do about Joe Packard?"

"That's up to you."

Jacob stood and stretched, "I will find Joe and talk some sense into his head. He's being manipulated into working for Gabriel and I don't want to see him sell his soul to the devil."

Clyde picked up his cigar again, "He already has." Clyde puffed some smoke, snuffed out the end, and blew out the candle. "He's just not dead yet."

After showing Jacob his room, he said he'd be up before the sun, then left down the hall. Jacob tossed his hat onto a nearby hook, kicked off his boots, then laid on the bed. The room was nice, yet small. He looked at the walls wrapped in a painted fabric and the bed nestled against the far wall near the window. The bed's comforter had a simple flower design and reminded him of the one Sarah had made several years after they married. His thoughts drifted to Sarah and Virginia having to fend for themselves while both he and Bill lay miles away. He didn't enjoy leaving them alone and hated that no other man was around to care for their needs. The trip back wouldn't take as long, as they had no cattle to slow their journey down. Jacob figured it'd take them two to three days of hard riding to get back to Purgatory. The mountains would slow them, but once home, he'd be able to hug both his wife and daughter and tell them how much he missed and loves them.

Jacob blew out the lantern and the room grew dark. His eyes adjusted to the moon light filtering in through the sheer curtain. He could hear the crickets singing their songs of praise, filling the night with their music. He closed his eyes and waited for sleep to envelop him and pull him into its embrace.

The world faded and for the first time in weeks, Jacob felt at peace.

CHAPTER THIRTY-TWO

ALONE THE last two weeks, Sarah busied herself tending the garden and completing daily lessons for the children. The days felt long and with each passing moment, she realized how much her heart longed to hug and hold her husband. The first time Jacob left on a trip, his father had died. It'd been six years since that day. Now, she sat in a quiet house with Virginia, contemplating all the horrible things that could go wrong on a cattle drive.

That's not what bothered her, that thought lived with Gabriel Grant. She detested the man and everything he stood for, all the horrible acts he committed, and the poor lessons in rearing his child. She opened a book sitting to her left and tried to push all thoughts of Gabriel from her mind. Glancing at the worn pages reminded her that Virginia's dress needed mending. The girl had a knack for destroying good dresses. The last one she'd torn on a branch while clearing a path to the creek.

Sarah closed the book and squeezed the bridge of her nose. Time for a walk. She glanced around the room at the children working on their homework. They were quiet, just what she wanted. Leaving Virginia in charge of the room, Sarah stepped out into the bright sun. She let its warmth wash her thoughts away. Last night's rain clumped the dust, keeping the streets clean. Sarah breathed deep as she approached Missy's Tavern before pushing the waist high doors aside. The tiny place was orderly. Several round tables filled the space, and the bar sat to the left. Sarah felt funny walking into Missy's and turned around. Good girls and liquor don't mix, at least that's what Daddy used to say. As she pressed back through the doors, someone called her name. Sarah looked around to see who spoke–that's when she saw Moira sitting at one table having lunch.

"Hi, Moira," Sarah managed.

"Sarah Creek, come in…come in. I'll have Missy fetch you some chicken soup."

"No, that's okay. I've already eaten." She closed the distance and sat next to Moira, "How are you?"

Moira sat there, munching away at a carrot. She didn't look up and kept her eyes to nailed to the table. Moira had become a good friend and someone Sarah connected with in this crazy town. From what she could gather, Moira hated being in Purgatory and if she had to guess, hated being Mrs. Gabriel Grant too. No use broaching the subject and Moria didn't seem much interested.

"It's tough, you know. I try to be the good wife and try to give my opinion and he…you know, he doesn't treat me like a lady. I'm a piece of property. All he needs is a pretty wife, skinny and ready for sex; then he shows me off like I'm his prized horse."

Guess she wanted to talk about Gabriel after all. Sarah didn't know what to say. The woman was spilling her heart, and she didn't know where to begin or how to comfort. Listening was a good way to begin.

"Moira, I'm sorry," that was it. Nothing else came out. All Sarah could muster was *sorry*?

Moira stifled a slight cry, "No need to be, dear," then pulled another spoonful to her mouth and played with a noodle before it slipped behind her lips, "Are you sure you don't want a bowl?"

Sarah declined again and assured Moira that she'd always be available to talk. Her mind drifted to the children working on their papers. She shouldn't stay much longer. She rested her hand on Moira's, "I can't imagine the life you're living. Have you thought about leaving him?"

"Oh, Gabriel would never let that happen. He owns me, like he owns everything else. And if I stand up to him, that's a whole other ball of wax. Besides, what good would it do? He is my husband, I love him and I do my best to honor him. I wish he'd treat me with a little more respect." She stood, "Now, you heard none of this from me...I shouldn't have said anything."

Sarah waited until Moira left before heading back to the school. She'd been gone too long. As she approached the schoolhouse, a man stood on the steps. He picked up his hat, placed it on his head, then flicked a cigar end to the street. She squinted against the sun to see Gabriel Grant step off the porch. She hoped he hadn't heard the previous conversation with his wife.

"Good day, Mrs. Creek."

"What do you want?" it came out with a rude snap and she didn't care.

He pulled another skinny cigar from a case and bit off the

end. He spit the loose tobacco and lit the cigar. He puffed and exhaled, "It's a beautiful day, isn't it?"

"School's not out for another two hours, Mr. Grant. So, if you're here for Felix, you must wait till his studies are finished," she said walking past him toward the door.

"Actually, I'm here for you," he pulled a folded piece of paper and handed her the letter.

She unfolded the letter and noticed an intent to buy. "What's this?"

"I'm purchasing the land the church and school sit on. I wanted to let you know that the end of the week will be your last day in this establishment."

Sarah stood dumbfounded. She tried to speak, but the words caught her throat and nothing came out. Closing the schoolhouse? What about the children? What about her job? It didn't seem to make any sense. "I...I don't understand."

"It's simple economics, Sarah. I'm buying the land and I will build something on it."

"What about the children?"

"They'll be fine."

"I'm sorry, but the land belongs to the people of Purgatory. You can't just buy land that the people own." The shock hadn't set in, but she knew it would.

He pulled another piece of paper and handed it to her. "Judge signed off on it and the deal is done. I'm sorry, but you must meet somewhere else. Maybe Missy will open her establishment for school."

Was he serious? A tavern was no place for children, and putting them in a place of sin seemed like a bad omen. Sarah stared at the two letters in her hand. She saw Judge Talbert's signature, Gabriel's signature, and the bank manager's signature. It looked legit and ironclad. She didn't know how the law worked or how they bought or sold land, but to her, it didn't look good.

"Can we talk about this? Can we wait until Jacob's back in town to discuss some options?"

"I don't think your husband will want to talk with me. Let's say he had a deal go south in Cedar Grove. Sorry, honey, this town is mine, and no one tries to gain the high ground around here. I won't let them." He walked away before turning on his heel, "Tell that husband of yours you don't screw with Gabriel Grant."

"He's trying to pay you back," she shot back.

"I don't care," Gabriel said and kept walking, never looking back. Sarah glanced at the papers in her hand. She gathered them into a ball and tossed them at the building. The ball of paper thumped and rolled to a stop by her feet.

CHAPTER THIRTY-THREE

AFTER SENDING each child home, Sarah and Virginia walked through the doors of the postal building. Skip, the only postman in town, sat behind his desk with a visor over his head and a pencil in his ear. Did Gabriel have an endgame in mind for the purpose of closing the church and school? The only course of action she had left was to send word to Cedar Grove in hopes someone could get ahold of Jacob and deliver the news.

"What brings you in today, Mrs. Creek?" Skip said before spitting brown tobacco into a bowl to his left.

"Is your telegraph still working?"

"Just used it this afternoon. What do you need? Or should I say who you try'n to contact?"

"I need to get ahold of Jacob. He's in Cedar Grove on business."

He scratched his head, grabbed a piece of paper, and said, "Okay, you're sending this to Cedar Grove. What do you want to say?"

Sarah hadn't thought it through, but she knew Jacob needed to know of Gabriel closing the school.

FOR JACOB CREEK IN CEDAR GROVE. STOP
GABRIEL GRANT CLOSES SCHOOL. STOP.
GET HOME SOON TO CONFRONT GRANT. STOP
THE CHILDREN NEED A SCHOOL. STOP.

Sarah thought for a minute, "I think that'll be all."

Skip scribbled down her notes and counted the words. Sarah hoped it wouldn't cost too much. But this was the fastest form of communication. She had to get Jacob before he left Cedar Grove. She watched as he did some quick math.

"That'll be fifty cents."

Sarah pulled out a few coins and slid them over to him, "Thank you. Will you come down to Momma's house to fetch me when you hear a reply?"

He smiled, "Sure thing. Anything for Momma's family. Did Gabriel shut down your school? Shame, those kids deserve better."

She appreciated the sentiment and mouthed a quiet thank you before finding the door and heading down the street to Momma's Lodge.

"What are we going to do, Ma?"

Sarah knelt next to her daughter, "I don't know. Your father will figure something out when he gets home."

"I hope Pa gets home soon."

She rubbed Virginia's shoulders, "Me too, dear, me too."

They continued toward Momma's, and Sarah's thoughts ran like a raging river. Jacob paid the money, and he knew full well that Jacob is a man of his word and would pay the remaining amount to the bank. Yet something Gabriel said bothered her. Jacob's deal went south? How? Her husband wouldn't do business with someone he didn't find trustworthy. Sarah was glad Bill went along for the ride and felt confident the men could take care of each other. They needed another miracle. They needed this war to end.

By the time she arrived at Momma's, the miners had begun their process of cleaning up for dinner. Momma always had the best cooking this side of the Wyoming mountains. But the one cooking she missed the most was her mother's. She had made the best apple pie and fried chicken. Sarah alone carried the tradition of the famous Callihan fried chicken after her parents died from typhoid, just after Jacob married her.

Sarah wanted her mother. She missed those moments of serenity and peace her Mother gave, even when times got tough. And times were tough, no doubt about it, but she trusted Jacob to pull through and that God would give them the grace to carry on no matter what life gave them. That's why she went to Momma's Lodge. She needed to consult with someone about options and what to do with the children. It'd leave them without a proper education. How would they manage in life? To most in Purgatory, reading, writing, and arithmetic seemed archaic and didn't pay the bills. Most of the men needed their sons to as workers on the farm. Too much work to do and not enough money to pay farm or ranch hands to work.

Momma stood on the porch demanding each man kick off their boots, toss them aside, and go get cleaned up. Several men happened by Sarah and she couldn't help notice the stench of coal radiating off their bodies. Each man had a black face and black clothing; the only thing that appeared clean were the whites of their eyes. A few tipped their hat and said, "Ma'am," as they walked by to purge their work clothes and eat a hearty meal to satisfy the long day of work.

"My Dear," Momma said, "Come, come. I heard what happened. I can't believe he's pulling this crazy stunt."

Momma said it loud enough that several passersby stopped and shook their heads. No doubt the town heard about Gabriel Grant and his pulling rank in town…again.

"Hi, Momma."

"Come here, let me give you a hug. I'm sure you need it."

Momma embraced Sarah in a hug that caused her to break into tears. Sarah, for the first time, allowed herself to release the frustration and anger in a torrent of sobs. This wasn't fair. Nothing was fair. She needed Jacob.

As Sarah and Momma walked into the Lodge, she could hear the men taking their baths, laughing, and probably making a mess of Momma's house. One man's laugh reached her and sounded just like Jacob. How Sarah wished she could embrace Jacob and let his warmth soothe her weary soul and melt away everything.

As they walked into the dining area, she saw Moira sitting and drinking some of Momma's tea.

"Moira?" Sarah said.

"Hello, Sarah," she exhaled, "I need to apologize for my response earlier. I don't know what Gabriel will do when he finds out I'm helping you."

Sarah pulled up a chair and laid a hand over Moira's arm, "We're here for you. I sent word to my husband in Cedar Grove. I'm waiting for a reply. So, we could wait for a while."

Moira's head dropped, and she sobbed. Her shoulders shook with each wave and Sarah's heart broke as she noticed a torrent of tears streaming down her new friend's face.

Momma sat on the other side and squeezed the woman,

who pulled her head into the embrace and let it calm her mind. "There, there, Child. Us women, we stick together and know that God's always on your side."

She sat up and wiped her eyes. She sniffled a thank you and explained why the fear of talking this over with Gabriel consumed her waking moments. Moira had known about Gabriel's plans for some time, but never had the nerve to speak up or say it was wrong.

Sarah felt for the woman. It's a hard life to live with a man who respected no one but himself. If anyone knew that it was Momma. Leonard had beaten and belittled both Momma and Jacob. The two didn't get a reprieve from his madness until Moira's husband put a bullet in him. Not that he deserved to die.

"How can we help?"

Moira looked up at Sarah, "I need you to pray for me. I need know someone's got my back; that everything will be okay." She smoothed her dress, "I just hate that my husband is treating your family like… like this. It's not right, and he needs to understand that you're all good people. Your husband may be a little stubborn, but that's what angers Gabriel. He feels Jacob is someone to beat, someone who needs a lesson taught, just like his old man."

Sarah never thought of it that way before now. In her mind, Jacob stood for his family, word, and reputation and to have someone belittle him because of that seemed incredulous, but he no doubt was stubborn as a mule. If anyone understood that, it was Sarah.

"We can do that."

Moira mouthed thank you, again, "I have no friends and no one to talk to."

Momma stood and grabbed a plate of scones. "You do

now, Dear. Here have a scone with that tea, it'll make you feel better."

All three women laughed.

It felt good to laugh and Sarah couldn't remember the last time she had had a chuckle, though the seriousness of what Gabriel was doing loomed like a bear's encroaching shadow. She needed Moira's help, no matter how good it felt to laugh.

"Moira, we need your help. The children of Purgatory need a good solid education to succeed in this life. Without that, they'll grow up illiterate and never achieve a higher status in life. I understand that most work on their father's farms, but having solid reading, writing, and arithmetic skills will help them further their life."

She knew Moira understood, but standing up to Gabriel would be a challenge.

"Have you heard from Jacob yet?"

Sarah shook her head. It'd been six hours since sending the telegram. She hoped he'd hear soon and reply. "I don't think we have the luxury of waiting on my husband. He's in Cedar Grove and I don't know when he'll be heading back this way. By that time, the school will be closed and who knows what Gabriel will do next."

"I don't want to cross my husband. If he finds out I've talked with you and Momma regarding the school..." Moira let her voice trail.

"Then play it as you normally would when you've disagreed with something he's done," Momma said.

Sarah pleaded again, "Think of Felix and the other children. Gabriel loves education and I know he prides himself. Jacob said the library was impressive." She placed her hand on Moira's arm again, "Please, if you don't do this for me or the children, do this for Felix. He deserves just as much a good education as the next child in town."

Moira nodded her head, "All right, I'll see what I can do. I make no promises. Gabriel is a man of his own doing and he needs no one to tell him what to do after he decides." She stood and straightened her dress. "Give me some time to convince him."

"Okay. But I don't feel we have much time, Moira."

The road ahead would be long and tough, but with God's grace they'd make it through. Now they could only wait to hear from Jacob on what was happening in Cedar Grove.

CHAPTER THIRTY-FOUR

CLYDE AND Jacob left Cedar Grove after speaking with the Marshal. Tan arrived from Cheyenne a few days before Jacob with written testimonies but little evidence. Jacob's main concern rested on what Gabriel had done in Purgatory. Evidence of the barn burning and harassment seemed to be the most current cause for someone to raise an eyebrow in Gabriel's direction, but if they could nail Leonard's death, they'd have him.

Tan mentioned Gabriel had a body count in his path, but not a single corroborating piece of evidence could prove that the tycoon ever pulled a trigger to enact his will on the citizens of Wyoming. Gabriel hired out the dirty jobs, with the law backing everything he did. Jacob worried the Marshal wouldn't be able to put together a case for a federal judge to even consider.

Now the threat of losing the school and the church bothered him. Gabriel hadn't heeded Jacob's warning of leaving Sarah alone. When word of a telegram reached him, Jacob mounted and was ready to leave town. He read the note and sent a quick reply.

I'M ON MY WAY HOME. STOP.
I HAVE THE MARSHAL AND LAWYER WITH ME. STOP.
BE HOME SOON. I LOVE YOU. STOP

Jacob breathed deep. This would be a long ride home and he had a few words for Gabriel Grant. Not that he'd do anything rash, he'd just let Gabriel know you don't mess with someone's wife. He held the reins a little tighter and clenched his teeth. Gabriel Grant needed to pay for what he'd done.

Maybe, for once, something could go his way, and maybe having the Marshal was the answer God had all along. The Creeks had lived under Gabriel Grant's thumb far too long and it was high time he answered for the pain and suffering he'd caused the people of Purgatory. Momma. She didn't deserve to have her husband taken by a lead bullet, but the tycoon didn't care and killed Jacob's father anyway.

Last night, Jacob had learned what little evidence the U. S. Marshal's office had against Grant and thought through the previous night's conversation.

"Can this evidence get him off my back?" Jacob asked after several minutes of listening to Clyde and Tan talk.

Tan spit into a nearby bucket, "I'd suspect, if we can gain a little more evidence in Purgatory, we can put him on trial and wipe your debt clean. How much do ya owe the man?"

Jacob said, "I owe the bank two-thousand. Gabriel owns it and is using my debt to threaten me and my family."

"Banks don't matter to this case. You'll still owe that amount. But knowing that Gabriel could be behind bars should give you the relief you need."

Jacob nodded, then ran his fingers behind his neck to

smooth out the tension. "What can I do to help?" He wanted rid of Gabriel and wanted to be free. Oh, how sweet that could feel. No more worrying what he'd do to Jacob if payment didn't surface soon. Trusting in the Lord and Tan seemed the only course of action he could imagine. He'd rather play odds with the banker than Gabriel Grant.

"I need you to stay out of our way. We'll be working with the sheriff and the local judge. I understand that Judge Talbert might put up a challenge?"

"Yeah. He kinda helps Gabriel run the town."

Clyde piped in, "That could pose a problem." He turned to Tan, "Any chance of getting a Federal Judge from Cheyenne to sign off on a warrant to search Gabriel's home?"

"If we're leaving tomorrow, I don't see how we'll have time to wait, being the fact..." turning to Jacob, he added, "you need to be back to help your wife with the schoolhouse issue?"

Jacob nodded a quick yes.

"Okay. We'll leave at first light and I'll deal with the Judge. If he doesn't like it, that's too bad, I'll pull rank. I work for the United States government. I answer to the Governor of Wyoming. Sheriff Ballot won't be an issue; he has no choice but to comply with me."

"Fair enough," Clyde said and stood.

The three men shook hands, then left the following morning.

Jacob stared at the two men ahead of him. Grateful for the entourage, he wished there was another way to gain the high ground against everything they'd been through. First the nagging and threats, then the man burned down the barn and now, he was shutting down the schoolhouse. The Sheriff might know what Gabriel was up to, but if not, how would he keep the town from rising, demanding a new school house?

And that's the other thing that bothered him. They used city taxes to fund the building, the men had put their hands to work, and they had built a beautiful one-room building next to the church. He remembered that day; even his father had helped put up a few boards in his sober moments.

Tan slowed his horse as the sun dipped behind the hills. "Guess we'll stop here for the night."

Clyde and Jacob agreed and dismounted. They lit a fire, ate, and pulled out their blankets for a cold night's sleep, though Jacob wasn't sure if he'd sleep at all. His thoughts made their way to Sarah and Virginia. His heart broke because of his absence while they sat frustrated and worried. He should've been there, but also understood this trip had to happen. Without the knowledge he now possessed, Gabriel could run the town of Purgatory into the ground for his own financial gain. Heck, he owned most of the town.

They'd be in Purgatory midday tomorrow and he couldn't wait to see Sarah. All he wanted to do was kiss her and tell her everything would be okay. God's got this and they needed to continue having faith that all things would work out. Yet, it seemed as if God was silent on this matter, and Jacob wished he could hear a simple answer to give him solace.

Jacob leaned his head back on the saddle and pulled the blanket up to his neck. He gazed at the stars twinkling above and smiled at the night's stillness. He had the law, and that gave him peace. The pull of exhaustion pulled him into sleep's embrace.

Before sleep enveloped him, one thought ran through his mind. *Don't worry, Sarah. I'm coming and we'll get through this together.*

CHAPTER THIRTY-FIVE

OIRA SAT at a small table in their staff kitchen. The walls and the floor were tiled and unimpressive compared to the rest of the home. In fact, it lacked the lavishness of carved wood and silver accents the main dining room bore. She thumbed a cup of coffee and allowed thoughts from her conversation with Sarah and Momma to consume her. Truth to tell, agreeing to speak on their behalf to Gabe brought an uncomfortable horror to her mind. There's no way he'd ever consider this request to keep the schoolhouse and build his hotel elsewhere.

Holding her breath, her heart raced deep inside her chest. At one point, it seemed as if it might pop right out and land on the table, beating what little life it had left. Moira puffed her cheeks, releasing held breath, then wiped her sweaty palms on her black skirt.

A staff member walked into the room and stopped short at the sight of Moira sitting in the kitchen. "I'm so sorry, Ma'am. I'll leave you alone," she said, looking down and away.

Moira glanced up, "No. Katy, that's okay. I'm just think-ing. Have you seen Gabriel this morning?"

The woman thought for a moment, "I think I saw him heading toward his study. Except I think he shut the curtains. I'm not sure he wants interruptions." She hesitated, "I'm sorry, I shouldn't have added that last part."

Moira smiled at Katy, "Don't worry about it. I'll go see for myself."

"Anything else I can get for you, Mrs. Grant?"

"No, thank you," she pulled back from the table, then headed down the long mahogany-lined hallway. She watched the red carpeting as she meandered down the hall. A few housemaids busied themselves, shining the silver in the dining room. Grateful for their staff, Moira always felt they were more like family than the help. Gabe never saw them as family and wanted them to clear the family area of their presence during the holiday season. He preferred them seen and not heard. And they stayed away from him in the staffing quarters unless called for, but Moira knew they respected her and she liked that about their staff.

Moira noticed the study's curtain was closed, but saw the light coming from underneath. The door was open. She breathed a sigh of relief. If the door had been closed, she'd wait until Gabe finished whatever business he attended to before confronting him. She prayed a silent prayer; not that she was religious, but figured if God existed, he'd need to give her strength to help him see from the children's perspective.

She pushed through the curtain and watched her husband write something down in an open journal. Moira didn't know if she should cough, say something, or just wait. Either he didn't notice, or he didn't care. He kept writing. She placed one foot in front of the other and a board creaked.

Gabe looked up and smiled, "Hello, my Dear."

"Hi," she dropped her shoulders. He seemed to be in a good mood. Pulling back the green chair, she sat.

"Give me one second," he finished writing his thoughts, closed the book, and pushed it aside. After he replaced the pen into its holder, he crossed his fingers and leaned forward. For the longest moment, he didn't say a word; he looked at her and grinned. She stiffened as fear crept back into her soul. "What do I owe this privilege of you visiting my study?"

Moira avoided contact with Gabe while he worked. This room served as his private office, devoid of all familial life. He kept it that way unless either she or Felix needed his attention. Today was one of those moments and she hoped to God he'd listen. After all, this was business, and this room was where that happened.

She glanced out the door, contemplating if she should abandon this fool's errand before turning back and smiling. He was in this study and that set her at ease. Gabe had another study off their main bedroom where he could work, and the smoking room where most of his financial deals happened; it sat just down the hall from the main study to the right. That room remained a men's only room. Moira knew better than to enter it while he smoked with clients or when Judge Talbert came over. She avoided it on most cases. That's his room.

Just say it and get the words out. That's what she kept telling herself, anyway. "I heard about you closing the schoolhouse." Phew, it's now in the open.

He didn't flinch or move, "I see...your point?"

"Do you have plans in place to build a new schoolhouse elsewhere in town? And what about the church?"

Gabriel sat back and popped open the cigar case. He

fetched one out, snipped off the end, then lit it on the nearby candle. "It's all taken care of, no need to worry. The children will meet in the courthouse. There's plenty of room and we seldom have any cases needing to use the large space. The Judge signed off on it a few days ago."

"So you're not closing the school?"

"Don't be an absurd. I'd never put our children at risk just to get even with the preacher," he smiled, "I love revenge."

Seriously? Revenge? What did the Reverend do to Gabe other than taking his time to pay? He'd done better at paying back the thousand dollars than his father did. Yet, she feared Gabe would toss her out along with the garbage just by asking him to reconsider. The courthouse was no place for children.

"Gabriel, you can't be serious. The courthouse is a terrible idea. Now, I want you to listen before you react, this is just an idea." She braced herself. "Why not move your hotel to the vacant lot?"

A fire lit through his eyes and Moira knew she had stepped over the line. He stood and a low growl escaped his clenched teeth. He flattened his palms on the desk and in a low voice said, "Woman, you better watch your tongue. I have half a mind to slap you where you sit."

She swallowed hard and shrank inside. All that courage washed like a sandcastle being knocked over by the tide with that one statement. All she wanted to do was run away and hide in her upstairs sewing room. This would not end well.

She watched as Gabriel moved around the desk toward her. He grabbed her by the shoulders and tightened his grip.

"I will not be moving the school from the courthouse. It is where it is and that is final. Do I make myself absolutely clear?"

Moira nodded her head and fought the tears. She tried to

find another course of action before her strength to fight waned, "But what about Felix and the children? I feel that… I mean, hasn't this gone far enough between you and the Reverend?"

That's when the slap happened. The back of his hand whipped hard and stung against her smooth skin. She cradled her face and knew it reddened.

"Gabriel, please…"

He slapped her again, knocking her to the ground. The chair fell on top of her legs. A torrent of tears flooded her eyes, and she tasted blood from her cut lip. Moira pulled herself across the carpeting, trying to escape another blow she'd undoubtedly receive. A housemaid walked by and saw her lying on the floor. Moria pleaded with her eyes and the maid swiftly ran away. She couldn't blame them, they'd endured the wrath of Gabriel Grant before and knew better than get involved in their marriage.

"Gabriel, please…"

He bent down and sat her up. "I'm sorry, but you needed a lesson taught. I've decided. The schoolhouse is mine and I will take the church. I'm already in talks with the Judge about the land. Cross me again, woman, or question my motives again…because when I'm through with you, you'll wish for a slap. Now, get to whatever it is you do and leave me alone." He stood and grabbed the cigar that had fallen on his desk. He puffed a few drags and exhaled, "And, it has not gone on long enough. He took out a loan from the bank, I bought the bank, now he owes me more." He rounded the desk and sat, "Now, leave."

Moira stood and felt the swollen and cut lip, then held her breath before leaving his study. Each step to their bedroom sent waves of pain through her head. She sat at her vanity and looked at the bruising that crawled its way up to her eye. Her lips and cheek were puffed and a large cut split her lip. She pulled off her skirt and blouse and let them gather on the floor, then Moira crumpled onto the bed and sobbed.

<hr>

CHAPTER THIRTY-SIX

<hr>

JACOB WALKED through the door of his home to find Sarah and Virginia peeling potatoes at the table. Two long weeks apart and Jacob's heart rejoiced to be home. The journey ahead was long and with two men for support, no doubt they'd give a final blow to Gabriel Grant for the murder of Leonard Creek and harassment of the Creek family.

He watched them for a while before speaking, "I guess we're having fried potatoes and chicken for dinner?"

Sarah turned around at the sound of his voice and smiled. Virginia, already up, crossed the room and threw her arms around him. He held on tight.

"Daddy! I can't breathe."

"Oh, sorry. I missed you that much," he released her and embraced his wife before kissing her deeply, "And I missed you that much."

"Ewww," Virginia said, and they laughed.

"I wasn't expecting you for another day."

Jacob hadn't either, but after learning about the school

and Gabriel's insistence of closing it down, he rode hard to get back to comfort Sarah. She didn't need to go through this alone and he had every intention of speaking with the Sheriff. Course, he didn't plan on doing that alone; Marshal Bennington and Clyde would be with him.

"I had to get home. I'm so sorry I wasn't here."

"Jacob, how do we stop him?"

"The Marshal has a plan."

He saw surprise glint in her eyes, "A Marshal? What's going on, Jacob?"

"After I contacted Clyde out in Cedar Grove, he learned of a U. S. Marshal named Tan Bennington, from Cheyenne, who's been investigating Gabriel Grant for several crimes. Sarah, he's broken so many laws and the problem is, he has Judge Talbert in his back pocket to clear him of any wrong doings. It's time for Sam Ballot to do his job."

"When are you speaking with the Sheriff?"

"I'm planning on meeting up with him on Monday regarding the church. At least that building is still usable." They could use the church as a schoolhouse and turn it back into a church for Sunday service. That's how things used to be before the town grew to needing a schoolhouse. The problem, Jacob feared, was that the church and the school shared the same plot of land. As of now, it seemed as if Gabriel was taking the land to build his hotel.

"Jacob, he said he's going after the church too."

Jacob gritted his teeth, "Did he say to vacate as he did the school?"

"No. He told me I had to find a new place for the school."

"Okay, we'll worry about the church later. The school comes first."

Sarah breathed a sigh of relief and told Jacob about her

meeting with Moira. The hope was that Moira could talk her husband into changing his mind about letting the children use the schoolhouse instead of moving it to the courthouse. Though she'd put her faith in Moria, Gabriel wouldn't budge and everyone knew that. She was the last effort they had by using conventional means and Jacob figured that now, with a lawyer and the law in town, Gabriel had to comply.

After finishing up with Sarah, he went outside to talk with Bill regarding the use of their ranch for a schoolhouse, if the church wouldn't work and if it came to Gabriel taking the church. They agreed it'd take work, and they'd need the townsfolk to help pay for its construction, but with a few hands and the congregation, they'd be able to build a new place.

What Jacob needed was sleep. He never slept well away from home. Clyde was nice enough to open his ranch house, but taking the time to rest before tomorrow would prove worthwhile. He had one problem in the name of Joe Packard. No one had seen or heard from Joe since he abandoned them and had his little pow-wow with Clyde.

It wouldn't take long for Gabriel to learn of the trick Clyde played on Joe, and Jacob feared the worst for the man. You don't mess with Gabriel Grant. You don't play games and if you do, you end up dead. Jacob hoped for Joe that wasn't the case. Maybe Joe was staying away and for good reason. The moment he stepped foot in Purgatory, Gabriel would come looking for him.

Jacob also feared having Clyde Heller in town. It might incite the violence he was trying to avoid. He considered himself a peaceful man and did everything he could to pursue peace—however, Jacob feared his actions resembled that of his late father. Quick to anger and ready to shoot off his mouth before thinking it through. Not that it was always bad to be quick, but sometimes using your head to process your ideas before getting yourself into trouble went further to release tension.

After coming back in from talking with Bill, Jacob headed for the bedroom for much needed sleep. Sarah followed him and helped him get undressed. She pulled the covers over his chest after he laid down. "I'm so glad you're home."

He smiled, "Me, too. I'm sorry to be long and that you had to deal with this by yourself. I will say, good thinking using the telegram to get your message out."

Her eyes brightened, "You got my message. I didn't think you received it and thought I missed you."

Jacob placed his hand on hers, "I responded as we were heading out of town. You didn't get it?"

"No, but I never checked back in with Skip at the Post Office. Now, get some sleep and I'll have fried chicken ready when you get up."

CHAPTER THIRTY-SEVEN

GOLDEN SUNLIGHT filtered through the windows of the tiny community church in Purgatory. The place filled, and soon the sound of the small congregation singing hymns of doctrine filled the church. It had been weeks since preaching a sermon or standing at the pulpit, and for the first time a few months, Jacob felt a veneer of peace.

Sarah sat in the front with Virginia, and his heart melted knowing he had a strong wife and a beautiful daughter. Without their strength, he never could have made the journey to Cedar Grove to seek help.

While everyone sang, he looked around for Clyde. The small man seemed interested in hearing Jacob preach, but had decided not to attend.

The hymn ended and Jacob stood, "I'd like to open to the Gospel of Saint Mark in the eighth chapter, the thirty-fourth verse. 'Whosoever will come after me, let him deny himself, and take up his cross, and follow me. For whosoever will save his life shall lose it; but whosoever shall lose his life for my sake and the gospel's, the same shall save it. For what shall it profit a man, if he shall gain the whole world, and lose his own soul? Or what shall a man give in exchange for his soul?"

It sure seemed to be a good fitting passage after everything they'd been through. Gabriel's antics seemed to know no bounds, and the man tried to get everything his way. It was always Gabriel's way. Well, Clyde, Tan, and Jacob had other news for him—no more and it stopped, now.

"My friends, never allow yourselves to go to the place where you reject God or get angry at him. If you try to save those around you from the eternal damnation of hell, you are doing your job as good Christians. However, if you try to win the world over by your own achievements and desires, you can lose your own soul. God does not want us to die and give our soul to the devil, no He wants us to live our life for the sake of the Gospel.

"It's about showing love and respect. It's about not allowing anger to seep into your soul and drive your mind mad with false hope and unconnected ideas about faith. When we do that, we lose. Vengeance is the Lord's and if we take the reins of our life, without giving them over to God, we lose.

"But imagine with me. Someone comes along and kills a chicken on your property. Do you go after them for their grievances? Or do you talk it over and come to an agreement? In most cases it's the latter, but when they don't listen or refuse to own up to their sin, you have every right to seek outside help and guidance.

"This is where God comes in. We must implicitly trust that God has our back, and he knows the outcome of our choices before we act. Therefore, Jesus told us to pick up our cross and follow him. No matter what life throws your way, we can know that God can save our soul because we trusted that he would meet our needs and keep us safe. He has our best interests at heart. Even if the road is tough and you lose everything, know that God is still on the throne and he will never fail, reject, or abandon you. Great is his faithfulness."

"Amen, Reverend."

The back door to the little church opened, letting a swirl of dust move like a small tornado up the aisle. The sound of heavy, black boots echoed in the tiny room. He was wearing his usual tailored business suit and, today, a black, wide-brimmed hat. His jaw was set with a wide smile

"Howdy Reverend… folks," Gabriel Grant smiled, "I didn't interrupt yer Sunday service did I? Oh shoot, looks like I did." He cackled and took off his hat, "I'm sorry about the intrusion. Ya'll can head back to your Bible soon enough; have something to say to the Preacher. My bad, Reverend Creek."

Jacob stared Gabriel down, "Please Gabriel, sit–join us, I'm starting up my sermon."

His cackling laugh rippled through the air and gave Jacob gooseflesh, "No...no, no, no. I have to say I'm buying this piece of land ya'll are sitting on–so this here is my rightful property, and I'd appreciate it if you kind folks would move locations by Sunday, this time, next week."

It took every ounce of self-control to keep his calm. "Mr. Grant," Jacob started, "this here property belongs to the good people of Purgatory, as does the schoolhouse. You can't possibly expect us to pick up and move?" Jacob closed his Bible, "And besides, there has been no notice of eviction given." He intended to take control of the entire piece of land, claiming both the church and schoolhouse. The audacity and now his congregation would be affected by the feud Leonard started.

A few nods and vocal approval rippled through the congregation.

Gabriel Grant let out another loud laugh, "You don't get it Preacher, this is your notice of eviction." He turned to the congregation, "Now I've been more than fair, have I not? I'm giving you seven days to vacate." Turning back to Jacob, he added, "I'm a very reasonable man, Reverend."

Gabriel placed his hat back on his head. "Now if you kind folks will excuse me, I have some official town business to attend to." He pulled a piece of paper from his jacket and tossed it to the ground, then left.

Gabriel was done.

What was there to say? It wasn't like Gabriel Grant would allow anything other than what he stated to have a rebuttal. They would have to move out. No question about it. There was no other building in the town of Purgatory to house both a school and a church. Guess his conversation with Bill might need another visit. He hoped Tan and Clyde had a plan.

"Reverend," came the voice of John, a local rancher. "I just sold three cows to the butcher this last week. I can give my proceeds to the cause of building a new church if that'll help."

Jacob looked the faithful attendee over, searching his heart and intentions. The man was a good and upstanding individual in the community. He knew that John would stand by his side no matter the cost, even if that cost would be to give his own money to help the greater good of those in Purgatory. Nothing would give Jacob greater pleasure than to take the man's money, but principle was principle. How could he justify moving locations when even the Sheriff didn't bother showing up to help give a notice of eviction?

"John, I appreciate the kind offer. However, this is our church. I will not stand by and allow this man to run us out of the Lord's house," Jacob sighed. "Folks, let's go back to the Bible and seek its answers."

Jacob stood outside the front doors of the church following his sermon. Many shook his hand; while others complimented him on the fine sermon he deliberated that morning despite being interrupted. He glanced up at the siding. The building needed a new paint job, and Jacob had wanted to get that accomplished in the next several weeks, but now that may not happen. Oh well, he must trust the Lord knew what he was doing.

One member took his hand. Missy. She was a good friend and strong as she was beautiful.

"Reverend, good sermon today," she said in a soft tone, "If you need anything, anything at all, you come on over to my establishment. I'll see if some local folks can help get us a new church building."

Her smile could energize the sun for a million years. "Thank you, Missy," Jacob placed his other hand on top of hers, "I'll keep that in mind." He let go of her hand and watched her leave.

"Now if you're not careful Mister… I'd think you're eyeing up another woman."

Jacob turned to his wife and smiled, "Not in a million years. Missy was complimenting me on my sermon and offered to help raise funds for a new building." He leaned forward and kissed his wife, "Now, what do ya say we get on that wagon over there and make some of that fried chicken of yours."

"Didn't I fix that for you yesterday?"

Jacob laughed and said, "Yup. And I want more."

Jacob picked Virginia up and set her in the back of the

wagon. In a single bound, he was up with reins in hand for the ride back to Creek Ranch. He snapped the leather straps against the backs of the two horses and the wagon jolted forward.

CHAPTER THIRTY-EIGHT

S ARAH TUCKED Virginia under the warm quilt that wrapped around her mattress, then grabbed the lantern and walked out of her room.

"Ma, what will happen to the schoolhouse?"

Sarah turned around, "I don't know, dear. God has it under control. Now go to sleep, this isn't the time to be jabbering, it's time to rest."

"Yes, ma'am," she replied.

Jacob listened to the exchange. He loved his family, and was grateful that Momma had given them what was left of his father's ranch. How much of it mattered if he didn't have a church, or Sarah a schoolhouse, to call their own? They had this land and the cattle. They had each other, and they had Momma.

Sarah climbed down from the loft and grabbed a blanket. Jacob had built the loft for storage, but once Virginia saw it completed, she had asked for it as a room. She was not like Sarah. Her personality was that of a ranch girl. She loved the animals. Every morning, Virginia would make her way to the barn and help Jacob and Bill feed the animals. Her love for life filled the darkest days with hope and rays of light. They were in darker days.

"Is she sleeping?" Jacob asked.

Sarah placed the lantern down on the dresser. "Yes, she's all tucked in, not sleeping of course. She's like her father, always thinking about tomorrow."

"That's my girl."

"She certainty is," she pulled the ribbon out of her hair and combed out the day's snarls. "Jacob, what are we supposed to do with Gabriel Grant? He can't force us out of our church and school, can he?" she asked, sitting on the bed next to her husband.

Jacob blew out a puff of air, "I don't know what to do. The Lord is silent on the matter and I wish I could find the answers." He jogged his fingers through her thick hair, then kissed her neck. "Maybe I should go talk with the Sheriff tomorrow, see if he knew what Gabriel was planning."

"Honey, is that such a good idea? Gabriel and Sam Ballot are close friends. I'd rightfully assume he sanctioned Gabriel's appearance today."

"I pray to God he didn't. I'm a man of peace, Sarah, and I want no bloodshed over this thing. I know Gabriel's not afraid of using brute force, but who knows which of my flock he'll go after first. He won't stop until we concede defeat." He took hold of Sarah's hand and kissed the back, "I'll see the Sheriff tomorrow and see if we can take care of this peacefully. We'll find a way. Besides, I have Clyde and the Marshal to back me on this one. They've been invaluable and have given me much-needed peace. They might be the answer I've been looking for."

Sarah pulled the blanket onto the bed and crawled in next

to Jacob. She nuzzled up to his back and tucked her feet behind his knees. He felt her hot breath tickle the back of his neck and realized how much he had missed her the last several weeks. Jacob had slept several nights in his chair. He had spent many nights praying that God would give them an answer. The problem: it seemed as if God remained silent and left Jacob to his thoughts.

In the morning he'd ride out to Purgatory and meet with Tan Bennington and Clyde to come up with a plan. He hoped the Marshal knew how to confront Judge Talbert. That man would be the linchpin in the whole thing. If he sided with Gabriel, Tan would need to get reinforcements and a federal judge to issue a warrant for Gabriel's arrest. Jacob wasn't about to acquiesce and move on. He had to fight. It was a matter of principle. At least that's what he told himself. This fight didn't belong to him alone. He fought for the town of Purgatory. Jacob needed to fight and needed to win.

"Jacob, remember that you have to trust God for his peace and his guidance. You said as much this morning."

"I know. I'm struggling and I need direction. First the school. Now the church. We'll get through this and I know God has our back." He turned over. "I know I have to trust God and know he's fighting this battle for me. Just wish the battle were over."

Sarah kissed his lips and caressed his cheek, "It will be and soon, I hope." She paused a beat, "Jacob, what if we lose everything on account of Gabriel's unrelenting disdain of you and our family? I know I just said we have to trust God, that's what my heart tells me, but my mind also worries about the future."

He tucked his arm under his wife's head, pulling her close. "I've thought a lot about that. This has to work. The Marshal says he has evidence that could arrest Gabriel Grant. This needs to happen." They lay in silence for several minutes before he continued, "I'm meeting with the Marshal and the Sheriff tomorrow. We'll see if we can resolve this within the letter of the law.

CHAPTER THIRTY-NINE

JOE PACKARD rummaged through his store. Gabriel could trace back Joe's decision to swindle Clyde Heller from his land. What he didn't count on was the fact that Clyde bested him and still took the money for a piece of land as worthless as fool's gold. Joe couldn't find the courage to speak with Gabriel, but what good would it do? Gabriel had already noticed Clyde's deception. And that's why he stayed away from Purgatory and Gabriel. He didn't arrive until late in the day after dusk.

He tossed aside a few crates that held some cans and a few sacks of four. The stupid Mercantile caused him more grief and didn't pay his bills. He wouldn't have come back to the store if it weren't for the deed to the property, but he knew full well he couldn't stay and that Gabriel would come looking. Before one of his many meetings with Gabriel, he had over-heard him talking with someone that the previous preacher was left in the mines before the collapse. The whole thing had been orchestrated by Gabriel's men to appear as an accident. He never told Gabriel.

Joe pulled out a piece of paper and jotted the story down. He'd take it to the church and speak with Jacob. It was the least he could do for betraying his friend and siding with the enemy. He looked behind the counter and looked through the small desk in the back of the store, where he put together his order to a distribution company in Cheyenne.

A few pencils had spilled onto the floor and he noticed a small piece of paper sticking out from a drawer. He yanked it open and found the deed to the Mercantile. Maybe Jacob could find some use for the place. Perhaps even the school. Then he'd pack up his family and they'd leave town at first light.

Joe stuffed the paper into his vest, locked the door, then headed to the other side of town where his house sat. But before arriving home, he stopped at the church and left the note-wrapped deed for Jacob. Back on the horse, he strode through town. A few casual drinkers milled around Missy's Tavern. How he needed some whiskey.

Milton sat outside smoking and tipped his hat, "How'ya do'n, Joe?"

Joe waved and kept trotting along. He passed by Momma's and hoped she didn't see him milling around town. He'd be home in an hour. As soon as he cleared the town, he kicked his horse hard and rode fast. When he arrived home, the place sat dark. Only a single lantern illuminated the main window. He couldn't see his wife Jenny anywhere through the dark glass. He dismounted and pulled the saddle off the horse. The horse spooked at something and Joe calmed her down, "Easy, girl." After securing her in the barn, he placed he saddle on a nearby fence. He'd have to remember to take care of that in the morning.

He had to talk with Jacob before leaving town. The nice

thing was that they'd ride through town and past the church. It wouldn't take but a moment to speak his mind, tell the Reverend about the deed he'd left, and get out of Dodge. Course, Joe had no clue where they'd go. His first thought would be Cheyenne, but would Gabriel look for them there? It was a large enough city, and he could hide out there before deciding to head down into Arizona.

He tossed his saddle bag around his shoulders and made his way across the yard to the house. The lantern, still lit, told him Jenny hadn't gone to bed. Good. Maybe he could talk about his stupidity and beg for her forgiveness. He placed his hand on the door latch and noticed it already open. Funny, she never left the door unlatched while home alone.

He pushed the door and it opened with a creak. He placed his hand on the gun and slid it out of the leather fixed to his hip. "Jenny?"

No answer.

He pressed his way into his home and found it empty. No one home, just a lit lantern. That's odd, why would she leave the house unattended with a lit fire? He placed his hand near the kitchen stove. It felt warm to the touch. He cocked his gun, "Jenny?"

The door behind him closed with a thud, and Joe spun round to see Gabriel Grant standing there with Jenny in his arms and a gun to her belly. "I'd advise you to drop your weapon, Mr. Packard or your wife'll have less of a beautiful figure."

The gun clattered on the wooden floor as two men approached behind him and took hold of his arms. He help-lessly watched as Gabriel tied Jenny to a chair and gagged her mouth. A tear slid down her cheek as she fought the restraints. She screamed against the gag but he couldn't make out her words. Gabriel approached him, and with a quick motion, the tycoon's fist collided with Joe's ribs. Splitting pain shot through his chest and he collapsed to his knees, trying to breathe against the pain.

Gabriel circled, then pulled up a chair. He spun it around and rested his arms on its back, "Now, Mr. Packard. Do you know why we're having this little impromptu meeting?"

Another fist connected with his jaw; this time, by one of Gabriel's cronies. "You tell me," he said, then spit blood. "Call off your dogs." A second blow to his face. This time, he felt his jaw bite down on his lower lip. He spit more blood.

"Enough," Gabriel said, "I hear you found me some new land?"

"I can explain," Joe said, wiping his mouth.

"Clyde Heller paid me a visit. Remember him? Course you do. He said you tried to swindle his land out from underneath him. Course, I don't blame you, I told you to. But wouldn't you know, to my surprise, he tricked you into buying a worthless piece of crap? There's no water nearby. There's no town nearby. What am I to do with land of no monetary gain? I can't even build on it, let alone profit from any project."

"I didn't know," he lied.

"You didn't know, or you were too drunk and wanting your way with the ladies to even care?"

That last comment received a raised eyebrow from Jenny. He pleaded an apology with his eyes, "I swear, he tricked me into buying the land. I did what we agreed upon."

Gabriel stood and tossed the chair. "NO! I know you're planning on leaving town. I know you've contacted Clyde to work out some kind of deal. I know about the U. S. Marshal and the investigation into my enterprise." He stopped listing off things and crouched near him. "Joe, Joe, Joe. Let's see how your change of heart fixed this little mess of yours. In fact, I will give you a chance to repent, as the Preacher would say, and be baptized by fire."

Gabriel snapped his fingers and the back door flew open. Joe watched as they dragged in a bloodied and tied-up Clyde Heller. They tossed him on the ground and he slowly pulled up to his knees.

"Wooo hooo, isn't this fun? We have ourselves a little reunion. Let's have a party." Gabriel pulled a gun from his holster and tossed it to Joe, "We're gonna play a little game."

Joe stared wide-eyed at the gun. What did Gabriel have planned? He heard his wife scream behind her gag again and he stole a glance. "What game?"

Gabriel grinned, "I want you to shoot me. If you kill me, you're free. If you miss, you're dead. Simple game, isn't it?"

"What? You're insane."

"Let me put it this way. You've been busy trying to convince everyone you've reconsidered and desire to be free from owing me any more than you already do—so if you kill me, you're free." He spread open his vest and puffed his chest to make a larger target. "Give it a shot." Gabriel stabbed his heart, "Shoot me, Joe, and save your wife and your life."

Joe bent over and picked up the .45, cocked it, and aimed at Gabriel's chest. One shot, it's all he needed. One shot and he'd be free. One shot and he'd never have to worry about anything ever again.

"Don't miss," Gabriel cackled.

Joe stared at Gabriel's open chest and tightened the grip on the trigger. He heard Jenny screaming and heard Clyde's heavy breath behind his own gag. He looked at Clyde's wide eyes then turned to his wife as a tear slipped down his own face. "I'm sorry."

She nodded through her own sobs and mumbled something. He guessed she said it was okay. He did what he thought best for them both. A chance to be free and live the life they deserved.

Joe lowered the gun and the tension in his chest tightened. He spun on a heel, aimed the gun, and fired.

For a moment, no one moved except the smoke rising out of the gun. No one made a sound, and the air sucked from the tiny house. Joe watched as Clyde's body slumped over before toppling to the ground. A single bullet hole, where Clyde's left eye used to be, leaked a river of blood.

Joe dropped the gun and fell to his knees. God forgive him for killing Clyde.

Gabriel bent over, picked up his gun, and holstered it. He secured his hat and walked through the door before stopping, "Thank you." He looked at Clyde's limp form, "Well. That was interesting." He snapped his fingers and proceeded out the door.

The two men closed rank on Joe and his wife.

"Make sure you leave your guns," Gabriel said.

"You promised..."

Two shots.

Gabriel mounted his horse, "I said, if you killed me, you'd be free. You missed," but he only spoke that to himself.

The two men walk out of the house and mounted their own horses. One man pulled a torch from a nearby fire and tossed it onto the house.

THE RECKONING

To me belongeth *vengeance* and *recompence*; their foot shall slide in due time: for the day of *their calamity* is at hand, and the things that shall come upon them make haste.

— *GOD, TO MOSES*

CHAPTER FORTY

BY THE TIME Jacob arrived in town, the early morning rain had saturated the ground. It had been a dry summer for Wyoming. Everything in Purgatory relied on the crops the farmers brought in, besides the local ranchers and miners. If the drought had continued on much longer, several people would leave the town and head out to find better business. So the morning rain was good for everyone. It meant that business would increase. He prayed that the rains would continue.

The clouds hovered in the sky, creating an otherworldly look to an already gray and weathered town. Jacob rolled into Purgatory in his wagon. At the church, he had to drop off some new linen Sarah had made for the communion table. He loved how she cared for the church and how it looked to the congregants. Once he dropped off the linen, it was off to Sam Ballot's office to discuss Gabriel's actions the day before in service.

How disrespectful of Gabriel to just waltz into the church, while service was going, and say they had to move out.

Gabriel Grant or not, that was uncalled for. Talk about sending the message, *you're not wanted here, I'd like you to leave.* Everyone realized Gabriel Grant did not like Jacob and Sarah Creek. His first run-in with the tycoon didn't turn out so well. Thinking back to the incident at Missy's, Jacob realized he could have been killed that night. Sam Ballot's jail was just the next building up. Jacob thought through his words before heading into town. He didn't want to give Sam anything that would give credit to Gabriel's actions. Even though the two men were close, Jacob feared the Sheriff would favor Gabriel Grant. At least the Marshal and Clyde Heller would be there to lend their support.

He knew God would provide a way where there seemed to be no way, but things hadn't worked out yet. If they had to move from their building, then by God's grace, they'd find a new place to hold their Sunday services, not to mention school for the town's children. Did Gabriel really care that little about the future of the children? That's what bothered Jacob and Sarah more than losing the church building. They could have church in a tent, but Purgatory's future rested in the hands of the children and they needed a building for their studies.

Jacob opened the door to the Sheriff's office, "Hello? Sheriff Ballot?"

The young, spry-looking man, cleaned and freshly shaved, walked into the main office from the back holding area. His set jaw and wide-brimmed hat, along with the golden polished badge, gave Jacob the sense that Sam Ballot took his job seriously.

"Sheriff, I'm glad you're still here." He hadn't seen the Marshal or Clyde and wondered if he'd be doing this meeting alone.

Sam picked up a coffee decanter from the stove and

poured a fresh cup. "What do I owe this pleasure?" he picked up another cup and offered it to Jacob.

"No, thank you." Jacob took off his hat, "I'm here about what happened yesterday at my church, Sheriff."

Ballot took a sip. "I heard about that, appears Gabriel paid you a visit." Another swig. "Shame to have it happen that way."

"Happen what way? Sheriff, he barged into the middle of a church meeting and told me to get out of the building by next week...that he's buying the land. How can he do this? I thought the land belonged to the people of Purgatory?"

Sam Ballot stood there drinking his coffee, probably thinking through his thoughts. "Reverend, it's a terrible shame to have this happen to you, it really is, but the fact remains that Gabriel Grant now owns the land your church is sitting on and you'll just have to move."

Had his ears deceived him? "You can't do this." He pressed his Bible tight against his chest, hoping and praying to keep his mouth shut.

Ballot set his coffee cup down with a bang, then picked up his hat and popped it on his head. "I'm sorry, Jacob. Now if you'll excuse me, I have a meeting with Judge Talbert to complete the sale of your property."

"Sheriff, please...think about the children. Where are they to hold their classes? You have a son, he's in my wife's class, how can you jeopardize your own son's future to that...man?" Gabriel seemed more monster than man.

"I didn't even think about the school." He placed his hand on Jacob's shoulder, "I still have to talk with the Judge. He's supposed to sign off on the land today, maybe I can persuade him to reconsider."

"Thank you, Sheriff. That's all I can ask for."

Ballot patted Jacob's shoulder, "Now, if you'll excuse me."

As Ballot stepped through the door, Marshal Tan Bennington stopped the man before he ran right into him. "Excuse me, Sheriff, you're just the man I'm looking for." His eyes caught Jacob's, "Mr. Creek, good to see you. Have you seen Clyde this morning? He was supposed to meet me at Missy's Tavern."

Jacob shook his head, "I've not."

Sam Ballot seemed eager to leave the premise. He clearly didn't like the Marshal and Jacob knowing each other. Jacob saw that much. Maybe this would help the man keep the law and not thwart the investigation the U. S. Marshal's Service had into Gabriel Grant.

"Can I help you, Marshal?" Ballot said, seeing the large man's silver badge.

"As a matter of fact. We have been talking to you regarding a Mr. Gabriel Grant. I believe you know him."

"Everyone knows him. He owns every business in town. I've had a lot of dealings with the man." He cleared his throat, "Though strictly professional is how I would say our relationship stands."

Jacob tried to stifle a laugh, but it escaped and Tan shot him a look.

"May I come in?"

Ballot stood back and allowed the Marshal into the room. "Certainly. Would you like coffee?"

"No, thank you. Where's Mr. Grant now?"

Ballot glued his eyes to the floor and fidgeted with his shirt buttons. "I'm not really sure."

Before the Marshal could speak, Freddy toppled into the office breathless. For several beats, everyone stared at the new member barging in. He gripped the door frame, panting, before speaking, "Sheriff, Jacob… It's Joe…Clyde…they're… You've got to come… Joe's place, just outside of town."

Jacob approached the man and knelt next to him. "What about Joe and Clyde?"

Freddy looked up with sadness in his brown eyes, "They're dead."

CHAPTER FORTY-ONE

JACOB COULDN'T look. The scene before him was too grotesque to comprehend and too vivid to ever forget. Joe, his wife, their daughter, and what looked to be Clyde were all dead. The house continued to smolder and the stench of wet wood filled the air. The Marshal and Sheriff Ballot were talking in hushed tones. He could tell from Sam's face he didn't want to be on the property any longer. Jacob walked up the blackened steps and into the burned house. The three bodies lay on the ground, burnt to the bone. There could be no way to determine if they died before or after the fire. That's when he noticed both Clyde and Mrs. Packard. Something odd about the way they lay. He crouched next to Mrs. Packard and could make out the fine details of a kerosine rope that survived the fire, binding her at the wrists.

He walked over to what he guessed was Joe's body, based on the holster and boots still attached to his blackened legs. The interesting thing about this body: no rope, his hands were not tied back, and a gun lay near his body. Jacob checked the gun; no bullets and one empty casing.

"Marshal," Jacob said stepping into the light.

The two men stopped talking and walked up the steps.

"I've found something you might find interesting." After all three were inside, he showed how both Mrs. Packard and the little body, assuming it was Clyde, were bound and, pointing to Joe, he added, "this one had a gun and no rope."

The Marshal stooped down to examine Clyde's body. "He has a single shot to the head. Could have been by the gun you found."

Jacob looked at Joe's body again. "He has a bullet to the head."

"This one too," Sam called out next to Mrs. Packard. He stood and dusted off his chaps. "Looks like this is case closed. Joe came home and found that Clyde had killed Mrs. Packard then set fire to the home. Looks like Joe fired his gun, killing Clyde, and then died in the fire." He thought for a moment, "Makes sense."

Jacob and the Marshal exchanged glances.

"What about the fact there are three guns?" Jacob said pointing to two other guns laying near the entrance to the Packard home.

Ballot shrugged his shoulders. "I don't know, but that's the story, and it fits the crime." He turned to the Marshal, "Thank you for taking the time out of your busy day to help us out on this one. I know it's above your pay grade to deal with petty local murders."

It took every ounce of self-control for Jacob to not punch the man. "You're serious? You're seriously suggesting that Clyde killed Joe and his wife? I highly doubt that. Someone tied them, and all three were shot point blank in the head." He cringed at the next thought, "And that little girl upstairs, she died because Gabriel Grant set fire to this place."

The Sheriff looked sick. "I...I...We don't know that Gabriel did this."

"Marshal? Help me out here," Jacob said.

Tan Bennington stood and picked up one gun. "Sheriff, it's time to arrest Mr. Grant." He held the gun in his hand and peeled off a small medallion, "This is Gabriel Grant's crest. It's a gun that either belongs to him or one of his hired men."

Jacob's heart sank. It was true. Gabriel was a murderer. He always figured it, and always knew the man had killed his father, but to kill a woman and child in cold blood? He headed down the stairs. "Marshal, thank you for everything. I need to go be with my family."

The Marshal nodded.

Jacob mounted his horse and took off toward Creek Ranch. He did his best to keep his mind fixated on other things, but the truth was his new friend and a family were dead. Nothing could change that. Nothing could bring back Joe and his family. They didn't deserve to die like this. He pulled his horse to a stop and dismounted. His breath became sharp, and he felt his chest heave. Vomit shot out of his mouth. The acidic taste burned against his throat. Jacob wiped his mouth and grabbed his canteen, gulping down water to be rid of the sour taste. Dropping to his knees, Jacob sobbed for several minutes before mounting his horse to continue the journey home. Only one thing gripped his mind; he needed Sarah's comforting embrace to wash away the sickening vision of Joe and his family lying dead in their home. This was not what Jacob wanted for Joe or Clyde. He never wanted them to die.

By the time he arrived home, Sarah was sitting on the porch. After dropping his wet coat and hat, he made his way to to the porch to sit next to Sarah. He pressed his wet face against her, "They're dead, Sarah. Gabriel killed Joe and our lawyer."

"Oh, Jacob," Sarah cupped his face and kissed his head, "I'm so sorry. Have you talked to his wife yet? Does she know?"

Jacob shook his head, trying hard to force back the tears that dripped from his eyes. It was all a horrible dream, it had to be and Jacob craved to awaken from his slumber and find that they really weren't dead. But he knew better. Now, Marshal Tan Bennington was the only hope he had to put Gabriel Grant behind bars. "He killed the whole family, Sarah. They're all dead." Fresh tears formed curved rivers down his cheeks as he allowed himself to cry.

She placed her fingers to her lips and let out a slight cry, "What are we going to do, Jacob?"

She was frightened and worried for their family, and rightfully so. A tear slipped down her cheek. If Gabriel could kill a family, what was stopping him from killing theirs? Nothing was beneath the man, nothing. It was in the Marshal's hands and Jacob prayed to God that he could talk some sense into Sheriff Ballot. They needed the Sheriff on their side.

Jacob noticed Sarah holding a small piece of paper, thumbing at it, "What's that?" he said, able to calm his mind.

She unfolded the piece of paper. "I found this at the church this morning. It's from Joe. He left it on one of the Bibles."

Jacob took the paper and opened it. His eyes fell on a property deed and quickly looked over the note. What he read knocked him over.

Jacob, I'm so very sorry for everything. I only tried to take care of my family and I knew it was wrong. I felt I didn't have a choice. Once you're indebted to Gabriel Grant, there's no escape. You're a better man than me and I hope you find this deed as a token of my apology and appreciation for you. Perhaps you can use this for the new school house.

Also, Gabriel had the previous minister killed. I was there when he trapped him in the mines, then staged the accident which killed him. I'll testify in court, but it should get him arrested for murder.

Take care, my friend. I'll send word after we're settled—I can't tell you where we're headed because I fear for my family's life and wellbeing.

Your friend, Joe

Jacob folded the note and sat his back hard against the house. He turned to Sarah, "We've got him. Joe just confessed that Gabriel killed the previous Reverend in the mines. He agreed to testify. This should give us enough to have him put away." He held up the note, "Maybe this note can serve as a signed confession. I need to take this to the Marshal, he'll know what to do next."

Sarah bit her lower lip, "Thank the Lord. He is good."

Jacob stood and pulled her up, "And his mercies endure forever. This is the break we're looking for. That and the murder of Joe." He stopped smiling and let his face fall. For several moments he stared at his feet. "Joe didn't deserve this."

"No one did," Sarah admitted.

CHAPTER FORTY-TWO

JUDGE RAYMOND Talbert sat at the bar drinking down the last bit of rum. It was his third glass of the late morning. Each sip Raymond took slapped against the back of his throat like fire. He considered himself the most well-respected man in town. Maybe that was why no one voted him out. Oh wait, no one ever ran against him. Purgatory was his home, and he loved and hated the town all the same. The town was quiet, so he sat and drank, hating every blasted person. He swore. There were only two people he didn't totally despise, Gabriel Grant and Sheriff Sam Ballot.

Raymond pulled out his pocket watch and realized he was late for a meeting with the Sheriff. He swore again, then slid his large form off the stool, allowing his fat to settle. He didn't care about his weight; it was part of the job. What judge didn't have a gut the size of Wyoming?

By the time he arrived at the courthouse, Sam Ballot sat behind his desk. "Get out of my chair!" his garbled voice rumbled.

"You're late," Sam stood, allowing the big man to slide behind the desk and sit, "What took you so long?"

The judge wiped spittle from his beard, "Was having lunch." Raymond pulled a file from his drawer, "Let's get this over with."

Sam chuckled.

Raymond looked at him and growled. Maybe he despised the man after all. More annoying than pleasant—really liked no one, and right now the Sheriff's smug face forced him to take another swig.

"I ran into Reverend Creek just before coming over here."

That caught Raymond off guard. He placed the quill down and took off his round spectacles. "What did he want?"

"Oh...for me to talk you out of signing the property papers for Gabriel."

"I don't like it. I don't like it one bit. Sam, you've got to do something, something to shut the Preacher up."

"Gonna be hard. There's a U. S. Marshal in town. He will try to pin Joe's murder on Gabriel."

Judge had heard about the Marshal being in town, but not the murders. "You talking about the Mercantile guy, Joe?"

"The one and only."

"You say Gabriel killed him?" He didn't like that either, in fact, being associated with Gabriel came with a price and Gabriel Grant could come begging for payment at any time. The deal: get Raymond elected the first time, and then when Gabriel needed help, Raymond was to reciprocate in like kind. No doubt the tycoon would call on Raymond to do something if this went south.

"That's what he speculates. The preacher found bullet holes in the whole family."

The news kept getting worse. "How's he involved?" And

killing women and children didn't seem like Gabriel's style—maybe the man had reached a breaking point.

"Like I said, he came by my office this morning to talk about the church and school building."

"What's he expect me to do, reverse my decision? I've already decided," he coughed hard and felt the rum gurgling against his stomach before belching.

He needed another drink.

"I will say this though, Jacob had a good point. We should find another suitable place for a schoolhouse. We don't need a church building, but we do need a schoolhouse. And with Gabriel taking the whole piece of pie, we're left without either."

"Who cares about the children—they can meet here in the courthouse for all I care. And for the church, he can meet anywhere he wants. It's a free country." He re-dipped the quill into the well, "Besides, the good Reverend doesn't want to keep crossing paths with Gabriel. You know that as much as I do."

"I do."

"Good. Watch him, and make sure he does nothing stupid, like approach Grant. Let's keep this between us." Raymond slurped back another drink he'd pulled out of his lower desk drawer. "I'm only doing this to keep the peace." He signed the last document. "I don't want to end up dead, like Joe or the previous preacher, just because I crossed Gabriel Grant."

"You won't."

Raymond swore and leaned back, spilling some scotch onto his desk. "And how, pray tell, can you guarantee that?"

The words caught in the back of Sam's throat. He knew he couldn't guarantee anything to the Judge. He also knew the man Gabriel Grant was. Gabriel wouldn't take no for an answer, and anyone who crossed him ended up lynched or shot. Neither of which excited Raymond. Poor Joe, however, got the short stick on whatever deal it was that Gabriel came collecting. He felt bad for the family, and it made him sick that the little girl was dead, but he'd crossed Gabriel and had paid the price. Raymond wasn't about to make that mistake.

He looked at Sam as he finished signing the documents. The man had done his best as the town's lawman to keep the peace, and if this would keep the peace, then so be it. Let the rotten tycoon have his precious land–it didn't bother him anyway, as long as people got along. Now, with Sam in the picture, things would work out, as long as the Preacher didn't get in the way. He would hate to have the town crying for the hanging of the man who killed the Reverend in broad daylight. He shuddered at the thought. Gabriel would need him to be free of this mess and continue on making money so he wouldn't have to.

"So, how can you guarantee that Gabriel Grant won't kill me, Sam?" Raymond's breath came in deep, heavy heaves as he grabbed another drink.

"You're going to kill yourself with that poison you keep throwing down the hatch." He grabbed the papers off Raymond's desk, "I can't say, but Gabriel won't kill you for just hearing out the good Reverend."

Raymond let a few expletives fly, "Sam don't go lying...I am a judge and I know when a man is lying." He cussed again, "Now take the papers over to Grant. The church and school property are his for whatever business he builds upon it."

Sam looked the papers over. "Seems everything is in order." He turned and headed to the door before stopping, "Raymond, let's pray we did the right thing."

"I hate this blasted town anyway, so what matter does it make if I signed these papers? I want to keep the peace here in Purgatory and you better have the same mindset." Raymond turned his back to the Sheriff, bottle in hand, and took another swig. "And don't tell Gabriel anything about what happened to Joe and his family."

Sam stood there and Raymond could feel him breathing.

"That'll be all Sheriff, good day," he took another swig.

CHAPTER FORTY-THREE

J ACOB CREEK, Marshal Tan Bennington, and Sheriff Sam Ballot sat at a table in Missy's Tavern. The place was filled with the usual crowd looking for good food and, since it was the only watering hole in town, beer. Each man had a mug and Jacob asked for a bowl of Missy's home-made soup. She poured the soup into a bowl and set it down for him to enjoy.

"Jacob, I never thought I'd see you step back through these doors, after what happened your first night back in town..." Missy trailed off before motioning to several hats by the door, "and thank you gentlemen for removing your hats. It's never polite to eat with one's hat on." She smiled and kissed Jacob on the cheek, "Enjoy, boys."

He watched her leave before pulling his thoughts back to the current discussion, what to do with the evidence regarding Gabriel Grant's murder of Reverend Johnson. He understood the evidence regarding Joe and Clyde seemed to hold merit, but the eyewitness evidence regarding the previous Reverend seemed to hold more weight with arresting someone. Sure,

Bennington could arrest Gabriel with conspiracy to commit murder, but would the charges stick with Judge Talbert in office? That's what this meeting was all about.

"So, how do we take down Gabriel Grant?" Jacob asked after shaking off her kiss.

Sam sat back, not wanting to be involved. He chewed his steak to keep from speaking and Jacob wondered how deep the Sheriff was into Gabriel's pocket. It appeared that Sam was there because the Marshal told him to be there. In Jacob's mind, Sam Ballot had a responsibility as the town's lawman to uphold the law he swore to uphold.

The Marshal folded his hands and leaned close, "I looked over the note you gave me, Jacob, and I don't see how this could be Joe's eyewitness account." He held up a hand, "I'm not saying it's not, but the fact remains, Joe Packard is dead and any evidence he carried around in his mind is now gone. If he knew who gave up Gabriel as the murderer, we'll never know who that man could be. He's gone like yesterday's wind, unless we poke around town. I don't think Gabriel would like that and would pay off anyone we could talk with from speaking."

Jacob shook his head and said, "We can't allow him to get away with any of this."

Sam spoke, "You know I've been one of Gabriel's biggest supporters in this town. We've let him have his way, I'll admit as much, but he legally procured the deed to the church property. The Judge signed off on it this morning and because Gabriel's also the Mayor, there's nothing we can do. He's legally in his right to take the land."

"Sheriff's right," Tan said.

"So, what, we let him run over this town and kill whoever he chooses?"

Tan held up his hand again, "Let's not become rash. We still have the little evidence regarding the murders of the Packard family and Clyde Heller," he turned to Sam.

Ballot leaned forward, resting his elbows on the table. "I've not talked with the Judge about Joe, both he and Gabriel are attached at the hip. They help each other out. After he shot and killed your father, Jacob, I was the arresting officer. I was only a deputy, but since I released him from prison, he considers me in his pocket." Sam bowed his head, "I know I've not been at my best in keeping Gabriel at bay, he's power hungry and when the Mayor says jump, you jump. I rather like my life." Sam glanced down at his lap and Jacob saw how conflicted the man was. Did Sam believe it was time to be free of Gabriel's hold over his life and vocation? Looking up, Sam continued, "I have, in my office, some of the evidence we collected in the mines, after the Reverend was killed."

Jacob saw him shift in the seat and look toward the door, as if expecting Grant to waltz in at any moment, "Sam?"

"I'm afraid. I'm afraid that if I'm involved with any of this, Gabriel will have me killed. I don't want to die."

The man sat there terrified of Gabriel Grant. Did he have everyone in this town so petrified with fear that no one dared speak against him? Laughter rippled through the Tavern as the pianist replayed the only tune he knew. Jacob's heart tightened in his chest. It was now or never. They had to arrest Gabriel, today. He feared the church won't last another week and for everyone's safety. Trying to undermine Gabriel's enterprise in Purgatory was the awful thing that killed Joe, and Jacob knew others would soon die if they left Gabriel to roam the streets and carry out his business.

"Don't worry, Sam. The Marshal is confident that we can put Gabriel away." Jacob turned to Bennington, "Right?"

The Marshal nodded his head before speaking, "Okay, here's what we're going to do," Bennington leaned forward and narrowed his eyes. "Jacob, you're going to head over to Gabriel's office and confront him about the church. Sam and I will remain behind a few minutes to avoid suspicion. I don't want this to take long, but Sam, I'll do the arresting and we'll house him in your jail until I arrive back here with a paddy wagon from Cheyenne and then we'll process him there for trial–but I need him to confess to killing Joe, otherwise this won't work. I'll be gone roughly a week, maybe more."

Sam's eyes widened, "Will I be safe with him in my jail?"

"Sam, get a grip," Jacob said, "the Marshal will be back soon." He looked at the two men across the table, "Let's do this." Jacob scooted back, "It's time to make Gabriel pay for killing Joe." Jacob got up and made his way across the tavern toward the door, where he grabbed his hat. He turned to look at Missy serving a customer.

She smiled and nodded, "Goodbye, Jacob."

Jacob waved, then faced the door. His stomach rolled inside and his heart twisted into a knot. This had to be done and his family needed reprieve from Gabriel's clutch. Time to stand up for a town controlled with fear because nobody ever stood up to Gabriel Grant. The power, money, and leverage he had to force people to do the unthinkable baffled him. Maybe, he and his late father weren't all that different. The only difference being, Jacob was using the law and not a six shooter to get his message across.

He walked through the doors and allowed the sun to wrap its warmth around him. Then he stepped off toward the edge of town.

CHAPTER FORTY-FOUR

FOR THE FIRST time since his father's death, Jacob's heart felt strong. No more worry, no more doubt. They were washed from his mind in a baptism of righteousness. Gabriel was about to experience the justice of God. Jacob and Sarah had waited a long time for God to fight their battle, and today the battle was won, if all went well. The moment he walked onto the street, everything changed. He would be free from this man's grip in a matter of minutes.

God, I need wisdom and continued strength.

Gravel crunched under his boots. A horse squealed as he moved down the dusty road. He didn't look at the horse or the master trying to calm the animal. His eyes focused on Gabriel's office. Before stepping onto the wooden porch, he turned around and saw Momma standing there. Her hands clasped in prayer and he couldn't tell, but it looked as if tears welled in her eyes. She nodded her head and Jacob walked into the building to confront Gabriel Grant.

The Mayor sat in his large chair, sipping a glass of brandy. The stoked fire warmed the cool day. Jacob stared at a pile of papers and guessed they were the same papers Judge Talbert signed off earlier today. Victory must have taste like the brandy Gabriel held. He knew the man forced his hand to find a new place to hold worship services, but that didn't really concern Jacob—not any more—and soon Gabriel would be behind bars, no longer to hurt anyone else.

As Gabriel gulped down the last drops from his glass, his Adam's apple budged, "Come in, Jacob." He set down the glass, "What what can I do for you on this crisp day?"

"Mr. Grant."

A crooked smile crossed Gabriel's face. He got up and extended a hand of invitation to Jacob.

Jacob accepted the handshake, "I'd like to speak with you...come to some agreement regarding the church and school."

"Have a seat, Reverend, and we'll talk."

While sitting, Jacob started, "Gabriel, you and I both know the town doesn't like you taking over the church and school land to build a hotel. That is what you're planning, isn't it?"

When the Gabriel didn't disagree, Jacob continue, "Let me get right to the point. You and I both know we need a church in town, or the people will tear themselves apart. We also need a schoolhouse—the children don't deserve to have that taken away from them—I ask you to reconsider building upon the site. There is a vacant lot next to the property, why not build there?"

He snickered, "Because I don't own the lot next to the church. I own the church lot, so it makes it mine to build what I like."

Jacob's mind flashed hot, "Give me a break! Someone else owning a piece of land has never stopped you from buying out the land before. What gives you the right to buy the land if you never owned it before?"

"Mr. Creek, I own it because you never paid me back; the original loan your father took, paid mostly by others, not you, and the loan you took from the savings and loan, a bank which I now own."

"So what you're saying is, you killed my father, burned down my barn, and killed Joe and his family, all to get even with me?"

Gabriel leaned back and grabbed a cigar, "Now I wouldn't say it's all your father's fault, is it my Bible-thumping friend?" he lit the cigar and breathed deep. "As for Joe, rest his soul, he should have listened. Now, you will lose your land and you will pay back every cent you took from me, or the bank...same thing. If not, it will go worse for you than it did Joe and his family."

Jacob's anger flared while he stood, trying to remain calm. "I don't scare easily."

He drew in deep and blew out smoke.

"Good evening, father."

Gabriel turned toward the door as his son, Felix, walked in.

"We're finishing up, just wait out the door and I'll be along shortly." Turning back to Jacob, he said, "Mr. Creek, there is a lot of profit to be had in the grand Territory of Wyoming. Congress has not put a stipulation on me buying up land, so I can do what I want, and not even the Governor can stop me." He re-poured the brandy into his glass. Done with the conversation, Gabriel held up the glass in salute, "I want my share of the profits."

"And you'll do whatever it takes to get your way. It doesn't matter who gets in your way, does it? You'll shut them up any way you want," a beat, "including Joe and his family."

Gabriel paused for a moment, and Jacob saw a new resolve spill out of the man's eyes. "Tell you what, Mr. Preacher man. If you give me the amount of the loan you took from the bank, I'll call it even, you can keep your pathetic little church, and I'll just swindle one of your parishioners to sell." He rubbed his soul patch, "How about Missy Cartwright's Tavern? That establishment will make a fine renovation for a hotel."

Jacob stood up, resting his hands on Gabriel's desk. He leaned in close and breathed deep. It was one thing to rest everything that had happened on both Leonard and him, but going after Missy? "Leave Missy alone," he said, gritting his teeth, spittle landed on the deed.

Gabriel backed off at Jacob's outstretched finger for a moment before leaning in till Jacob's finger rested on his forehead. "Now, now...isn't it against the Bible or something to be threatening?"

"I have not threatened...yet! But leave Ms. Cartwright alone."

"Alright, alright, Preacher...I'll leave your girlfriend alone if you pay up and I'll call it even."

"Let's get one thing straight, Missy is not my girlfriend."

He cackled rudely, "Oh, my mistake, your mistress."

Jacob's mind exploded like gunpowder. He flew over the desk, grabbed Gabriel by the shirt, and shoved him hard against the wall.

Crack.

A shelf fell from its brackets and crashed next to Gabriel's leg. Jacob saw a nail sticking out from the wall and shoved Gabriel's shoulder against it.

Gabriel screamed in pain and swung a fist that connected with Jacob's face. Fire rippled through his cheek as teeth cut the soft flesh of his lip.

"ENOUGH!"

Both men stopped as Marshal Tan Bennington stepped into the dank room, Sheriff Ballot close behind.

"Sheriff, thank God you're here. The Reverend walked in here and attacked me without provocation."

"Shut up!" Jacob balled his fist and drove it deep into Gabriel's face, driving him backwards against the wall.

"Jacob, I said enough!" Bennington said.

Jacob pulled Gabriel to his feet, "Marshal, he's all yours."

Marshal Tan Bennington walked around the desk with a pair of cuffs, "Mayor Grant, I hereby place you under arrest for the murders of Clyde Heller, Joe, Jenny, and Marisa Packard."

Gabriel's eyes widened. He didn't expect this. The door creaked open. Jacob turned and saw Felix poke his head out.

"Daddy?"

Gabriel turned at the sound of his son's voice, "It's okay. Go tell your mother what's happened. Have her go to Judge Talbert. You hear me, boy?"

Felix nodded and Jacob crouched next to him, "I'll make sure he's taken care of, okay?"

Gabriel growled, "Sheriff, what's this all about?"

"I'd advise you to remain silent. We can talk at the jail, okay?"

Jacob smiled as he approached Gabriel, "I hope you rot in that cell for killing my friends and my father."

"Come on," Bennington said, "let's go."

"This isn't over, Preacher! You've just made a grave

mistake. I'm coming after you. You hear? I'm coming after you!" Gabriel screamed as the Marshal led him outside.

Jacob smiled again. Nothing in this world gave him more pleasure than seeing justice served and God answering his prayers. Now, for the first time, Purgatory could sleep knowing that Gabriel Grant sat behind bars for ruining many people's lives.

CHAPTER FORTY-FIVE

"THAT'LL DO IT," Bill said hammering in the final nail, securing the hinge to the new barn door. He stood back, admiring his work. Trying it, the door closed with ease. He pulled down the latch, turned, and smiled at Jacob, "I think she's a beauty. Better than the last barn."

Jacob agreed. He gazed at the tall structure. The rough-hewn wood craved red paint to complete the look. He'd take another loan from the bank. The past two days came as a relief to Jacob and Sarah. Every waking moment worrying about Gabriel Grant and his next move had stopped them from living life. Sarah relaxed into her normal routine and no longer worried about Gabriel sneaking up on her and Virginia. And for Virginia, nothing changed. She understood Jacob's sadness but couldn't comprehend the inner workings of his stress.

His eyes followed the beams to the gable, gazing at the incomplete roof. He dashed off toward the work shed. Bill said something, but he didn't hear. Light peeked through small windows in the dark building and Jacob wondered where he last laid the item. He shoved a few things aside and in the back corner, poking out like a cattail above junk, sat his cow-topped weathervane. Clambering for it, he heaved it up and proudly displayed it to Bill as he exited the shed.

"I thought we lost that," Bill exclaimed.

Jacob grinned ear to ear, "Nope. I've been saving this puppy for this occasion." He grabbed the ladder and clunked up each rung. Upon reaching the top, he steadied himself with his left hand and slid the weathervane into a shaft before securing it with a nail. Satisfied it freely spun, he lowered himself to the ground. "There, now she's complete."

"She's a beauty," Bill said for a second time.

"Thank you for all of your hard work. I know it hasn't been easy around here and I know I've been a little preoccupied," he held up a hand, "not that my actions were justifiable, I got lost in the moment's heat."

Bill shook his hand, then rested a comforting hand on Jacob's shoulder, "But you did nothing rash."

"No, but I didn't trust God either."

"You know, that's one of my favorite passages from the Good Book." Bill's eyes looked up, trying to recall the passage, "Trust in the Lord with all thine heart; and lean not unto thine own understanding. In all thy ways acknowledge him, and he shall direct thy paths.

"You know, Jacob, God's got your back and if you continue to trust him, your path will be made straight by the Lord."

Jacob knew it to be true. His will crowded out God's and all that anger, all that rage needed to go somewhere. Worry kept him from truly allowing God's full peace to rest on his soul. Even though Gabriel was in prison, not able to hurt anyone, that anger still grabbed his heart and wouldn't let go, not until Gabriel Grant was in Tan Bennington's custody. Arriving in the next few days, the Marshal would be removing Gabriel Grant from their lives for good.

He kicked the dust and watched it swirl off his boot's tip. He loved Bill and trusted the man's years of wisdom. No way he'd ever pay back all the elder did for the Creek family.

"Thank you, Bill. I thought I was the preacher around these parts."

The two men laughed and looked at the barn one last time before heading to finish mending the south fence. Several broken beams lay in a pile of ruin from the fire that had wrecked a lot of the surrounding fence running along three sides of the barn. With a new barn, Jacob needed the ranch back up and running again. Without a functioning ranch, there were few ways to make ends meet. He had paid most of the bank back their money before needing another loan to keep the ranch running. He might get with the banker, but knowing how he treated other customers when they defaulted offered little comfort. He looked out at his land and ran his fingers through the scruff of his face. Maybe it was time to sell some property back to the bank to make ends meet.

Jacob and Bill pulled several beams aside, tossing the damaged pieces and keeping any that looked usable. Only three posts needed to be dug and set, a nice little blessing after all they'd been through. He grabbed the post digger from the shed and worked the earth, softening it. Bill managed a spade into the hole and swept out the loose dirt so Jacob could set a new post. They took several hours to complete the work, but the fence looked great. Another week or two and the place would be back to functioning. They still needed another horse for Bill. Freddy had none to spare and no one around the area seemed interested in parting with theirs. The other piece he needed to solve was getting some more cattle. They had fifty good head of cattle left, but soon he'd have to purchase some to replenish what was sold to Clyde Heller.

A wave of sadness washed over Jacob's soul. He'd never meant for Clyde to die by Gabriel's uncontrollable rage. The little man had so much to teach Jacob and now he was gone. He wondered what would happen to Heller Ranch in Cedar Grove.

After a short break, Jacob and Bill talked through some new ideas they each had for the property and how they could help Heller Ranch in Cedar Grove. The place needed tending to, and Jacob couldn't spare a single man to help care for Clyde's place. The problem was that Clyde had no family to share his future with and soon the Governor's office would come collecting. Something inside Jacob desired the cattle. Adding back his two-hundred head, plus whatever Clyde had, would give him enough cash flow to keep this ranch going. The only problem: money. That single thing leads to more people failing in life than success. The more you had, the more you could help the town; the less you had, the more dependent on others you became.

It was a vicious cycle and Jacob hated every moment of lacking funds to accomplish the simple task of running his family ranch, especially now that he sold most of his cattle just to satisfy Gabriel's greedy hand.

"I think I will call it a night," Bill said, pulling Jacob from his musings.

"All right. Sounds good. Sarah's got something cooking by now."

Bill turned to leave, then stopped. His hand rested on Jacob's shoulder. Something in his eyes pulled at Jacob's heart. For a moment, his world stilled and he knew Bill had something important to say, "Jacob, you know I care about you, Sarah, and Virginia. You guys are like family."

"I appreciate that, Bill."

"After Claudia died, I never thought I'd find peace again. I never understood what a family could look like. We never had children of our own and I never got upset at the Good Lord for denying me that pleasure, but it's something I've never understood until now."

"Bill, what are you saying?"

"Jacob, for years I felt alone, tired, and worn from years of hard work." He spread his hand at the ranch, "I love this place and I always will and I'll work here until my dying breath." His eyes welled with tears, "I love you like a son, and that Virginia is the closest thing to a grandchild I'll ever have."

A scraping sound caught Jacob's attention as Bill's boot played with a rock. "I've fallen in love with Joanna. I know I said I'm okay with our platonic relationship, but the events of the past few weeks have shown me how much she means to me—how much your family means to me." His body stilled, and he looked Jacob in the eye, "Jacob, with your blessing, I'd like to marry your mother."

Jacob felt his face flush and his eyes blurred with tears. A few escaped and crawled down his cheeks. Everything from the past several weeks washed away, and Jacob looked at the man who was more a father than Leonard ever was to him. "Bill, it would honor me if you married Momma. She's my everything and I have always considered you to be the father I never had."

Bill staggered for a moment and pulled his arms to the side, figuring out how to give Jacob a hug. He fell into Jacob's embrace and laughed, then cried, then they both laughed, "Thank you."

"When are you going to ask her?"

"I know Momma's a busy woman and she'll want something quick. I want to head into town and ask her tonight. Jacob, would you do the honors of marrying us in the sight of God and man?"

Jacob's heart leaped, "I would be honored."

Bill shifted and turned to walk away again. He stopped and turned around, "Thank you, again. I'm so honored that you said, yes."

Jacob shook his head and smiled, "Would you get out of here, ya big goof? Make Momma's day. I can't wait to hear how it went."

CHAPTER FORTY-SIX

JACOB KICKED off his boots before settling into his favorite chair by the fireplace. His thoughts drifted to Bill and Momma and he smiled at the happiness that wrapped its arms around the Creek family. The first time he met Bill had happened after his father hired him as a ranch hand. Most of the property's work landed in Bill's lap as Jacob's father spiraled further into his alcohol addiction. He watched the alcohol suck his father deeper into anger, resentment, and fear of everyone around him. When he took the money from Gabriel Grant, he changed the course of the Creek family because of his hot temper. He never should have provoked Gabriel Grant that night.

Jacob and Sarah were living in Salt Lake City they received word of Leonard's death. After leaving Sarah behind in Utah, he traveled to Purgatory and learned from Bill of his father's murder. One thing bothered Jacob: if Gabriel killed Leonard over the money, why didn't he kill Jacob to satisfy the debt? Thankful it never went that far, but Jacob's thought lingered. None of that mattered any longer; Gabriel was behind bars where he belonged.

Sarah busied herself at the stove frying up lamb she bought from the market in town. Her dark hair rested on her back as she swirled around the kitchen fixing up dinner. Jacob didn't mind lamb, but his favorite was Sarah's fried chicken, recalling the first time she made it for him. Jacob loved her version, but she told him over and over it didn't hold a candle to Momma's chicken. Bill was in for some great cooking. When would they wed and where would they live? Here on the ranch—Jacob still needed him here to help run things—or would they live in town at the Miner's Lodge?

He tried to push the thoughts aside and realized he never told Sarah the good news. Pressing up from the chair, he strode across the room and wrapped his arms around her waist. She stopped cooking to turn into his embrace. Her warm smile and tender touch on his arm sent ripples down his neck.

"Well, hello," She said.

"Hi," as he drew her lips to his and kissed her deeply.

"What was that for?"

"I love you."

"Well, I love you, but if you want dinner to taste decent, I need to get back to work." She turned, and he caught her arm again, "Yes…?"

"I have great news."

"If it's about Momma and Bill, I already know."

Jacob let go of her arms. Confounded with the news, he hesitated speaking except for a few odd syllables which escaped his throat.

"You're wondering how, aren't you?"

Jacob nodded, "Yeah…"

"As I did the wash yesterday, I found a ring tucked inside Bill's pocket. I asked him who the lucky lady was, and he gushed."

"Gushed?" Jacob laughed, what an odd word, "So, he spilled the beans, as it were."

"As it were."

"Wow!" he pointed toward the stove and Sarah jumped at the sight.

"Look what you made me do. The lamb's overcooked. Guess you'll have to settle with no pink in the meat tonight."

Jacob frowned, "He's asking Momma tonight for her hand and asked if I would marry them."

Sarah's expression brightened, "Really?"

"Right now. We'll hear all about it after Bill gets home."

"Jacob, you're not going to wait up to talk to the man, are you?"

He hadn't considered that Bill might be longer. Guess it seemed right, the two were about to be engaged and Jacob couldn't be happier. Momma lived a hard life: cleaning, cooking, and caring for those miners was all she had, next to trying to take care of the ranch while Jacob and Sarah lived in Utah. But all was changing. They came back home, Momma now had Bill, Gabriel was behind bars, and all was right with the world.

"Does Virginia know?"

"Know what, Daddy?" Virginia said, looking up from her book.

He floated over to where she sat and knelt down. He cupped his hands around hers. "I have some exciting news for you."

She nodded, "Yes, Daddy."

"How would you like another Grandpa?"

Her smile brightened, "How do I get one of those?"

"Well, what if Bill became your new grandpa?"

"Really?" she squealed with delight, "I love Bill."

Jacob grinned, "Well, he's about to marry Momma."

Virginia leaped up, knocking him over and then wrapping her arms around his neck. After composing herself, she nodded her approval and said, "I always knew they should be married."

They all laughed. Virginia went back to her book, and he watched her for several minutes while Sarah finished up dinner. It wouldn't be long before she set food on the table. Jacob stared off toward the window facing the barn and watched the moon shine through the curtains. Wandering over to the door, Jacob opened it. The cool air swirled around him as Sarah rummaging around with some dishes, setting the table for dinner. Jacob stepped onto the front porch, closed the door, and leaned against the roof's support beam.

The night air pebbled his skin, and he pulled his collar tight. The new barn looked white as the moon cascaded its rays across its rough walls. Maybe he'd choose white as the color instead of red. It looked nice against the moon. He imagined the color against a blue sky and he felt pleased. Bill never thought red looked good on barns, preferring white or no paint at all, and Jacob hadn't agreed, until now.

He watched his clouded breath push into the night and disappear with a swirl. It wouldn't be long before the leaves changed and winter started its grip on the land. Sarah always loved autumn. The warmth of the day and cool of the night excited her. After they married, they'd spent countless autumn nights sitting and dreaming under a large oak tree at their place in Utah, dreaming of their future together. They dreamed when it seemed life became impossible. They dreamed even after Leonard died. As of late, dreaming seemed to evade him as Gabriel consumed their thoughts with frustration, anger, and for Jacob, hatred.

As a tragic as losing Leonard was, Jacob had never felt comfortable dreaming he'd be back in Purgatory. It never felt right and even though the church needed a new minister, which he took, he wondered if the whole thing was a big mistake. Maybe none of this would have happened if he never stepped foot in this god-forsaken town.

Tap, tap, tap.

Jacob turned at the sound and Sarah waved at him to come inside. The warm house thawed his skin as he stepped through the door, and the tingling sensation climbed his arms and burned at his ears. The food smelled even better inside and Virginia sat in her usual spot. Jacob took his chair at the head of the table.

He beamed at his family for a moment before he grabbed his wife's hand, "Let's pray."

CHAPTER FORTY-SEVEN

A PLATE OF BEANS and overcooked beef landed on the dusty jail floor. Gabriel stared at the rations slopped onto the metal plate. His stomach churned at the sight. How he wished a juicy steak, prepared the way he liked, replaced the refuse Sam threw together. How was he supposed to eat this? He sighed and picked up the plate. It stank and the burnt texture of the beans gagged him.

"You call this food, Sam?"

Ballot looked up from the desk as he shoveled a forkful into his waiting mouth. Chomping down, he frowned, "What, you don't like it? It's my specialty."

A growl escaped Gabriel's throat as he shoved a spoonful into his mouth. He swallowed the bite without chewing and the texture turned gelatinous as it hit his stomach. The taste could have been better, and it wasn't prime rib, but he figured he should eat anyway.

The cramped cell had become claustrophobic after two days with nothing but thinking to do. A thin straw mattress on a wooden bench sat to the back of the cell and set against the opposite wall was a bucket to urinate in. It only took a few hours before he kicked his boots off and shed his black coat. Never had two days felt so long.

He managed another swallow before giving up and tossing the plate through the cell door. The food hit the floor with a splat.

Sam startled then pushed from his desk. "What is your problem? After everything I've done for you, you mess my jailhouse? Come on, man. I'm trying to do you a favor and keep you company. Lord knows if one of my Deputies were here…" Sam let the thought trail, "I fixed this for you and this is the thanks I get."

Gabriel snarled, "You could have kept the Marshal from arresting me. You could have warned me what the Preacher and Lawman were up to." He settled into the mattress, "I'll be out of here before you can even blink."

"The Judge hasn't set bail yet. So, I don't think you'll be heading anywhere soon. I don't like it either, Gabriel, but I am a lawman and I need to protect and serve my community."

Chuckling, Gabriel quipped back, "Then protect and serve. I'm sorry I'm such a burden."

Sam finished cleaning the mess. "I'm sorry, Gabriel. I really am. But it seems you got yourself into this mess."

Gabriel let silence settle between them for a few minutes. The Marshal would return in a few days to fetch him and haul him back to Cheyenne. A prospect he didn't like one bit. They'd hang him for sure for Joe's death. As the plan formulated, he sat up. "Sam, is there any way you can settle our little matter here in Purgatory? I'd rather have a jury of my peers oversee the case and I'd love for Judge Talbert to be presiding."

Sam Ballot laughed and tossed a rag into a nearby bucket.

He meandered back to his desk, sat, and shoveled another mouthful into his waiting mouth. "The Marshal has tied my hands on this one, Gabriel. Clyde's from Cedar Grove and a current resident in Cheyenne. Truth to tell, this is no longer a county matter, it's a territorial matter. I know the Governor wouldn't want the case here, he'd rather see it tried in Cheyenne. Sure, we could try you here in Purgatory for the murder of Joe and his family, but because Clyde brought big business to the Capitol, they'll try the case there."

Gabriel's heart sank. Before he could speak, someone walked through the front door. Sam got up and walked out of sight. Hushed voices reached him and he couldn't make out who Sam conversed with. Sam returned and Gabriel's eyes widened as Moira followed behind and approached the jail cell. The last place he needed Moira to see him was in jail.

"Hello, Gabriel," her words were just above a whisper.

His own words stuck and he felt a lump form in his throat. He swallowed hard against the dry vocal chords and tried to hide his shame. The last time she saw him behind bars, Sam had arrested him for the death of Leonard Creek. This time might be different and she'd never see him again.

She wore a soft maroon dress with a laced V pattern that angled from her waist to her neck, which formed a collar that sat tall against her slender neck before stopping just under her chin. A matching hat perched itself upon a bun, the hat tied in a neat bow under her chin. He reached into her dark eyes and saw her sadness and anger. No doubt this conversation could end their marriage.

"Hi," he said through a dry throat.

"What have you done? They say you killed a family—a woman and child—and set fire to their home? How could you? Who are you?" Moira slammed her gloved fists into the bars.

Words escaped him and he tried to speak, but nothing would come. No words, no thoughts, just self-pity.

"What if someone killed me, or Felix?" She wiped her tears, "How could you? What if that were me?"

"Moira, I tried to spare you from my business."

Anger flashed in her eyes and a low groan vibrated from her chest. "Spare me the indulgences. If your business is about killing, then we have nothing in common. You were a good man. You were kind, gentle, and headstrong. I loved that about you," she leaned closer and stuck her nose through the bars, "but you used me. You berated me. You told me to do everything at your beck and call. How dare you? You push me around, slap my face, and force me into submission. No longer, Gabriel. Maybe it's best if you rot in prison. Maybe it's best if you don't come home."

"Moira…" it was all he could manage, no other words would form.

She pulled away from the cell. She walked backward a few paces and turned around as fresh tears fell.

"Moira, I'm sorry!"

She kept walking. She didn't look back. She didn't say another word. She was gone.

Gabriel sank into the thin mattress and let a few tears creep their way to the corners of his eyes. He wiped them and noticed Sam watching. He looked away at Gabriel's glance.

Just as the empathy for his wife emerged from his heart, the anger toward Jacob Creek filled the void she left. No doubt he'd lost Moira. He'd be lucky to get her back. This hadn't been part of the plan. No, his plan would play out in the next day. He laid back down and laced his fingers behind his head. Oh how sweet vengeance would be, and Jacob would feel the wrath for playing these cards.

The day of reckoning was coming. Gabriel's plan would unfold just as he foresaw. He knew Jacob's ruse at the office would trap him long enough for the Marshal to get enough evidence. He did not expect that Sam Ballot would be part of the Preacher's charade. At least now, Gabriel could finish what he started. The Preacher would pay. His friends would pay. And everyone in Purgatory would know that you don't mess with Gabriel Grant and get away. No, no, no—the fun's about to start.

Gabriel closed his eyes and waited.

It wouldn't be long now.

CHAPTER FORTY-EIGHT

THE SUN CLIMBED in the early morning sky as Jacob pulled fresh straw and hay bales down from the hayloft. They tumbled through the air before thudding on the floor below. He tossed two more bales before climbing down. Tugging at the strings, he heaved each into a stall and broke the rope tying each into a square. Satisfied straw now covered the floor of each stall, he then filled each trough with fresh hay for the animals to eat. The crisp air did its job of keeping him cool, but the work forced his skin to perspire. He wiped his brow and shoveled more hay into a nearby stall. The main door creaked against the wind and Jacob turned to see Bill's silhouette.

"Hey."

"Jacob, Missy's here."

"*Missy?*" Jacob didn't think she'd ever been on the ranch before and not since the baptism. What brought her to the ranch today? Pulling off his gloves, Jacob tossed them onto a nearby bench before dusting his pants and shirt. He didn't want her to see him dirty and sweaty.

"Missy say why she's here?"

"Nope. But she seemed shaken. Sarah's with her right now."

"In the house?"

"Yup," Bill grabbed a pitchfork, "I'll finish up here. Go find out what she needs."

Jacob headed toward the house and turned his head, "I still need details on what happened last night with Momma."

Bill chuckled and tossed hay, "I'll tell you later."

Jacob laughed to himself as he stepped into the house. It took a moment for his eyes to adjust to the dim lighting. Everything darkened then lightened as his eyes figured out he was indoors. Sarah and Missy sat with tea warming their hands. Virginia sat in the corner with her dolly. He walked over to his daughter and placed a hand on her arm, "I need you to go outside for a bit."

"Why?" she asked, tugging against the doll's hair.

"Off you go. I won't ask again."

She shrugged her shoulders, pulled herself up and meandered through the open door. She closed it behind her and Jacob moved to the table and sat.

"Missy? What brings you to Creek Ranch today?"

Her hands tightened around the flower patterned cup. Her breathing stilled and Missy averted her eyes from meeting Jacob's. He noticed her countenance seemed sour and sorrowful at the same time; something bothered her, or she wouldn't have made the trek out to the ranch. She sighed in the deafening silence and spoke after several passing minutes.

"The Judge forced me out of the Tavern last night. He said if Gabriel remained in prison he could no longer employ me. So, the Tavern is up for sale and if I want to remain the sole runner I also need to be the sole owner."

Jacob felt his throat tighten, "Who's running the Tavern?"

She let a tear slip from her left eye, "I don't know. Far as I know, it's closed until further notice."

So, Gabriel Grant still pulled strings from behind iron bars. His face flushed hot and his ears burned with fire. No doubt they turned red and Sarah would have to calm him down. He turned to his wife. Her face was ashen and quiet. Jacob placed his hand over Missy's and caressed her thumb with his. "We'll get through this. Sarah and I will help you out if we can."

She tried to smile through tears, "Thank you, but you guys are just in as much debt and Lord knows the bank will continue to come after you for the rest of the monies you owe to Gabriel."

"Missy, we will get through this. We'll pray that God will intervene," Sarah said.

This time Jacob cupped both her hands, stared into her green eyes, and smiled, "That's right. I'll help you any way I can." A thought crashed into his mind like a locomotive. Maybe he'd be able to get Judge Talbert to reconsider the Tavern. Lord knows he had to reconsider the church and school house now that Gabriel was out of commission. If he wouldn't listen, Jacob would just head to Cheyenne and hire another lawyer to help. The problem with that idea was money. They were indebted to the bank and the money he received from Clyde Heller had paid for the barn, upgrades, and only part of the loan. He hoped it would have taken the bulk of the loan, but that wasn't the case. At least it was the bank he was indebted to now since Gabriel was sitting in Sam Ballot's jail, unable to hurt anyone.

But there might be another solution and Jacob thought it might work. "Missy, let me talk with the Judge and see if he'll let you keep running the place until you can gather enough money for a down payment to buy the place. You should have it. You've worked hard to keep that place running. No one knows you better than the people of Purgatory. If anyone should understand this, it would be the Judge. He buys from you every day. Doesn't he?"

Missy shook her head. "It was a standing agreement between Gabriel and the Judge. He could drink there anytime and I had to wait on him, no matter what he wanted." Missy sobbed as a torrent of fresh tears ran down her cheeks, carving out little rivers. "He…the Judge…he…he used me. I became his…" The words caught in her throat and she sobbed again, "I was his…" Missy cupped her face, "I'm so sorry."

Sarah pulled Missy close and hugged her tight. Jacob's heart ached for Missy. What the Judge did to her boiled his blood. The man needed to be behind bars as much as Gabriel. Forcing your way on a woman should get a man hanged. Jacob wanted to tie the noose himself and watch the fat man's body twitch under its own weight. Maybe talking it over with the Judge wouldn't work. He pulled up resolve and decided he'd travel to Purgatory and give the Judge a piece of his mind.

"Missy, I'll ride to Purgatory and talk with the Judge. I'm sorry he's done that to you. You don't deserve it. You're a pretty woman who deserves a man to treat you with respect and kindness. For all I know, the Judge is just as guilty as Gabriel and should be hanged for what he's done to you."

"Jacob!" Sarah scolded.

"I'm serious, Sarah. He deserves a noose for what he's done to Missy. I'm done being the nice guy. Everyone tramples on the nice guy. I have my faith, I have my family, but people like Missy need someone to stand up for them. Who's that going to be with a crooked Judge?"

"Jacob, you can't be Purgatory's savior."

Missy's eyes widened at the exchange. Jacob noticed but didn't pay attention.

"Listen, we all have had enough of evil people having their way in this town. It's a real purgatory here. Once you arrive, you can never leave. Your faith will be tested, tried, and pressured to fail in this town. You'll be burned alive if you live long enough to see another day. And besides, I've been used and abused more than anyone in this town and it's time for me to take a stand against evil.

"In all honesty, I don't care what I have to do to prevail against the evil that plagues this town. It's as if the Devil himself has come to roost. You can't even take a piss without either the Judge or Gabriel Grant giving you permission. I'm done being the good Reverend. It's time to take a stand, and you're either with me or not, but I'm going to town to give the Judge a piece of my mind."

Missy lifted her head, "I don't want to cause either of you trouble. I've done enough by coming here. I'm sorry. I should go."

"Missy, I'm sorry," Jacob said.

"You should stay for the day. You can help me with a few things around here. My husband can go calm down elsewhere," Sarah glared at Jacob.

The icy stare made him avert his eyes toward the door. He longed for the barn. He no longer wanted to be part of this conversation. Maybe he'd just grab a horse and head to Purgatory now. The barn could wait.

"Missy, we'll make this right," he turned to Sarah, "I'm

sorry. I'm just so frustrated with everything. It seems to never end."

"I know," she placed her hand on Jacob's leaned forward and kissed him, "I shouldn't have pressed it. Get out of here. Go talk to the Judge. He needs a good whooping," Sarah smiled.

Jacob tried to smile, but it faded as his heart was set on confronting the Judge and seeing the man pay for his treatment of Missy.

CHAPTER FORTY-NINE

JUDGE TALBERT settled his fat into a nearby chair. As he sat, his beer sloshed around, splashing onto the table. He cursed and wiped it with a sleeve. The glass thunked onto the table and he let a chortle escape his throat. Sam stared at the large man whose jowls shook with each syllable and chuckle. Judge slurped his drink before slamming it onto the table again.

Sam pushed his away, his appetite lost.

"You gonna drink that?"

Sam pushed the beer closer to his friend, "It's all yours."

"Thanks," he said before chugging the glass and wiping the foam from his fat face.

Sam sat, worried about whether they had made the right choice in arresting Gabriel Grant. Things never went well for those who crossed him and the last thing he wanted was Gabriel retaliating against him. He preferred to keep his head and his life. Marshal Tan Bennington was due back in two days to pick up the tycoon for transfer to Cheyenne. Yet, his thoughts kept bothering him about the Judge. Gabriel had that man wrapped around his golden fingers. No doubt Gabriel gave them special treatment to do what they saw fit. They both enjoyed the luxury money bought and Sam did as he was told, kept his head down, paid his dues to Gabriel, and the money kept flowing his direction. He tried to get involved by offer his two cents, but either Gabriel or the Judge did not see his contributions in keeping Purgatory safe. To them, Sam Ballot was a hired gun who wore a badge.

The real question of the day: would Judge Talbert follow through with keeping the law? Would he transfer Gabriel into U. S. Marshal Service custody?

Sam leaned back and fiddled with the table's edge. "So, is everything squared away for transferring the prisoner?"

The Judge stopped eating a chicken wing, "Prisoner? Gabriel's a friend and you refer to him as a prisoner?"

"I'm trying to keep this professional."

"Ha!" he laughed. "You lost being a professional the moment you got into bed with him." He sunk his teeth into the meat and pulled some off the bone, "We all did."

Sam couldn't argue that point. They all owed Gabriel. He could have run them out of town years ago. Do right by Gabriel and you lived well; that is, until you cross him. Sam shrunk into his chair. Look where that got Joe and his family? They wound up with a bullet to the head. He didn't feel good. His stomach churned against the beer and food and he wanted to vomit.

"Listen," Talbert said, "we all need to get used to the fact that this town is no longer run by Gabriel Grant. His enterprise is over. Doesn't mean I don't like it, he did so much good for the community."

"You sound like you wish things were different."

"Sam, don't you see. He will not be around much longer. Maybe we can all have a piece of the pie now. I'm now running this tavern. I already ran Missy out of here." He blew his nose, "And since she found religion, I don't enjoy having my way with her anymore. She won't take my advances or my sweet talk'n."

Sam had to laugh, "Sweet talk'n, is that what you call it? Com'on Talbert, you only ever forced yourself on her, and you know it. And you know what? It's disgusting. She's a pretty thing and you go and..." He pushed away from the table, "I'm done with this conversation."

Talbert huffed and slammed his fist into the table, causing the glasses to bounce. "How dare you insult me like that?" he snarled, "When do you need those transfer papers?"

"Tonight."

"I'll have them on your desk first thing." He held up his mug. "Can I get another beer for me and the Sheriff?"

A thin and pretty lady walked up. Her blond curled hair bounced with each step. She wore a white baroque pearl necklace. It hung just below her neck and highlighted the softness of her skin. Her laced corset wrapped around her body before fanning out at the waist. She grabbed the two mugs and off toward the bar for a refill. Her rose scented perfume covered the area and Sam felt mesmerized by her beauty before a loud cowboy behind him replaced the thought.

"That fire was intense. Can you imagine how the bodies would melt under that kind of heat?"

"Yeah, and Gabriel made us stay until no one survived."

Sam's eyes widened, and he noticed the Judge listened in. "Can you believe this?" he said.

The Judge shushed him, "I want to hear more."

The one behind Sam spoke, "Don't think anyone survived the bullets. I know the short midget man flopped dead like a codfish. I know Joe didn't fare too well with my bullet."

The other man snickered, "I know that whore of a wife sure enjoyed hers." He lowered his voice, "I didn't feel right about the little girl. Why'd you kill her anyways?"

Silence and then, "I like little girls," he cackled.

Sam had heard enough. He looked at the Judge, who nodded in approval. He pulled his gun, stood, and tapped the man behind him on the shoulder, "Boys, I think we need to have a talk outside." The man didn't move. Sam kept his gun with enough pressure on the man's back to stop him from going for his own. Sam reached down and slipped the man's gun from the holster. "I'd advise you to drop yours as well," he said to the other.

Man number two stood and reached for his weapon.

"Careful," Sam said.

Number two yanked the gun from the leather, cocked and before he could fire, Sam pulled his trigger. The bullet slammed into the man's ribs, which exited his back. He toppled backward and fired his own gun. He missed, and it hit wood somewhere behind Sam. A few screams and people ducked for cover as Sam cocked his gun and fired again. This time, the bullet ripped through the man's neck, sending flesh and pink mist into the air. He staggered forward, grabbed the chair, then toppled over, gasping for air.

Sam let go of the man he held, "Sit down."

The man sat.

Sam approached the wounded man and watched as he stopped gagging against his own blood.

"What's your name, son?" he asked, turning back to Number one.

"Jimmy."

"Well, Jimmy, today's your lucky day. You get to live. But you're under arrest for the murders of Clyde Heller, and the entire Packard family." He pointed his gun at Jimmy, "Let's go."

CHAPTER FIFTY

GABRIEL STRETCHED against the iron bars. He grew tired of the six by seven cell. The food grated on his nerves and he felt ill each time he forced some kind of slop down the hatch. It took every ounce of self control to not curse at Sam, Purgatory, and his wife for leaving him abandoned. Sure, maybe he did this to himself, but that was beside the point. He pressed his back against the bars to release the tension building between his shoulder blades, cursing the uncomfortable mattress and the god-forsaken cell.

He paced a few laps around the tiny cell before sitting on the bed to read a book that Sam brought him from home. He leafed through a few pages and quickly grew tired of staring at the same book for so long. He missed his library. He missed his luxury living. He missed his wife and wondered, since their last conversation, how much she actually missed him. It didn't matter, it wouldn't be long now.

Last night, while Sam slept, one of Gabriel's hired hands had paid a visit. The plan was simple, talk about the killings and see if Sam would bite. Sure, they'd get arrested but

Gabriel told them he'd pull a few strings and they'd be free. Talbert owed Gabriel one. If Gabriel hadn't paid off a few voters to re-elect Judge Rex Talbert, he would've lost. It worked and Gabriel told him the day would come when all things were paid. A lesson the Preacher nor Leonard ever learned. How he wished a gun and a bullet would shut the Preacher up. What a glorious day that would be.

The door to the Sheriff's office opened and Gabriel heard hushed voices from behind the wall. He strained his ears to make out who and then smiled because Jimmy had found the Sheriff. Or, more likely, the Sheriff had found Jimmy. The two men rounded the corner and Sam opened the cell next to Gabriel's. He shoved Jimmy's back and slammed the jail door. He placed the key in and locked it tight.

Sam stopped at the sight of Gabriel, "I'm sure you're happy now, aren't you?"

Gabriel pulled closer by grabbing the bars. He pressed his nose through, "I have no idea what you're talking about, Sheriff."

Sam just glared at him, "Then why the smirk?"

"Happy to see you is all."

Without a word, Sam walked back to his desk and pulled out papers from a drawer and wrote. Gabriel guessed prisoner papers for his release. He smiled to himself. It was a glorious day. He managed back to his bed and sat. Jimmy sat against the opposite wall with his head in his hands. Gabriel should feel sorry for the poor man. But he followed orders and when the Mayor says jump, you jump. That's what Jimmy did. Gabriel always enjoyed a good lapdog.

"Gabriel."

He stole a glance at Jimmy who looked up.

"How are you going to get me out of here?"

He chuckled, it was a good question, "You'll just have to wait and see."

"You got me into this mess, you better get me out, or so help me God."

"God can't help you now. Only I can."

A few minutes later, Judge Talbert walked into Sam's office. He couldn't make out what they were saying, but Sam just handed the Judge paperwork needed to free him.

Talbert looked it over and Gabriel saw the fat man frown, "What's the meaning of this?"

Sam stood and paced. His arms flailed about. "I cannot in good conscious release Gabriel. He was the mastermind behind Joe's murder."

"I told you. Jimmy's going to pay for the murders. The dead man was the orchestrator. What part of that didn't you understand?"

"I'm not releasing him. If you won't do what the law demands, I will."

The Judge shoved the papers at Sam and pushed the man into his own chair.

"How dare you," he growled, "I'll have your job for this."

Talbert let his fat settle and walked toward the jail cell.

"Talbert!" Sam, now wielding his gun, aimed it at the Judge's back.

Gabriel found the whole exchange amusing. What would Judge Talbert do? How would he get out of this pickle? And Sam, he didn't think the Sheriff had it in him to betray the man who helped get him elected. That man being Gabriel. So much for loyalty.

"I'd advise you to lower that pistol," Talbert said. He fiddled with the keys he pulled from a nearby wall. He approached Gabriel's cell, "Hello, Grant." He slid the skeleton key into the slot, and the door opened with a clink. Talbert swung the door open and Gabriel stepped through.

"Gabriel, you better get your butt back into that cell."

Before Gabriel could say a word, Talbert reached behind his belly and pulled a .38 caliber pistol. He handed the gun to Gabriel.

"What are you two talking about?"

He could feel the man's fear and the tension in the room escalated. Gabriel placed his hand on the Judge's arm, "Thank you." He leaned around the fat man and fired the gun. Sam Ballot blinked. The bullet passed into his heart. The look of shock and surprise reached the Sheriff's eyes. He looked at the blood running down his chest. His gaze clouded as he tried to cock his gun but slumped over, dead. Satisfied, Gabriel handed the gun back to Talbert, "Get Jimmy out of there."

The tiny man whooped and giggled, "Sheriff got that one real good. Nice one, boss."

Gabriel stepped over the Sheriff's dead corpse before stopping at the door. "I'll meet you at your office, Judge. And thank you for everything. I couldn't have done it without your help." He grabbed his hat. "Coming, Jimmy?"

The small man pulled on his hat and followed Gabriel out the door, dancing.

CHAPTER FIFTY-ONE

I T WAS LATE afternoon by the time Jacob arrived in Purgatory. He couldn't leave right away, as Bill required his help to hold up a beam to reset the work shed's roof. One thing bothered him the whole ride into town: why would the Judge care if Missy ran the tavern or not? The man oozed debauchery from every pore and didn't care who he abused. Unfortunately, Missy received his wrath and desires. Glad he didn't carry a gun, otherwise he might take action against the Judge and put a bullet between his legs. The man deserved that much, and Jacob imagined the shock on Talbert's face after he lost his...

Jacob regretted the thought and his heart sank to his toes. How could a man of God justify such thinking? Didn't the Bible say, "as a man thinketh in his heart, so is he: Eat and drink, saith he to thee; but his heart is not with thee?" Did Jacob's heart belong to God? Sure didn't seem that way.

Jacob stared ahead at the vast hills. The trees swayed against the cool breeze. Trying their best to stand against the wind, they held their strength. Something Jacob felt he lacked.

He had tried, really tried over these past few weeks to entertain thoughts of God fighting his battles, only to have that idea squashed by his actions. Not that he directly hurt Missy and took away her tavern, but pursuing Gabriel, with no thought about anyone else, caused her to lose the one thing she loved. It didn't seem fair—though life rarely was.

Town's sign rose from behind the hill, and Jacob knew it'd be moments before he stood in front of the courthouse confronting Judge Talbert. He was doing this for Missy. The other thing was that Jacob didn't want to become a man who cared more about his well-being than anyone else. But here he was, fighting for Missy when he should just let it alone. And maybe he simply made mountains out of mole hills, but the Judge needed to understand one thing: Jacob wouldn't back down until he gave in and let Missy back through the doors.

Jacob defended her honor. As a woman, Missy deserved as much. He cared for her, desired that she have a good life, and would make that a reality. She didn't have much, just what she'd made of herself in the tavern. Which is why he needed to fight for her benefit - Missy wouldn't.

As he descended into town, he passed by Freddy's place. The skinny man sat on a rocker smoking. He waved and called Jacob over. Leading his horse up next to the blacksmith's shop, Jacob nodded toward the man.

"Jake. How ya do'n?"

"A little on edge, today. I don't feel like getting into it right now."

Freddy, nodded, "No prob. You hear about Missy?"

Jacob hung his head. So much for staying out of the conversation. "Yes, that's why I'm in town. Going to give the Judge a piece of my mind."

Freddy tossed the cigarette with a flick and stood. He

steadied Jacob's horse and said, "Do yourself a favor, don't argue too much with the Judge. He holds a lot of power in this town, now that Gabriel is out of commission."

"I'll do what is necessary for Missy and this town," he shot back.

Freddy cursed, "Alrighty, but don't say I never warned ya."

"I have to go. I want to catch Talbert before he heads home for the night." He slapped the reins to keep plodding up the street. By the time he reached the tavern, Jacob noticed a small commotion coming from the Sheriff's office. A small crowd had gathered, and he saw several of the men had their hats off and others were flailing their arms about.

He slowed to a stop at the Sheriff's office, "What's going on?"

Otis, one of his parishioners, turned, "Reverend, it's the Sheriff. Someone has shot him dead."

The news shocked Jacob. *Sam?* He dismounted and pushed through the crowd. One man stopped him, "I wouldn't go in there, Rev. It's not a pretty sight." Jacob ignored him and pressed his way through the door. There, laying in a pool of sticky blood, was Sheriff Sam Ballot's dead body. His skin was already pale and blue. Jacob reached down and touched his neck. Cold. He'd been dead for a few hours, at least.

He looked up toward the jail cells and saw Gabriel's wide open. He wasn't there, he was gone. Jacob pulled up and walked to the cell. Everything remained where it sat. A book, a blanket, and a waste bucket. Gabriel got up and left? Someone had to have opened the jail door and let him out. Jacob grabbed the door and held the cold iron. He felt strong enough to bend the door in half. Anger rose in his chest. He slammed the door and it vibrated against the violent onslaught.

"Where's Gabriel Grant?" Jacob seethed.

Otis, now inside the jail, said, "It's a shame, Ballot was a good man."

Jacob grabbed the elderly man by his bony shoulders, "Where's Gabriel? Has anyone seen him?"

Otis shook his head, "I've not seen him. Course, I wasn't the first person here. Without a sheriff, who'll keep our people safe?"

That question was the least of Jacob's worries. Why wasn't anyone concerned about Gabriel Grant? Now freed, there was no doubt he'd pay retribution to Jacob for placing him in prison. Jacob feared for the safety of his family, and his own life was now at the mercy of Gabriel Grant. He lifted his eyes to the crowd, "Did anyone see where they went? Did anyone see who came out of the jail after someone shot the Sheriff?"

Everyone shook their heads. They hadn't.

Jacob pushed his way back outside and looked up and down the street for any sign of Gabriel Grant. The man was gone. Time to get the Judge involved. He grabbed his horse and shot down the street. The Purgatory courthouse sat at the end of town. The church and the courthouse stood on either end of the town, bookending Purgatory in legal and religious traditions.

He dismounted and scampered up the steps with the determination to understand what had happened to the Sheriff.

CHAPTER FIFTY-TWO

GABRIEL BREATHED a sigh of relief. He was free. Not just free, but cleared of all charges. In time, they would bring the Sheriff's murderer to justice. And that's where Jimmy fell into his plan. The poor sap didn't stand a chance to escape this one alive. He'd shot Joe and his family, and it wouldn't be a stretch to say he overpowered the Sheriff and killed him before the Judge freed Gabriel from prison. At least that's the story he'd tell the fine people of Purgatory.

Judge Talbert settled his fat into a tight-looking chair. He leaned back and popped open his brandy. He offered Gabriel a glass and the two men toasted his release from prison and talked through plans on how to give Gabriel what he wanted—power. Gabriel would re-assume his position as Mayor of Purgatory, and he would take the spots for the church and school. No delaying the inevitable; then he'd run Jacob Creek out of town or shoot him in the head. Either way, he'd be rid of the Preacher and his righteous indignation.

"You think he'll leave Purgatory?"

The Judge sat back and swished his glass around before

sipping it. "I think anything is possible. The thing is, once he figures out I have released you from prison, the man will be hell bent on doing anything to have the Marshal reconsider keeping you a free man."

"And if I offer him something he can't refuse?"

"That would be?"

"A church building, outside of town. I have a piece of land I'm not doing anything with. Course, he'd have to build the church himself and I own the bank. So, he defaults, I'll push him out of town." He waited for Talbert to take the bait. And he did.

Talbert shrugged, "That's a real long shot. Besides, the Reverend doesn't want a new place. He wants you gone. Heck, he's already turning this idiotic town against us." He leaned forward, allowing his elbows to dig into the desk, "I don't get it, Gabriel. Why are you so fascinated with the Reverend? Didn't he pay you back?"

"He did. But I own the bank. I own this town. Nobody blinks unless I say they may blink. I helped Preacher get his loan, and I bought his church land. I own him! And then you know what he did?"

"I'm sure you'll tell me."

"He tacked on another loan to build his barn because the sale of his precious cattle wasn't enough to pay me back for him to rebuild." Gabriel smiled, "Of course I set this whole thing in motion by burning down the man's barn."

The Judge shook his head, "Cost of doing business with you. Never let me get on your bad side."

Gabriel cackled, "Don't be an idiot." Jimmy sat outside the Judge's office, "Come on, we've got business to attend to. We have a schoolhouse and church to shut down."

Jimmy sat up and giggled, "I like children."

The Judge looked disgusted. "You have my permission. Burn both buildings. That'll get things moving in your direction and force the Creeks out of our town."

Gabriel smiled, "Thank you," then turned to leave.

"And, Gabriel, no more dead bodies. Lord knows we have killed enough people."

"Fair enough. But just so you know, I've wanted to take out the Sheriff for a while."

"You're sick, you know that?"

Gabriel heard a door open. Someone was coming.

"TALBERT!" Jacob Creek's voice echoed off the walls.

The Judge looked shocked and Gabriel felt his heart quicken against his chest. "I can't be here when he arrives."

"If you hurry, there's a side door to the building, but it's in the courtroom. You can use the door from my chambers into the courtroom."

Gabriel grabbed Jimmy by the shirt, "Let's go." He kept an ear for Jacob to see where the conversation would go. Would the Judge admit that Gabriel had killed the Sheriff? If so, Talbert was a dead man. He pulled the door, so it left a slight crack to listen.

"Come on, boss."

"Shut up, Jimmy. I want to listen."

He watched Jacob enter Talbert's office. Determination fired in the Reverend's eyes as he pushed the door open. No doubt he'd heard about the release and seen the Sheriff's dead corpse. Shame, really; the Sheriff was a good advocate and ally, but he'd defied Gabriel and received a bullet as a thank you for his service.

The Judge settled back as the chair squeaked under his weight. "What do I owe this privilege, Reverend?"

"Did you hear the Sheriff is dead?"

A pause, "No, I didn't. What happened?"

Good boy, Gabriel thought.

"Someone shot him dead at the jail. Someone let Gabriel Grant go."

"Well, don't know anything about the Sheriff, but I was the one who released Gabriel."

Another pause. Jacob chewed over what the Judge had said. The question lingering in Gabriel's mind: would he buy it? The man's face turned red, and he balled his fists, "You what? The Marshal will be here tomorrow to see that Gabriel is taken for trial. Why would you let him go? You know he'll come after anyone who's crossed him. He'll come after me!"

True, and the Reverend was about to find out how much he'd pay for his insolence. Talbert thinks he's going to offer the Preacher land. What an idiot. Gabriel just used him for his own gain. He knew full well that Judge Rex Talbert hated his guts and wanted him gone, but truth to tell, they needed each other. They had a symbiotic relationship, and Talbert wouldn't be where he was without Gabriel's influence. He kept Talbert around because he allowed Gabriel to do what he pleased.

He waited for the Judge to respond, "Well, I can't tell you everything, it's an ongoing investigation. I can tell you this, a man came forward claiming he had something to do with the deaths of that tiny lawyer fella from Cedar Grove and the Packard family. What a shame they all had to die the way they did." He leaned forward on his fat elbows, "You think this guy could have killed our beloved Sheriff?"

Don't sap it up too much or the Preacher might get suspicious. The last thing Gabriel needed was the Judge to thwart his plans to get even with Jacob Creek. He looked at Jimmy, who looked bored and didn't care to be there. He kicked the man's boot and whispered, "Time to go."

He shut the door to Talbert's office, and they made their way through the courthouse and out the side door. Two horses sat at the ready and Gabriel pulled himself up. Jimmy followed suit. He led the horse to the right and behind the buildings.

He saw the schoolhouse at the edge of town. The children were gone by now and it was time he'd made a final statement to Jacob: you don't mess with Gabriel Grant or there would be consequences.

He smiled. This would be fun.

CHAPTER FIFTY-THREE

JACOB BALLED his fists with the urge to crawl over Judge Talbert's desk and knock him in the jaw. He had had every intention of confronting the man regarding Missy, and now, with Gabriel Grant at large, those thoughts lost ground. He pushed thoughts of Missy aside and concentrated his mind on getting the Judge to tell him where Gabriel was. Jacob paced in front of the desk, trying to calm down.

"I'm going to ask you again, why did you release Gabriel Grant from prison? I know I don't know how the law works, but I know this, if they jail a man for murder, you cannot just release him if it directly involves him. There's evidence found at the Packard farm of Gabriel's involvement. You have to at least consider the evidence. At least wait until Marshal Bennington arrives back in town to make that decision."

The Judge seemed to consider the issue. He pulled a cigar and lit the cut end. He pulled smoke into his lungs before exhaling. "Reverend Creek," he said, tapping the ash against the side of his desk, "I'm fully aware the release of Gabriel

Grant elicits provocation for you and others, but I cannot ignore eyewitness accounts."

Jacob leaned forward. What did he just hear? "And that's stopped you before? Eyewitnesses saw Gabriel kill my father. The rules of a duel were not followed and are illegal. You of all people should know that."

Talbert leaned back, "I remember hearing a story of a former United States Vice-President Aaron Burr having a duel with Alexander Hamilton. Now, Hamilton and Burr were rivals. They hated each other's guts. In fact, Hamilton supported Thomas Jefferson in the race against Aaron Burr. He never forgave his former friend for siding with Jefferson."

"What's this have to do with Grant?"

He held up a hand and puffed another round of smoke, "Let me finish. After years of failing in the political arena, Burr wrote a letter to Alexander Hamilton challenging him to a duel. Hamilton accepted. They met over the border in New Jersey. Both men were handed pistols and given the rules of a duel.

"Now some people say Hamilton missed Burr with a bullet; however, the rules of a duel state that one person shoots, then the other takes their turn. Burr fired and shot his former friend and political rival." Talbert placed his cigar in a glass ashtray and crossed his sausage-like fingers, "What I'm saying, your father fired first and missed. Gabriel is an excellent marksman. Because of these rules and because of my desire to keep the peace, Gabriel was released from all charges for killing your father. There was nothing I could do."

Jacob gripped the chair. He sat down. The clean nature of the Judge's story was nice; however, the fact still remained that Gabriel Grant had murdered his father. Sure, they didn't have dueling pistols, but they should have followed the rules. One shot! Gabriel fired twice, or so he was told. Once both he and Sarah arrived in town to take over the church, Gabriel couldn't stand their sight and demanded payment; when that didn't happen, he burned down the barn. He'd harassed the Creek family and now he'd be coming after Jacob to settle a score started by his late father. How could he win against such odds? Where was God and why was he so silent?

"Your Honor, you know full well the man that Gabriel Grant is. You know that he will not relent until I meet his desires. He will not rest and he will not stop until I'm dead of broke. He won't stop at the amount I still owe him. He'll take everything until I'm a broken man who has nothing left."

The Judge narrowed his eyes, leaned back, and poured another drink, "I'm very sorry. There's nothing I can do. You'll have to take this up with the United States Marshal's office. I know that's not what you want to hear, but my hands are tied. I'm sorry."

Jacob's nails bit into his palms as he balled his hands. He clenched his jaw so tight he feared a tooth might shatter. He stood and leaned forward on the desk, "Just wait, you will someday owe Gabriel Grant and when he comes collecting, you'll wished you listened."

"I already paid my dues, and Sam's dead," he slurped his brandy and grimaced. "Is there anything else?"

CHAPTER FIFTY-FOUR

"**D**O YOU HAVE everything, honey?" Sarah called after Virginia, who was still collecting her slate and desk items.

"I think so. I don't want to forget my chalk. It's kinda hard to do my homework without it." She tossed a few items into her sack and flipped it over her shoulder. "Okay, Mommy, I think I'm ready."

Sarah leaned against the door frame. It'd been a long day. First Missy early this morning, and now a group of rowdy children who wouldn't listen or sit down. The worst offender was Felix. She frowned, feeling bad for the boy. It wasn't his fault that his father sat in Sam Ballot's jail. Ever more so, Sarah's heart went out to Moira. The poor woman would have to raise Felix on her own. Maybe she'd head over tomorrow to help Moira handle a few things at home. Maybe she'd take a pie to give them something different from staff cooked meals.

Virginia hauled her sack and set it down with a thump. Sarah stared at the bulging burlap. "What, pray tell, do you have stuffed in this bag?" She reached down and picked up the sack. "Good, Lord, child. I don't think you need everything in this sack. Now, I want you to take out everything but your primer and your slate board."

She frowned, "Must I?"

Sarah shot a glance, and the girl understood, "I won't ask again," she said, driving the point home.

"Yes, Ma'am."

"Go on now."

Virginia hauled the sack back to her desk and unpacked the many items she'd stuffed into her bag. She pulled out her slate, several books, Sarah's board eraser, and other odds and ends. Her new dolly fell out onto the ground. Glancing back at Sarah, Virginia mumbled something and smiled. She tossed the doll onto her desk and continued pulling items out.

Shaking her head, Sarah wondered how much more could be in Virginia's little sack. The sound of boots caught her attention, and she cranked her head and shrieked in terror as she plastered herself against the door.

"I'm sorry, did I disturb you, Sarah?"

"I thought..." her eyes deceived her, but there he stood, "I thought you were in jail?"

Gabriel smiled. "Surprise, surprise, isn't it?" He grabbed her wrists and pinned them to the doorframe, "I do love a good surprise."

Sarah tried to wriggle from his grip, but the more she fought, the tighter his grip became. Where was Jacob? She knew he came to town and hadn't checked in. They were to have lunch, but he never showed. "What do you want?" She said, trying to keep her voice calm but failing.

Virginia looked up at the third person, "Mommy?"

Sarah pleaded with her daughter to stay back.

"Mommy!"

"Mommy's okay, just going to have a little chat with me."

Gabriel yanked Sarah from the door and tossed her. She flew down the stairs.

Virginia screamed.

Her shoulder hit first, followed by her leg as burning pain rippled through her shin. No doubt she'd scraped it against the steps. She tumbled as her hands dug deep into the gravel. Her palms burned from loose, bleeding skin. Sarah pulled up to her knees and balled her dress into her palms to soak up the blood leaking from her wounds.

"I'm sorry, was that too much?" His boots clunked against the wood as each step called out *I'm coming for you.* His eyes lit with malice and his mouth twitched in delight.

Where was Jacob?

"Mrs. Creek, I'm going to ask you a question and I want you to answer this in all honesty," Gabriel knelt, and she felt his hot breath against her neck.

Sarah held her tongue.

He placed his thumb under her chin and raised it so her eyes could look into his. "I'm trying to be nice and not lose my temper." A tear slipped and dropped onto her dress. "There, there," he said and wiped her cheek with his gloved hand, "I'm not the monster you think I am."

Gabriel snapped his fingers and a skinny looking man rushed into the schoolhouse. Sarah heard a scream followed by the sound of a slap. Through the darkened door the skinny man dragged Virginia by her hair and pulled her down the steps. That's when she saw the sparkle of a blade pressed against Virginia's belly.

All air escaped Sarah's lungs. She gulped, trying to steady her galloping heart. Her vision faded and her mind reeled against what was happening. Sarah's heart dropped to her knees as she reached for Virginia, "It's okay…"

Virginia's terror-filled eyes ripped Sarah's heart from her chest, "It's okay, honey. Daddy's coming."

Gabriel looked at his man and cocked his head, "Well, this is a predicament I didn't expect." He leaned in close enough to whisper, "He likes kids. A real good baby sitter. Now, I'm going to ask you a question, where is your husband? Where is Jacob?"

Sarah felt the convulsions grip her chest as bile burned the back of her throat. She clenched her jaw and had to get Virginia away from that man. "I don't know."

Gabriel stood, then turned to the skinny man, "I try to be nice and this is the thanks I receive." The back of his hand smacked Sarah hard, and she toppled over as pain rippled through her head.

She pulled up against the pain and felt blood drizzle from a torn lip. Fear clutched her heart and she couldn't inhale. She gasped to find the needed air to stop from hyperventilating.

"Do anything you want to me, don't hurt my baby," she pleaded, she cried, and he had to listen. "Please, Gabriel, you're a father. Don't hurt my baby."

Gabriel snapped his fingers, "Let the girl console her mother."

Skinny man hesitated, then raised his blade against Virginia's neck.

"I won't ask again. We're not going to hurt the girl," he looked at Sarah, "Okay? I won't hurt her."

He released Virginia, and she ran toward her mother. As soon as her daughter slammed against her bruising chest, Sarah toppled over and the two embraced. What did Gabriel want? What purpose would this serve? Jacob would kill the man for this. And that was the first time Sarah understood the anger her husband had toward Gabriel Grant. The man deserved a noose. She tried to get up, but the pain in her leg nailed her to the ground.

"What do you want?" Sarah asked.

Gabriel stooped down again, "I want to watch your husband burn." He stood, "Jimmy, burn it."

Jimmy grabbed a torch and tossed it into the schoolhouse.

CHAPTER FIFTY-FIVE

JACOB STOOD in the Sheriff's doorway. The undertaker had just removed Sam Ballot's body and Jacob felt the tinge of sorrow for the man. Sam got involved with Gabriel Grant and that involvement cost the man his life. He sat down behind the desk and rested his arms against the worn wood. Several papers scattered about and Jacob stared at the badge lying on top. He picked it up and wiped the blood off with a nearby towel.

Everything Gabriel touched died. How long would it be before he showed face in Purgatory? No doubt he'd come after Jacob and anyone else who'd betrayed him. Would Judge Talbert live long enough to see another election? Jacob didn't know, and hoped the large man would do the right thing and arrest Grant for the second time. One thing was for sure, the town needed a new lawman. The Judge gave Jacob temporary status as Purgatory's only lawman.

He pinned the badge, and its weight sagged the shirt. The jail needed scrubbing after Sam's demise. No doubt Momma would have an idea to get blood from floor boards. And now that he was acting Sheriff, he could figure out a way, within the law, to get Gabriel back behind bars. Could he arrest him and the Judge be okay with that decision? Only time would tell.

Picking up several papers, Jacob noticed the Sheriff had investigated the death of the previous Reverend. He rummaged through the drawers and pulled out a journal. He opened the notebook and found the date before he and Sarah arrived in Purgatory. His eyes widened. The Sheriff believed the Reverend's death involved Gabriel Grant.

Fanning the journal, he found an entry dated just two weeks ago. Jacob read the entry.

I was just paid a visit by mercantile owner, Joseph Packard, as an eyewitness to the destruction of the mine shaft out at Purgatory Gulch. He heard Gabriel give the order to make the explosion seem like an accident.

Jacob leaned against the back of the chair and felt his heart race against the ribs. Joe had been right. This confirmed his eyewitness account.

I asked Mr. Packard how he could hear this conversation. To his account, he hid behind a mining car as two men named Jimmy and Aaron moved into the mines to set some TNT.

A question formed, and he asked himself, "If Sam knew about Joe's account, why did he not arrest Gabriel Grant?" It made little sense. If Sam had done his due diligence and corroborated the story with evidence, they'd have enough to put Gabriel away. He rifled through more pages. Several regarding domestic disputes, drunkards, petty theft from a boy in town. The journal ended with no other entries regarding the death of the Reverend.

Jacob shoved his hand into the drawer and found another journal. He peeled back the strap and opened the book. More hand-written notes about several events and then midway through the book he found another entry dated a week ago. What he saw boiled his blood.

I presented Gabriel with Joe's account regarding the night Reverend Jones was killed. After being threatened with losing my job and Gabriel finding a man willing to do the job, I am to bury it and never speak of the former Reverend again. I asked him why and his response was that the Reverend had information regarding illegal movement of cattle belonging to another rancher. Therefore, I believe they killed him and why my life may be in danger. I have closed the case in fear of my life.

If you're reading this, I fear Gabriel had me killed.

Jacob pushed back from the desk, picked up a Bible that lay open, and leaned against the doorframe. Jacob was a minister of the Gospel. He was no lawman. He didn't know the first thing about arresting or bringing charges against someone. He thumbed the badge fixed to his shirt. "Guess I'm all Purgatory has now." Maybe he should talk with Momma or Bill; they'd know what to do with this information. Determined to keep the Judge out of this new investigation, Jacob pushed back from the desk and walked to the doorway.

He stepped foot onto the boardwalk and heard the commotion coming down the street. He strained his eyes and thought he saw smoke rising into the early evening air. That's when he saw a man running toward the Sheriff's office. His arms waved about and he screamed something Jacob couldn't make out. The waning light made it difficult to see who it was.

"Jacob!"

It was Bill, he knew that voice as it became clearer the closer the man ran.

"Jacob!" Bill grabbed the doorframe and heaved as his chest gasped for air. "It's the schoolhouse. It's on fire."

"Fire?" Jacob's heart skipped a few beats, "Sarah? Virginia?"

Bill shook his head, still breathing hard.

"Bill, what about my family?"

He grabbed Jacob's shoulder, "Gabriel has them and he's burning the schoolhouse."

CHAPTER FIFTY-SIX

As Jacob and Bill arrived at the schoolhouse, smoke already filled the air. The stench of burning paint and wood smelled sour in the early evening humidity. Gabriel held Sarah by the arm and another boyish-looking man held Virginia with a knife at her throat. Jacob's heart burst inside his chest and he came to a dead stop.

"Hello, Jacob."

He looked at his wife, then his daughter. Anger, concern, and rage knifed through his gut, "What do you want, Gabriel?"

"I knew you'd come."

He saw his wife's bruised face. Her hands were wringing against her dress, and he saw the bloodstains. Jacob reached for his gun and realized he'd never grabbed it. Bill didn't have his, either, and the two men exchanged a glance. Jacob clutched the Bible he still held tight against his chest. He clenched his teeth and his eyes focused on Gabriel, burning as hot as the fire. "What did you do to my wife?"

The tycoon looked down at Sarah and shrugged his shoulders, "Taught her a lesson you need to learn."

"Let them go. They have nothing to do with any of this. This is between me and you. Let them go!"

Gabriel released his grip on Sarah and told Jimmy to let go of Virginia.

Jacob ran and embraced them. "I'm so sorry, I should have been here. I was just sitting in the Sheriff's office. I should have been here." He wiped the dirt and blood from Sarah's face as a lump formed in his throat. Sarah sobbed against his shoulder. He hugged Virginia, and she collapsed into her own set of convulsions. Jacob's throat tightened as he fought the tears that burned his eyes.

"Okay, I've let them go. Time for us to talk."

Jacob stood, holding Sarah and Virginia's hand, "What do you want, Gabriel? I know about the Reverend Jones' death. The Sheriff recorded everything."

Gabriel pulled a gun from his holster. "Did he now? I guess it's all I can do to keep a man quiet. Guess he deserved what he got. Shame, he was a good lap dog," Gabriel said as he fiddled with his gun's chamber.

Jacob stiffened and wanted to shout and scream. The man hurt his wife, held his daughter at knife point, and burned the school house. What kind of monster was Gabriel Grant?

"Gabriel, your next words better be in surrender. Jacob's acting Sheriff," Bill said.

Gabriel's cackle rippled through the smoke that filled the surrounding air. The building hadn't fully caught on fire, but Jacob feared it would ignite soon enough. "Put down the gun and let's talk this over at the Sheriff's office."

"Bill, I don't think you're in a place to confront me."

Gabriel leveled his gun at the man, "This here conversation is between me and the Reverend."

Jacob held Sarah's hand, "Go with Bill and get Virginia to safety." He knew the two women he cared about needed to leave; needed to be safe. He looked up at Bill, who nodded in an agreement. Jacob stood, "Go. I'll be fine."

Sarah and Virginia remained frozen in place. Gabriel let out a few curses and taunts, which Jacob ignored. This all would end tonight. Whether he could pay, whether he would die, this would end tonight. He pulled the Bible to his chest again and realized how much he'd forsaken the Good Lord's Word. It never really became a part of his life, and he knew now that he had to trust God that would bring this whole mess to a conclusion.

Sarah accepted Bill's hand and Virginia stood, "Let's go, girls. I'll take you to Momma's." They followed Bill and Jacob's heart released its grip of fear. Now, it was just him and Gabriel. Time to bring understanding to the man. The only thing he wished he had was a gun. This would make arresting Gabriel for assault easier. Not that the charges would stick, but at least he could keep the man in prison long enough until Marshal Tan Bennington arrived to discuss what to do next.

"Okay, it's just us. See, they're leaving. I've kept my word," Gabriel said.

No sooner than Gabriel let the words into the air, Virginia turned on her heels and ran into the burning building. "My Dolly!"

Sarah screamed something, and Jacob's feet froze to the ground. He held his breath as Bill ran after Sarah, who also ran into the fire to stop Virginia.

Gabriel's gun sounded, and the bullet struck Bill in the

head. Bill's head snapped back before the man toppled forward, landing on the ground like a sack of potatoes. Jacob tried to yell, but the sound remained caught in his throat.

He ran forward and swung a fist at Gabriel. Pain rippled through his hand as Gabriel's gun clattered on the ground. He blocked one blow, then Gabriel's gloved hand collided with his jaw and sent him sprawling to the ground. He had to get to Sarah and Virginia. They needed his help, they would die in that fire. He pushed himself up to run as Jimmy grabbed his arms, holding him back.

Fire exploded out the front door and raged from the building as black, billowing smoke rolled upwards, darkening the sky—accentuated by Jacob's scream. It wouldn't be long before the entire structure caved in. The heat from the flames caused the windows of the little school to explode with a sickening shatter. Death filled the air with the smell of burning flesh. The screams coming from inside the building had stopped and Jacob's whole world crashed.

The shock of what happened slapped him across the face. His shirt was torn and dirty as Jimmy held him back by the arms. His knees dug in deep on the gravel ripping holes in his slacks. *Why? Why would God let this happen?* Is this what happens when you trust the Almighty? Fire knew no bounds, and it never set its captives free. Jacob tried, and he failed. He wanted to kill. He wanted to cry. He wanted to feel nothing at all because nothing else mattered.

Jacob gasped for breath.

The sound of his Bible clattering next to his leg caught his attention.

"Guess you'll be building that new school after all Preacher, the church is next."

The blow to the ribcage by Gabriel's boot shot a piercing pain through him as three ribs broke, sucking the air from his body. Jacob cried out as his lung rubbed against each broken bone, causing him to gasp for air, which sent another wave of searing pain over him.

Jacob wanted to join his wife and child inside the burning building. There would be no relief. His whole world just ended. Why did God forsake him? His wife, Sarah, and daughter, Virginia, were *dead*.

"You killed them!" he screamed in pain and grabbed at his side. He slowly stood to his feet. He lunged at Gabriel. His fist connected with the man's chin and Gabriel's head snapped back.

Gabriel wiped the blood from his lip and laughed. "Preacher's got some right hook." He picked up his hat and dusted it off, "I'm real sorry for your loss, but I warned you. Now, get off my land before I shoot you in the head."

"Shoot me dead. Let me die," his scream burned his throat like the fire burned his wife and daughter. He looked at Gabriel as tears formed in his eyes. What would it matter? Gabriel Grant should shoot him. There was nothing worth living for, anyway.

Sarah and Virginia were dead.

Another shattering pain waved across his jaw as Gabriel's fist buried into his flesh. Then another. Then another. Jacob peeled himself off the gravel and spat blood.

Gabriel pulled him up by the shirt, "I'm not going to kill you. But I want you gone. I broke you and your righteous indignation. I told you I was a god in this town. I told you this land was mine. I told you that your family was indebted, and you did not listen. I'm real sorry they died, but your stupid daughter ran into the fire. You could have remained some semblance of a life with your wife, but you didn't stop her either."

Then the sadness melted away. He closed his heart. God would no longer listen to Jacob's cries and prayers. Jacob would wait. He pulled himself away from Gabriel and dug his eyes into the man's soul and found he had none.

COLD RETRIBUTION

Say to them that are of a fearful heart, Be strong, fear not: behold, your God will come with *vengeance*, even God with a recompense; he will come and *save you.*

— *ISAIAH*

CHAPTER FIFTY-SEVEN

JACOB STOOD there, broken, bloodied, and bruised. The school house continued to burn against the darkened sky. The shattering of glass and laughter split the night as he saw the church also go up in flames. Flames reached the steeple and wrapped their tongues around the cross perched on top. After several minutes, the cross crashed to the ground, engulfed in the yellow fire. Jacob's ears buzzed against the raging migraine that ravaged his head, and then he looked down at Bill's unmoving body and his heart shattered like glass. Gabriel had shot his friend in the head.

His knees buckled and his body crumpled to the ground. *Why?* Why did God allow this to happen? What did Sarah and Virginia do to deserve such a horrible death? He'd never recover their bodies. He had no one to bury. He had no home to call his own. Jacob was a broken man. They were dead. Bill was dead. Nothing mattered.

Nothing.

A small crowd formed behind Jacob as several wanted to see what happened. Surely they didn't know about his family.

All they could see was Bill's lifeless form and burning buildings. Gabriel Grant had just let the entire town know he was in control and if you crossed him, if you made any move against him—you'd die! He heard the commotion as people gathered around to watch the buildings burn. Someone told people to disperse and leave before a hand landed on his shoulder. He looked up at Freddy. The man's face wore shock and sadness.

"Jacob, what happened?"

Jacob looked down as his throat tightened. He balled his fists and shoved them deep into the gravel, widening his already split knuckles. "They're…dead." He looked into Freddy's eyes as the man examined the scene.

"I'm sorry about Bill. Who else did he kill?"

Jacob slid his Bible over and picked it up, curling the book into his hands and squeezing the pages, "My family." Jacob gritted through teeth. All he envisioned were their bodies engulfed in flames, burning them in their horrified screams before it left nothing except charred bone.

The color drained from Freddy's face. He looked at the smoldering building, then at Jacob. "Sarah and Virginia?"

Jacob nodded, not knowing what to say. All words escaped him and killing Gabriel marched across his mind. Would he ever be able to pick up the broken pieces of his life? Would he ever be whole again? Maybe time would tell, but everything seemed like an illusion. His family wasn't dead, they were waiting for him at the ranch. He dusted his knees and walked over to his dead friend. He rolled Bill's lifeless body over while praying that, by God's grace, maybe Bill was still alive. The wound in his head left little sign that Bill lived. The back of his head had shattered from the bullet. He closed his friend's eyes out of respect and wiped fresh tears as they formed.

How would he tell Momma? She was all he had left. No one else mattered to Jacob, just Momma, and he concluded that Gabriel would go after her next. Resolve filled his heart and he stood to face Freddy. The man looked pained as sadness filled his dark eyes. "We have to get to Momma's. I don't want Gabriel going after her next."

Freddy nodded, "Okay. What do you want me to do? How can I help?"

"Help me keep her safe. Do you own a gun?"

"I don't like them too much, prefer a nice tomahawk, but yes, I have a gun."

Jacob held his ribs tight. Each breath and word shot waves of new pain through his body, "I need you to grab your gun and meet me at the Miner's Lodge." He grabbed the man's hands, "Can you do that for me?"

"I'll see you soon."

"Be careful," Jacob said as Freddy took off toward his shop and Jacob prayed he didn't run into Gabriel Grant in the meantime.

Jacob looked at the smoldering building, "I'm so sorry I couldn't keep you safe. Sarah, forgive me for what I'm about to do." Placing his hand against the ribs, Jacob made his way toward Momma's Lodge to warn her and tell her what happened. He feared this would paralyze his mother and she would stop living. She loved Bill and it pained Jacob that they all lost someone today.

As he passed by the tavern, Missy stood on the porch, looking in Jacob's direction. At the moment he didn't want to talk. He had to get to Momma's house.

"Jacob? Are you okay?"

He tried holding up his hand, "I can't talk. Get inside."

"Jacob, what's going on?"

Jacob felt a wave of fresh emotion squeeze his heart. He stopped and looked away. He couldn't bear saying their names at the moment. Not again. And he didn't. Missy saw the pain and hurt filling his eyes as he tried to hide it, but there was no escaping how fragile he felt.

Missy held a hand to her lips, "Oh, Jacob…"

"I'm sorry, I have to go," he pulled away and continued toward the Lodge. Nothing needed to be said, his actions told her who died. She had gone through enough, with no need to take on his grief and pain. As Jacob approached the Lodge, Momma was already on her porch humming a song. He slowed and winced against the pain robbing his ability to walk straight when he recognized the song. Momma loved this one. It was the first time following his father's death that he'd heard the hymn while attending church with her.

As he drew closer, she sang the words, "Safe in the arms of Jesus, safe on his gentle breast; there by his love o'er-shaded, sweetly my soul shall rest. Hark! 'Tis the voice of angels borne in a song to me, over the fields of glory, over the jasper sea."

Tears flooded Jacob's eyes. He sobbed against the sharp pain of his ribs and for a moment, the pain faded. "Momma…"

She broke into her own sobs and he realized she knew full well what happened. "Safe in the arms of Jesus, safe from corroding care, safe from the world's temptations; sin cannot harm me there. Free from the blight of sorrow, free from my doubts and fears; only a few more trials…" Momma fell to her knees as her voice broke into sobs, "…only a few more tears!"

The two embraced and Jacob welcomed his mother's loving arms. He melted against her and wanted to push so far into the earth that he ceased to exist. The words washed over him and he begged her to finish the refrain. He fought the large lump that formed in his throat as his chest heaved against the sobs that shook his body.

"It's okay, son." She finished the song, "Jesus, my heart's dear refuge, Jesus has died for me; firm on the Rock of Ages ever my trust shall be. Here let me wait with patience, wait till the night is o're; wait till I see the morning break on the golden shore."

CHAPTER FIFTY-EIGHT

TWO DAYS later they all stood on the hill overlooking where the church used to sit. Sniffles, cries, and whispered prayers made their way through the small gathering of parishioners and town folk. They faced the two caskets which contained Sarah's and Bill's remains, while a lone cross sat next to theirs, denoting where Virginia would have been buried. They never found her body. Jacob held his mother's hand as she pulled her black veil tighter around her neck. The air pebbled his skin, and he wished the sun would peek through the clouds for just a moment to honor their dead. But that wouldn't ever happen. Dark, grey clouds that filled his heart with anger now shrouded his life. Nothing in his life would ever bring comfort and healing to the pain that ravaged his inner man.

Pulling up his collar to protect his neck from the wind, Jacob wished this whole miserable moment was over. He didn't need those around him paying their respects and didn't need them to give him their unsolicited sympathies. He wanted to be left alone. Other than the night of their murders, his mother pulled on him to keep trusting in God.

But why?

Didn't God abandon him the moment they ran into the fire? They left Jacob to pick up the pieces of his broken life and make something happen. He gawped at that.

Jacob nursed the broken ribs and wished he didn't have to wince with every breath or movement. His eyes blurred with fresh tears. His body numbed against the pain that ripped his heart in half.

A tear slid down Jacob's face as the minister spoke his eulogy. Momma sent for him from Cheyenne and he came at once. Jacob turned to his mother and squeezed her hand.

Momma glanced up and smiled through tear stained cheeks. She placed her other hand on top of his, "We'll get through this, I promise." She squeezed his hand and looked back at the minister.

"We commit to the ground the bodies of Sarah Callihan-Creek, Virginia Creek, and Bill Erickson. We know they are counting their blessings in the presence of our Lord and Savior, Jesus Christ. For dust we are and dust we shall return."

Jacob and Momma knelt down and lifted handfuls of dirt. He held it for what seemed to be an eternity, then loosened his grip and watched the black earth fall onto Bill's coffin. It danced about before resting on top the wooden box his friend would now call home until Christ returns. He picked up two more handfuls and laid one on Sarah's casket and the other on Virginia's grave. As his hands touched the soil he prostrated to the ground and wept. His heart ached for them. After several minutes he stood and found only Momma and Freddy remained.

"I'm so sorry, son. You've had so much pain in this life. I

pray you find solace in God. I'm praying for you and I love you." She looked at the graves again, "I sure miss them."

The words stung, "Me, too. I need to find Gabriel. I need the man to pay for what he's done," he slammed his fists together.

"Remember, we have to trust God. I don't know why the Good Lord took our beloved, but we need trust that he will guide us and protect us."

He knew she was right, but hated it all the same. He huffed and blew air, causing his lips to flap and then clenched and unclenched his fists.

"Jacob, are you praying? Because that's the only thing that will get us through."

"I don't want your platitudes. I don't want sympathy. I want Grant to pay. He killed them, he took them from me."

"I know. Have you talked with the Marshal yet?"

Jacob looked away. "The Marshal is searching with the full force of the U. S. Marshal's service. I'm waiting, but if I wait any longer, I may just snap. I'll hang Gabriel myself."

She sighed and pulled closer, "Remember, the Lord is your rock and your refuge. In him place your trust and he will fight the battle for you."

His heart cracked and the lava began its slow rise. He felt his face flush hot and clenched his nails deep into his palms. He walked toward his horse, "Momma, I love you, but I can't do this. How dare you bring God into this conversation. He did nothing for me, he let my wife and daughter die. For all I know, God could have killed them himself. I have nothing left. I know you're hurting too, but don't put God back onto my plate. For all I care, God can shove off."

The moment the words left his mouth, he felt bad, and could see the pain and wounds he ripped open in his mother's eyes. A single tear formed and trailed its way down her cheek. She brushed her dress, "I think I need to be alone now."

"Momma," tears welled in his eyes and he knew what he said was wrong. She loved him. She'd lost her whole family too. And his words were raw and he was glad no one else was around.

Momma walked to the wagon, climbed aboard, then placed her head deep into her hands and sobbed. "Oh, dear God…"

He nodded a short smile and watched as Freddy, with a gun still strapped to his waist, jumped up next to Momma and lead her home, leaving Jacob alone. Looking at their graves for a moment, he finally mounted his horse and rode home, listening to the methodic thump-thump of Gypsy's hooves as they echoed through the night. Jacob mindlessly gazed at the stars pricking the night with light. Darkness had crept its way into his soul a little each passing day and he wondered if God pricked his heart like those stars. The glimpse of the man he was with Sarah seemed a lifetime ago. Gabriel Grant chipped away pieces of his life until he took everything from him. Chip, chip, chip, like a lumberjack pulling down a pine. The tree of life crashed to the ground of his heart and would never see the light of day again.

The ranch sat dark against the black night.

No light.

No sound.

No laughter.

Jacob put the horse away in her stall and silently brushed her down from the sweaty ride home. Jacob grabbed the lantern and made his way inside. He sat down in his favorite chair and numbly stared at the window, while ghosts of yesterday fluttered in his mind like a butterfly happily dancing about the sunflowers. He smiled at the memories and allowed his eyes to fill with fresh tears.

He missed them and suddenly realized that he hated being alone.

IN THE DAYS following their funeral, Jacob tried to find Gabriel Grant, but the man had disappeared.

"I want you to go home, Jacob. Get rest. Find closure," Tan said.

"I want Gabriel dead. Can you guarantee that for me?"

"There's a warrant out for his arrest in the murder of Bill, the Sheriff, and your family. Go home, Jacob. Let me handle this."

Jacob agreed and found comfort for his grief in the tavern. Whiskey became the only medium in which he drowned his sorrows and pain. Now here he sat, alone in a dark home with a whiskey bottle in his hand wishing for some kind of normalcy. He regretted the way he treated Momma after the funeral. He wished the whole nightmare would end and the dark storm that ravaged his soul would end.

Through everything, Sarah was the only one who brought him comfort and clarity in the midst of life's storms. He felt like the disciples clinging for their life while Jesus slept. Was Jesus sleeping now? If only someone would help him feel free of the pain. Sarah couldn't, she was dead and Jacob was alone.

A knock at the door interrupted his thoughts. It was light and soft. "Who is it?"

"Missy."

He got up and opened the door for her. She walked in and removed the shawl from her shoulders and untied her bonnet.

"Why are you here?"

"I wanted to check in on you. I felt bad that I haven't seen you since the funeral."

He smiled at that. It was sweet and Jacob was glad she came. "That's very kind." He glanced at the cold stove, "I'm sorry, it's cold in here and I have nothing to offer you."

She approached and pulled at his hands. He wrapped his arms around her waist and let his emotions run their course. They hugged for several moments and he breathed heavy against her and apologized for getting her dress wet from his tears. She smiled as he sat down. He didn't want to be alone. He needed someone there.

"Can you stay? I can't do this alone. I don't know what I'm supposed to do now that they're gone."

Missy kneeled next to his chair and rested her head against his knee. "I'm so sorry Jake. I'll stay as long as you want."

Grateful, he knelt and pulled her into an embrace. Then Jacob Creek wept.

After several minutes, Missy lifted his head and kissed his lips.

Jacob looked away, "I'm sorry. I shouldn't have."

Missy pulled his chin back and he gazed into her blue eyes, "You didn't," and they kissed again, but this time, he didn't pull away and Jacob wrapped his arms around her, pulling her close so he could feel warm again. He needed to feel love wash away the sadness even if for a moment.

CHAPTER FIFTY-NINE

Sarah and Virginia were alive and well. Sarah busied herself in the kitchen, cooking up a healthy amount of eggs, ham, biscuits, and gravy. The smell intoxicated Jacob as he propped himself up on the bed and smiled. It felt good to smile. Casting the sheets aside, Jacob shufflefooted to the kitchen and wrapped his arms around Sarah—something he'd done for years.

She smiled and kissed him on the lips, "Hello, you. I'm trying to fix you breakfast."

Jacob poured himself a fresh cup of coffee and sat at the table as Virginia busied herself drawing something on a loose piece of paper. "What are you doing?"

"I'm making a picture for you, Daddy," She smiled and continued to color.

"Can I see what you're working on?"

She giggled and lifted the paper. As he stared at the page, horror wrapped its talons around his mind and his heart leapt from his chest. He lifted the sheet from her little hand and saw a school building with colors of fire drawn around the structure. Sweat rolled down his face as her hand turned black and crumbled. He turned to Sarah who lifted a pan from the stove as her chest and body erupted into flames. Jacob tried to scream but couldn't. He grabbed at his throat to find that he too was on fire.

The scream popped Jacob's eyes open. He lay there, in a soaked bed filled with sticky sweat. He peeled himself from the mattress and crossed the room to a basin of water that sat on their dresser and he splashed the cool water onto his face. He sat back down and the realization that they were dead settled back into his heart. Balling his fist, he drove it into the soft mattress. *Why them?* Why couldn't God have taken him?

Jacob had never felt such sadness in all his life. It enveloped him and pulled him deeper into the pit of despair. Remembering Missy went home last night, he regretted what happened between them. How would that honor Sarah? Sure, it was just a kiss and he was glad it became nothing more. Shame filled his mind and he couldn't shake how wrong he felt. He used his sadness to feel close to someone, anyone who'd take the reality of what happened to his family away.

He pulled a fresh bottle of whiskey out of the cupboard, which Missy had brought, and poured himself a cupful. The golden contents sloshed around and begged for him to consume his sorrows in its harsh alcohol. Lifting the cup, he swallowed a mouth-filling gulp, allowing the burn to slide down and warm his chest. Whatever the stuff did, he felt its effects the moment the whiskey emptied into his stomach. His hands tingled and that's when his head spun light and dizzy.

Tucking the bottle under his arm, Jacob made his way back to the chair. He sat down with a plop and let the rocker lull his senses. Would the sadness ever end? Would he ever feel alive again? Day after day, Jacob pulled himself back to the night they died from the fire. The gunshot that killed Bill and his family running deep into the fire caused night terrors. He feared going to sleep–hated that his body craved its rest.

The house walls began their slow march, enclosing him–trapping him–into a claustrophobic state. Jacob had to get out of the house, had to do something constructive. That's when he realized Bill hadn't finished the south fence. Jacob pulled on some boots and yanked the door open. The sunshine caused his eyes to squint, so he grabbed his hat, pulled it on tight, and felt the ground crunch under his boot as he walked towards the barn. Several beams of wood sat alongside the barn. Grabbing a few pieces, Jacob tossed them down where Bill left off.

Several birds chirped nearby and a rabbit shot across the yard toward the fenced in garden–Sarah's garden. He noticed one beam had fallen, allowing the tiny creature to hop right in and have a tasty snack. Probably munching on some beans that needed picking. He could almost see Sarah bending over with a basket plucking the long green stems from the plant and tossing them gently into the wicker basket that Virginia held. The scene faded as Jacob hammered the board back in place. He patted the board with a 'that should keep the little critters out of his wife's garden' pat.

He grabbed the nails and worked on the south fence. Work felt good and made him feel strong. He didn't know how long he'd been working until his stomach threatened revolt if he didn't feed it something. Looking up at the sky, the sun already sat past halfway in the sky and Jacob needed nourishment, knowing better than to work into the night with an empty stomach. He listened to the clucking of several chickens nearby and longed for Sarah's fried chicken. Wondering if he could make it himself, Jacob grabbed an axe and found the chicken he wanted.

He lopped off the bird's head and let the animal bleed out. It took some effort to remove its feathers, as it was the messiest part of preparing chicken. He hated it, always had, but Sarah's fried chicken was worth the work. After butchering the chicken, Jacob placed the pieces of meat on a tray he'd grabbed from the house. Not knowing a thing about cooking, Jacob rummaged around Sarah's spices to find what she used to make her famous chicken dish and gave up, not knowing what she actually used. He grabbed the flour sitting nearby and saw a bowl of salt and some pepper Sarah must have recently ground. He coated the chicken with flour, added salt and pepper, and tossed it into the waiting cast iron pan he'd warmed on the wood-burning stove.

It didn't take long before the smell of burnt flour filled the house and Jacob cursed himself for trying to make something he enjoyed. He forgot the lard and figured adding it now wouldn't work. Plopping the pieces onto a waiting plate, he tried eating the meat and realized the breading and skin were too tough and way too black to eat. He peeled it off and ate the meat. That's all he ate. Jacob knew nothing about cooking. He sighed and shoved the plate aside and grabbed his whiskey and poured another cup.

The liquor sat in the cup and Jacob detested the substance. He grabbed the cup and threw it against the wall. Whiskey splashed onto his hand, rolled off the table, and soaked into his pants before the glass shattered against the far wall.

He picked up the plate and stared at it, "God, I don't understand!" He screamed at the chicken, hoping it would yell back

Did he have the courage to go after Gabriel Grant? Jacob

needed to kill him for killing Sarah and Virginia–for killing him. The plate exploded against the wall to his left after throwing it. Several shards made their way back to the table and danced about before settling in place. Jacob slammed his fist into the table, shoved his chair back and retreated to the bedroom.

Jacob stooped and slid out his gun case from under the bed.

CHAPTER SIXTY

THE GUN STARED back at Jacob, willing him to pick it up and put an end to everything. The reality of life ever being the same escaped his mind and begged him to join Sarah and Virginia in heaven. What did God demand of him now? What purpose, plan, or destiny did God have for Jacob now? Maybe God demanded justice for his family's death. If that were so, Jacob asked for an audible voice to give him instructions on how to proceed. None came and ever would, and the gun sitting in his lap told him as much.

He spun the chamber several times and watched it twirl before stopping to arm and disarm the gun with each spin. Jacob's shirt from the previous week sat in a pile near the dresser as the gleaming gold of Sam Ballot's badge caught his eye. He felt sorry the lawman had died standing up for the law. That same law always seemed to be on Gabriel Grant's side and the sheriff, until recently, sided with the tycoon. Judge Talbert might as well be married to Gabriel and always seemed to be at his beck and call. Maybe it was time for the law to deal with Gabriel Grant. Jacob's version of the law.

Standing, Jacob looked away from the badge that called to him to an image of their family mounted on the wall in front of him. They had taken the image in Salt Lake City before moving to Purgatory. Sarah wanted an image to remember their time. Jacob had hired the local photographer to set up a meeting to take their family portrait. A tear slid down his cheek and landed on the gun's barrel. He missed them and his heart tugged at his deep desire to be in their arms again. Nothing else mattered. Jacob desired heaven, needed heaven. He was not meant for this life and he needed God's amazing grace to pull him into eternity.

He lifted the gun and stared at its blue, case-hardened steel. The cherry wood grip fit deep into Jacob's large hands. His heart slammed against his chest and his breathing shallowed as he cocked the gun and fired the empty weapon against his temple. Air escaped his lips and his hand trembled as he dropped the bullets from his grip. They scattered across the floor while he kept one bullet at his fingertips. He chambered the round and the urge to be with Sarah and Virginia flooded his mind–this would be his defining moment.

Jacob spun the chamber closed and armed his .45 Colt revolver. His throat dried and he found it difficult to swallow. With clammy hands, he wiped them against his trousers and breathed deep. He held the gun to his head and the world closed in and stilled. It was just Jacob and the gun. His vision darkened, tears flooded his eyes and he let their torrent become a waterfall.

If the gun opened fire against his skull, he'd die and join his family with God. If the gun didn't fire, Gabriel Grant would die by Jacob's hand. His finger shook against the trigger, the deep groans crawled their way from his throat and filled the room with a roar, and then Jacob held his breath.

Time to meet God.

He pulled the trigger.

The click of an empty chamber stilled his heart and he breathed hard, gasping for air to fill his lungs. He collapsed to his knees. He was alive. The gun didn't fire.

"Okay, okay."

For the first time in a week, clarity filled his mind and a deep resolve filled his heart. God spared his life so that Gabriel could die. To Jacob, it seemed no different from what Christ did for him. He lived and Christ died so he could live. As long as Gabriel Grant lived, Jacob and his Mother were in mortal danger, so the gun begged for him to put an end to everything and the gun failed at its job. Like Gideon, he needed one more test. He aimed the gun at the mirror. If his real life didn't die, his life as a minister would and he knew full well that going after Gabriel Grant would put an end to that old life, the life that drew him to be God's spokesperson in the world. He spun the chamber once more, cocked, and pulled the trigger.

BANG!

The gun rotated in his hand as the mirror shattered into a thousand pieces. Satisfied, Jacob slid the gun into his belt. His black minister's shirt hung on a hook and his white collar curled on top of the dresser. They had to go and Jacob wanted no memory of the past. It took several minutes to gather everything he wanted to burn. The question wasn't whether he should burn his past, but how fast would the fire consume its contents?

He piled a few more logs into the stove and watched as the fire's fingers snaked around each new log and devoured them in a wash of red and gold. Balling his pants, Jacob shoved them into the narrow opening of the stove and watched as the flames ignited the fabric, melting away in a bright flash. His shirt went in next. The fire immediately latched on and sent a ball of hot cotton onto the floor. Jacob quickly put the flame out as his gaze fell to the collar he fingered. He'd spent his whole life worrying about saving souls when he should have been concerned about his own and protecting his family. His lust for justice had caused the death of his family, so he tossed the collar into the fire and he saw it crumple against the heat, then disappear into the ash below.

Jacob picked up his Bible. Every ounce of his flesh desired to see its pages crinkle against the flame; maybe if God were gracious, the pages would burn like Moses' bush in Midian. He thumbed the pages and the leather-bound book opened to the first page. His eyes fell on the note Sarah wrote the day they married.

> *To Jacob,*
>
> *I'm so proud of you and the man you have become. Life's been hard and the road has been long, but as long as you trust in the Lord, he will guide and direct your path. I know your hand will touch many lives with your obedience to the Lord. He is good and his love endureth forever.*
>
> *I love you, Jacob Creek. Thank you for being my best friend, and today we wed under God's holy covenant. Someday, you will make a great father and I know you are a man who fears and honors God with his life. Go get em for Christ.*
>
> *With love,*
>
> *Sarah Callihan (Soon-to-be, Mrs. Jacob Creek.)*

They'd married that afternoon. Smiling at the memory, he pulled the Bible close to his chest and closed the stove door, then made his way back to the bedroom and laid the Bible on the dresser. Jacob buttoned his shirt and fastened his belt. He picked up the holster and stared at the brown leather. Wrapping the gun belt around his waist, he slid his .45 Colt revolver into place and secured the hammer with a small leather strap. His hat hung near the door and he flipped it onto his head.

Several moments later, his horse was saddled and he looked back at the house. The realization that he may not see home again struck him hard, but nothing mattered any longer. His family was dead, his best friend and future father-in-law was dead, and Jacob had nothing left to live for.

Tonight, Gabriel Grant would die.

CHAPTER SIXTY-ONE

I T HAD BEEN three days since setting fire to the school and church buildings. Three days since the death of the Preacher's family. Doing the extraordinary to get his way worked and he never thought about the consequences, because they never mattered; however, why did the deaths of these two bother him so much? Gabriel Grant didn't intend to kill them, just shake them up and get the Preacher to see the problems he's created for himself. As a general rule, death didn't bother Gabriel; yet, he couldn't shake their deaths. If a god existed, this was his way of getting even for a lack of belief.

Gabriel stretched against the hard ground and let his fingers grip the tree behind his head before his back cracked. He pushed off the ground and stood. The woods were quiet other than birds and squirrels playing against the branches above. After leaving Purgatory the night of the fires, he couldn't bring himself to show face in town or at his own home. No doubt Moira hated him and would walk the moment he stepped foot onto their lush estate. Had he gone too far? It became the all-consuming question haunting his sleep, wishing he could take back their deaths.

Over the past week, Gabriel realized the pursuit of power and money drove people away and caused him to become a man he swore he'd never become. But that's what power and money did, they created change and demanded respect. As a young man, he'd longed for public office and desired to bring real change to the Territory of Wyoming. As he became more powerful and made a name for himself, having a job as a politician seemed inconceivable to him; that's why he strived for power and money. So politics became his life obsession and he helped keep the people he liked in power. One such man helped keep his name clean, and now he wondered if Judge Talbert would come to his rescue. Would he wash his hands of Gabriel Grant? He certainly hoped not.

The saddle lay next to the horse and Gabriel heaved it onto the powerful animal. It took several minutes to buckle and cinch it tight against the horse's ribs. Grabbing his coat, he slung it around his arms and buttoned it, then picked up his hat and pressed it onto his head. He had to get home and talk with Moira and explain what happened. Would she listen or understand?

Gabriel swung his leg up and pulled into the saddle. It was time to face his wife and have a nice talk with Judge Talbert to see what legal consequences the previous week's actions had caused. He rode through the forest for half a day's ride before making his way toward Purgatory. As he cantered past Purgatory Gulch Mines, several miners stopped to watch him. He tipped his hat and several men cussed and tossed rocks his direction. His hand slid down to his pistol and pulled it into view. He fired one shot into the air and they hurried back into the mines. After the dust settles from all of this madness, they'd fear him again and he'd once again become king of Purgatory. He would demand each man's respect. He already owned most of the town, so if anyone crossed him, they'd pay the price. That thought alone helped push what had happened to the Creek family from his mind as he settled on the idea of taking even more power.

As he made his way down the mountain, he could see Purgatory sitting comfortably against Encampment River in the valley. He veered the horse to the north and headed toward his estate which sat five miles outside the town limits. No doubt Moira was still there, being waited on hand and foot by the staff. He never understood her liking them. They should be seen and not heard. They were hired help, not friends. It took seven years for the house to rise from a hill that needed carving to fit the large 32-room estate. They spared no expense and everyone from the Governor to any congressmen or businessman who visited would leave impressed, wined and dined—and because Gabriel and Moira only had Felix, they had more than enough rooms to serve their prestigious guests.

The large brick house rose through the trees like an impressive castle waiting for her king. Gabriel smiled when he saw his home and his mouth watered for a cigar he'd acquired from a business expedition to Cuba. His horse snorted as they neared the carriage house. One of his staff walked out of the stable to greet him and asked if he needed a fresh change of clothes before heading into the house. Gabriel agreed and the staff set out new clothes in a changing room he had built on the upper level of the carriage house.

Once he was adorned in new clothes, he strode up the path toward the large red-brick house. When he went to open the door, to his surprise, he found it locked. Frustrated, he buried his fist into the door and after no one arrived, he pulled the string to ring the bell. A few more minutes passed and a click reached his ears.

"Master, so good to see you," his head Butler said, while keeping his eyes narrow for keeping him standing on the front steps.

"Let me in."

The man stepped aside and Gabriel walked to the right and into his study. He rounded the desk and sank into the chair.

The Butler approached, "Can I get you anything, sir?"

"I want to see Moira, now," the man hesitated. Gabriel stood and rested his knuckles against the desk, "Where is my wife?"

He stood there not moving as fear marched into his eyes.

"I will ask you one more time, before I put a bullet in your head—where is my wife?" Gabriel gritted his teeth, pulled his gun, and casually pulled back the hammer. It wasn't so much a question as it was a command, and his staff knew better than to keep something from him. He'd move heaven and earth to get what he needed from them, and if he had to shoot the man, so be it.

The Butler hugged the door's curtain, "She is staying at the other property in town. The boy—he's wandering the wooded area."

Gabriel slammed the gun's butt against the desk. The Butler backed further against the door.

"Would… would you like me to fetch them?"

"GET THEM HERE, NOW!" Gabriel fired the gun at his butler, missing the man's head by inches. The butler turned and ran.

CHAPTER SIXTY-TWO

JACOB BOUNCED in the saddle as he guided the horse up a steep embankment. Several rocks skidded down the hill behind him. Why he chose this route into town eluded him. But he needed time to process his plan of taking out Gabriel Grant. He clicked his tongue to encourage the animal forward. Her hoof slipped and she shook her head. Trails of air spilled out of her nose, swirling in the chilled air. He slid his hand down her neck, "Easy, girl."

Stilling his hand, he pulled the reins as she finished the leap onto flat ground. It'd be smooth riding here on out to Purgatory. He turned to look behind him at the ranch. The day he showed Sarah this view was the day he'd asked for her hand in marriage. Jacob slowed the horse and dismounted. He played with the ring on his finger, then tugged at his shirt, and pulled out a necklace which held her ring. He kissed it and stared out into the distance.

Ten years ago, he had taken Sarah to the far end of his father's ranch to this spot. A perfect hill which overlooked the valley and stretched as far as the eye could see. The ranch sat below them, nestled against the mountains, and in the distance, they could see the golden hue of the sun bounce off the mountain range like a bullet ricocheting off a rock. As the sun passed below the horizon, a purple and red glow emanated across the valley and accentuated Sarah's features. Her auburn hair had glowed like petals of a sunflower, and his fingers caressed her soft skin as her lips parted when he drew her to his mouth.

This was the moment, the moment he'd been waiting for. This was a bold statement from a boy who hadn't made his intentions known for years to the girl he loved.

"What was that for?"

"Sarah," he managed after clearing his throat, "I've got a question for you." He dug his perspired hands deep into the abyss of his pockets. "What would ya say if a guy like me asked a pretty girl like you to marry him?"

Sarah stood there, hand on her lips. "I would have to say, it depends on who's ask'n."

"What if me is ask'n ya?" *That came out all wrong.*

She giggled, obviously at his phrasing of the question. "Well, then my answer would be a *yes*." She grabbed his hands, "Yes, Jacob Creek, I'll marry you."

Jacob's outstretched hands were empty. Sarah's dead and the memory lingered in his mind like an evaporating fog. "Why, God?! Why did you have to take her from me?" God remained silent or refused to speak, and Jacob wasn't sure which. He placed the necklace over his head and tucked the ring back inside his shirt, held the reins, and stared once more at Sarah's ghost before pressing on toward Purgatory.

Two hours later, Gypsy's hooves echoed through the empty streets of town. The cold air bit at Jacob's skin as tiny snowflakes began their flitter to the earth. Momma's was ahead and he wondered if she was home—he hadn't talked with her since the funeral yesterday. As he approached the Lodge, he saw that Momma sat the front porch as usual, warming her hands on a cup of tea. It was probably Earl Grey, her favorite, with two lumps of sugar and a splash of milk. Jacob felt her icy glare and disapproval from across the street and he knew full well that Momma desired peace—for God's justice. His fingers felt for his gun and he saw it as God's justice. A .45 caliber bullet was slow, but it packed a nasty little punch. That's the justice Gabriel would receive.

Tying off his horse, Jacob dismounted and bound up the steps to greet Momma, "Hi."

Her cup clinked down and she stood, straightening her wrinkled dress. "What are you doing, Son?"

The question ripped into his heart. "Giving Gabriel Grant what he deserves."

"Does he deserve the justice you're planning on bringing him?"

It was a stupid question and he chided his mother for asking him. How could she stand there not desiring him to avenge Sarah's death? It seemed incomprehensible. "I…" The thought trailed off and remained hidden from Jacob's mind.

"Follow me inside. It's freezing out here."

They stepped through the door and Jacob thawed. "What were you doing outside, anyway?"

"Praying for you, that you wouldn't be so stupid as to go up against Gabriel Grant."

Jacob plopped into a nearby chair. "How can I not? He killed *my* family. Your *family*."

Momma peeled off her shawl and threw it on the hook by the door. She smoothed her hair and poured another cup of tea, "You want some?" When he declined, she poured one anyway and handed it to him. "Here, calm your mind, Jake."

"I went by the cliff that overlooked the ranch where I asked Sarah to marry me. It was a nice memory."

"Then hang on to those memories. Don't dishonor Sarah by taking another man's life. Remember what the good Lord says in Romans 11, '*Dearly beloved, avenge not yourselves, but rather give place unto earth: for it is written, vengeance is mine: I will repay, saith the Lord.*' Remember, Jake, God will repay the evil done to our family with good."

Jacob bore down on his teeth and felt his jaw pop against the building pressure. Through clenched fists, his nails dug grooves into his palms and he slammed his fist into the arm rest. "Don't you think I know what the scriptures say? I couldn't care less about when God will repay this evil with good. The only good I see comes out of the barrel of a gun." He pulled the revolver and set it on his lap, "From this gun."

Tears welled and Momma let them fall. "Jacob, I love you, but this *isn't* the answer."

Somewhere deep inside, Jacob knew Momma's words echoed truth and yet, he felt condemned just by thinking on the things of God. Nothing made sense anymore. God had called them to Purgatory. God made the way possible for him to return as the minister, and now one man threatened everything Jacob had worked hard to gain. Then a thought propped itself on the shelf of his mind—he was the sheriff of Purgatory. Not officially, but as acting sheriff. This could be his way of bringing Gabriel to justice.

He could kill Gabriel and explain to Marshal Tan Bennington that he died in self-defense. Would he buy that? Likely, Jacob would be arrested and stand trial for murder—as always, Momma was right. He knew it but the desire to put

Gabriel in his place outweighed his senses and Jacob tried to push righteousness from his mind.

"How can I move on with my life if Gabriel lives?"

"How did you move on after the same man killed your father?"

Jacob dipped his head, "I never got over how father treated me as a child."

"Jake, ask God to give you an answer. If you pray, he will listen. You may not find the answer now, but when the moment arises, God will be there to guide your hand, and gun if necessary. Remember the battle is the Lord's and if you trust in him, he will guide your path and and make it straight." She tapped her hand on the Bible's cover, "Be like Joshua. Be strong and courageous. Put on the armor of God so you can withstand the evils of this world."

Jacob sat there knowing Momma was right. He felt the Sheriff's badge pressing against his thigh. Reaching down, he pulled it from his pocket and fiddled it between his fingers.

Momma got up and sat next to Jacob's knee, "See this badge, this gives you the authority here on earth to see true justice served." She then placed the Bible in his lap, "See this? This is the badge for your soul. If you trusted this and his voice to bring your family to Purgatory, maybe his mission was to help you see deep inside your soul and deal with your own demons."

Fresh tears streamed down Jacob's face. He pulled out a handkerchief and blew his congested nose. He missed Sarah and Virginia. His thoughts had pushed so far toward revenge that he never saw God's version of justice. He thumbed the badge and knew it was time to bring that justice to Gabriel.

"Momma, I think I know how to draw Gabriel out."

"Just remember, trust your gut and trust God. Don't

succumb to Satan's temptation. Allow yourself to be the Sheriff Purgatory needs."

"I have to go." Standing, Jacob hugged Momma and kissed her cheek. He grabbed his hat and coat, "Pray for me."

"I will."

Then, Jacob left Momma alone.

CHAPTER SIXTY-THREE

OIRA GRANT sat in a high-back chair near the fireplace, in their smaller home near town. Its mauve fabric felt warm against the cold weather outside. She hugged the shawl tight that wrapped around her arms, keeping them warm. The past few days gave Moira no solace, knowing Gabriel had murdered Sarah and their beautiful little girl. When news reached her that Gabriel set fire to the school and church buildings, Moira understood her husband knew no bounds with the Creek family. Blinded by an unspeakable rage, he would pace the study, curse God or anyone who'd listen, while scheming ways to get rid of the minister and his family. Jacob Creek got under Gabriel's skin.

One of the housemaids brought her a fresh cup of tea and Moira entwined her fingers around the cup, letting its warmth tickle her fingers. November should bring thanks and praise for what God had given them, but now the weather served as a cold reminder of what Gabriel had done, the wrongs he'd done, and the countless lives he'd snuffed out in his quest for power. How many times did she come forward to help her husband with each run-in with the sheriff, even before Sam Ballot had the Sheriff's badge? The first time flooded her mind and she wondered if everything in their marriage was a lie.

After purchasing the Purgatory Gulch Mines, Gabriel made their residence in the struggling town of Purgatory. The mines had just opened and people tried to discover what gold lay beneath the ground. Once the gold rush happened and every man desired to strike it rich, Gabriel took his cut of the profits. He became filthy rich and bought up property in Purgatory and the surrounding areas, including the land their estate sat upon.

He spotted the land during a survey and wanted to buy it for their home. The local rancher had wanted nothing to do with Gabriel Grant and refused to sell the property.

"I'm sorry, Mr. Grant. The land isn't for sale. I've worked my whole life for this property. Now, if you'll excuse me," he turned to leave.

Moira placed her hand on Gabriel's, "Let him go."

"Moira, this land is for you. We'll have our babies here. Can you imagine the beautiful home we could build? Money is no object. We'll be the envy of everyone; not even the Governor could imagine such wealth and opulence."

She didn't like that then or cared much for it now—Moira despised the home. Two days later, they'd found the rancher's body gored to death by his prize bull. The man's brother had accused Gabriel of fixing his brother's death and pulled in the Sheriff to investigate. Sam Ballot had hauled Gabriel to jail while Moira came to Gabriel's defense to convince the sheriff to release the charges. He did and the man's widow sold the land. She sighed and leaned back into the chair as the distant memories flooded her mind. The poor woman had used the money to pay for her husband's funeral before leaving Purgatory altogether. Moira always wondered what happened to the woman.

The tea grew cold and she placed the cup on a nearby end table. Smoothing her dress, Moira proceeded down the hall to fetch a blanket from her bedroom. A rush of air pebbled her skin the farther down the hall she walked. Someone must have left a window or door open, as the hall never felt so cold. Rounding the corner, she noticed the head butler shutting the door behind him. He rubbed his hands together.

Looking up, he saw Moira staring at him, "Ma'am."

"Gerold, what brings you here? Not enough work at the Estate?"

He shoved his hands deep into his pockets, "Ma'am, it's your husband…he requests your presence."

Moira crunched her teeth. So, Gabriel showed face after all. Should she confront her husband? Maybe the time had arrived for her to take Felix and move–get away from everything in Purgatory and start a new life somewhere else, like the widow. She could always visit her ailing mother in Cheyenne. The last thing she wanted was Gabriel to raise Felix and help harden the boy's heart anymore than he already had.

Moira stood there unmoving. Her feet were stuck to the ground like clay. Afraid to go and afraid to stay. There was no way to tell what Gabriel would do, but one thing was certain, he would do anything to protect his interests and would stop at nothing until he got what he wanted: his family. The past several months led her to believe the man she once loved and called husband had died long ago–replaced by a monster who only knew of creating a life of vengeance in Purgatory.

It was time to leave Gabriel; she felt that much resolve and today would be that day. "Fetch my cloak and take me to the Estate, it's time I confront my husband."

The man stood there, unmoving.

"Today."

The ground loosened its grip on the butler as he took off down the hall to fetch her cloak. Upon returning with her cloak, Moira instead decided to go alone and he cautioned her about going to the Estate without someone there for her. Moira placed a hand on his arm and assured him she'd be okay and to not worry.

"And I think it'd be best if you didn't return. Stay here the night and I'll be along to fetch my things either tonight or tomorrow," the man nodded and opened the door. Moira stepped through into the cold evening. "Thank you."

He nodded, "My pleasure serving you, Ma'am."

The door clicked behind her and she pulled her coat tight to keep from freezing. It would be a long ride, but she needed the time to process and think through how she'd break the news to Gabriel that their marriage was over. For far too long, she'd accommodated and turned a blind eye to his business practices, but after the death of Sarah, nothing mattered any longer—maybe that was the one grievance she couldn't forgive.

She kept her head down, walked past the courthouse, and into the chest of Jacob Creek. Moira stilled as she glanced into his eyes, which were filled with sadness and anger. His hand pulled a gun from the holster hugging his hips, "Hello, Moira."

"Jacob," she tried to keep her voice from shaking.

"Let's have a chat about your dear, old husband." He motioned his gun toward the waiting horse, "Get on."

She hesitated, "Jacob, what's this about?"

"I don't have to answer to you." He pointed his gun at the animal again, "I said, get on."

"Can you at least put the gun away? You won't need it."

Jacob's eyes narrowed at the gun, then his face softened as he shoved it deep into the holster. "Okay, sorry. I need your husband to think I'll go to any length to get revenge for my family."

"I don't like him any more than you. Sarah was a friend, but is this the way you want them to remember you?"

Jacob snapped, "I already had a nice talk with Momma, I don't need another little chat from you. Now, get on the horse before I reconsider holstering the gun."

Moira pulled up on the horn and climbed into the saddle. She slid toward the front and wrapped her hands into her dress to warm them.

"Where's Gabriel?" Jacob asked, climbing up behind her and grabbing the reins.

"He's at the estate."

"Good. Time to pay him a visit."

Moira stared straight ahead. What was Jacob's end game? Did he plan on killing Gabriel? Is this the vengeance Gabriel sought against the Reverend, and now Jacob was bringing that vengeance to him? Yes, his family was dead. Yes, nothing could bring them back. But going up against a man who built his life on the backs of others, fast as lighting with a gun, and determined to win hardly seemed the Christian thing to do for a Reverend. She feared Gabriel would kill Jacob also and the town would pay for Jacob's sin against her husband.

She didn't know scripture that well, but there was one thing she remembered from childhood: Joshua had to trust God before the walls of Jericho fell. Moira glanced back at

Jacob's set jaw and knew God was the furthest thing from his mind. This man, whom she respected, sat ice cold with every intention of killing her husband. Moira's skin pebbled and with each beat, her heart thumped against her breast. Suddenly, she felt warm against Jacob's icy countenance.

CHAPTER SIXTY-FOUR

THEY STRODE their way through town. Several onlookers peeked through shop windows as they passed by. Several had heavy eyes. Maybe they knew what was about to happen. Everyone knew Gabriel had killed Sarah and Virginia, and the news about the previous Reverend made its way to the paper. No one wanted Gabriel around any longer. They all feared the worst was yet to come–they feared cold retribution at the hands of crazy tycoon. How anyone could vote for such a man, to keep him in power, was beyond Jacob's understanding.

He felt Moira's body stiffen as they drew deeper into town. It wouldn't be long before they passed the remains of the schoolhouse and church. The two buildings brought about a deep chill in Jacob's soul that matched the air's icy temperature. Using Moira as bait to lure Gabriel from hiding might be a bad idea and it worried him it all could backfire. He didn't want anymore bloodshed.

"You okay?" he asked.

She nodded, "Mr. Creek…"

"Please, call me Jake."

"Okay…Jake, what do you plan on doing to my husband?"

Letting the air settle between them, he sighed. He had to tell her the plan—what he was thinking—because if she died from of his lack of communication, he would be no better than Gabriel Grant. Jacob recalled the verse, *an eye for an eye.* But Jesus followed that up by saying, *But I say not you, that ye resist not evil: but whosoever shall smite thee on thy right cheek, turn to him the other as well.* The Bible never lied and Jesus was always right. He gripped the reigns tighter and marched out of town, past the burned buildings. His heart tugged at their sight. Looking away, Jacob fixed his mind on what would happen when they arrived at the Grant estate.

"Moria, I will arrest your husband for the murder of my family. The Judge placed me as temporary sheriff while the Marshal's out of town. And I will do my darndest in upholding the law—do things the right way."

"You're not going to kill him?"

"If it's all the same to you Ma'am, I want to see him dead so it can satisfy my pain. You of all people should know what he's capable of…"

She nodded her head with an emphatic *yes.* "So, what's your plan?"

"I need to use you as bait, to draw out your husband. No doubt he'll do everything he can to keep you safe. If he thinks your life is in danger, he'll come running."

"I know I'm particularly mad at him for what he did to Sarah, but you think he'll meet you face to face?"

"I'm counting on it." Jacob slowed the horse and hushed his voice, "Looks like he has several men guarding the gate." He halted the horse and dropped to the ground. "We stop here. If we take the horse in, they'll shoot at both of us." He offered his hand and Moira slid off the saddle.

Jacob checked his revolver, holstered it, and then slid the Henry rifle from its scabbard. Chambering five rounds into the rifle, he pocketed several more shells into his jacket, and tugged at his gloves to tighten the leather around his numb fingers. Just enough feeling to pull a trigger, but he couldn't stay in this weather much longer. Moria had to be freezing in her dress and cloak.

He swung the gun over a bush and peeked through the scope. Three men stood by the gate and it appeared two more near the carriage house. "How many men do you have on the property with guns?"

Moira seemed transfixed and out of focus.

"Moira…"

She flinched, "Sorry, I don't know. It varies. Only six armed at all times."

A smile formed across Jacob's lips. Though he'd never fired his gun at another human, he had plenty of practice growing up with both a rifle and his six gun. He didn't intend to kill anyone, but if they got in his way, he'd drop them. Jacob pulled the badge off his shirt and fixed it to his leather long coat. No mistaking him as law now.

"Okay," he said, nodding in the gate's direction, "are you ready?"

"Do you promise to keep me safe?"

"Stay behind me, and you'll be fine. If the shooting starts, stay here until I come back for you."

She looked nervous and he didn't blame her. "Okay."

"Okay. Here goes nothing." Jacob steadied the rifle against his shoulder and stood. The three men noticed him right away. He walked toward them. They shouted something but

Jacob couldn't make it out. "Hello, boys," he said the moment he knew they'd hear.

The man to the left of the gate pulled his gun, "Mister, I suggest you head back to town. No one is allowed on this property. It's a private estate."

Jacob stopped and leveled his gun, "I suggest you drop your gun. I have a legal matter to discuss with Gabriel Grant."

The middle man pulled his gun, "The law ain't welcome here."

Jacob heard the distinct sound of a hammer being pulled back. His rifle remained ready to fire. The two men raised their arms. "If you fire, I'll drop you." Someone opened fire and a bullet whizzed by Jacob's ear. He dropped to his knee and returned fire. The bullet slammed into the man who fired. He toppled over and the other two took off for cover.

Three more bullets scattered dirt and Jacob rolled out of the way. He found a tree to squeeze behind. Gun at the ready, he rotated around the tree and fired. The gun bucked against his arm as the bullet slapped the metal gate. He levered another round and fired. This time, a second man dropped to the ground, dead. Where was Moira? Jacob looked in her direction and saw her form hugging the ground. *Good girl.*

"You better drop that gun, Mister."

Gravel crunched behind the tree as the third man closed rank. He placed the gun on the ground and tossed it to the side.

"Smart. Now come out from behind the tree."

Jacob stood and lifted his hands, "Okay, you've got me. I know you have at least two other men closing ranks to protect the door. So, it's just you and me."

"Keep those hands raised."

"All right, don't get any itchy trigger fingers. I'm coming around the tree," he did with his hands raised.

The man eyed him up and down. He saw the badge and his eyes widened, "Take off your gun belt. You can talk with Gabriel without your gun."

Jacob narrowed his eyes, "Not going to happen."

"TAKE OFF YOUR GUN!"

Jacob made his choice and lowered his hand while keeping his eye on Gabriel's hired gun. His fingers glanced the grip. The man lifted his gun and Jacob saw his finger twitch against the trigger. His hand wrapped around the .45, drew and fired. The bullet pierced into the boy's chest and blood trickled out like a river from his shirt. He wavered, then crumpled. Jacob kicked the gun away. "Stupid move, son."

A hand touched his back and he spun and pulled back the hammer, only to release his grip on the gun and holster. Moira stood next to him. Tears filled her eyes.

"He was just a boy."

He looked at the boy's dead body. If only he could rechamber the bullet. Jacob wondered if coming in guns blazing had been the best course of action. "I'm sorry, he left me no choice." He grabbed her hand, "Let's go."

CHAPTER SIXTY-FIVE

KEEPING LOW, out of sight of the two men guarding the house, they approached the north side of the estate. The last thing Jacob wanted was for them to see him coming. No doubt the two men left heard the exchange of gunfire and knew their comrades were dead or disabled. The young boy's image flashed through his mind and Jacob had to push it aside–couldn't afford the distraction. He'd pay his respects later.

As Jacob and Moira neared the home, his heart raced. Adrenaline surged through his veins and he wondered if this was how his friends felt as they served during the war of the Northern Aggression. Jacob pressed against the red brick to remain hidden from the west entrance. He peered around the corner and saw one man standing guard.

"His back is to us," Jacob whispered.

"Are you going to kill him, too?"

He understood why Moira asked. Maybe he shouldn't have brought her into this mess. "If I don't have to. I didn't want to kill anyone, that's not what God would want." He knelt down and took her hands, "Moira, I'm sorry. My original intention was to come here and kill your husband. I've been so angry at God and Gabriel for their deaths that I felt I had no other choice." He glanced around the corner again, "Wish me luck."

Jacob leaned away from the wall. She followed and he held out his hand, telling her to stay put. A second man stood near the entrance and Jacob prayed he wouldn't catch sight of him encroaching his buddy—the last thing he wanted was for the man to turn around. The one with his back to Jacob shifted his weight and Jacob stilled. When he didn't turn, Jacob pressed forward. He stood behind him, his heart slamming against his ribs, and then he held his breath. And that's when Jacob lunged forward and wrapped his arm around the man's neck. The guard kicked hard against the gravel before his body stilled. Jacob hauled the limp man back toward the north side of the building and tied his hands.

"How many staff do you have?"

Moira looked at the unconscious man.

"Moira!"

"Um…I'm sorry. This is all just so much."

"How many?"

"7, I think. Three are at the home in town. You're not going to…"

"No. I don't want them getting in the way. Let's go." They pressed around the corner as the man standing guard turned and drew his gun. Jacob saw the fear in his eyes. He slowed. "I advise you to drop your gun. I'm here on official business to arrest Gabriel Grant. I've already taken out your friends, you don't want to try anything stupid."

"How do I know you're not going to kill me?"

"Drop your gun and leave us be."

"Mrs. Grant, are you okay?"

She looked at Jacob and he nodded for her to continue, "I'm fine. I'd do what the Revere...Sheriff suggests."

The man's gun rotated and he holstered the weapon. "Okay. I surrender."

He grabbed the man by the shirt, "Where's Gabriel?"

"I, I don't know. Inside somewhere. He might be in his study."

"Let me go inside first," Moira said. She stepped through the door and when no sign of Gabriel showed, she motioned for Jacob to join her.

Jacob pulled his gun, "Thank you," he said, and buried the gun's handle into the man's skull. The guard collapsed in a pile and he walked up the stairs and into Gabriel Grant's estate.

They pressed down the hallway toward Gabriel's study. Green light shown through the door and Moria approached; she stilled and looked back at Jacob, who stopped just behind the door jamb. "Okay. I'll talk to him first."

The door creaked as she stepped into the study with green walls that rose high before she disappeared into the room. "I see the woman of the house has returned." Gabriel's voice echoed.

"Hello, Gabriel."

Jacob heard shuffling and a chair stutter across the floor. "I heard shooting. Are you okay?"

"I'm fine."

"Did they kill the Preacher?"

Jacob figured that was his cue. He rounded the door into the room, pointing his gun at Gabriel. The book shelves rose high, each shelf filled with many books. In the center of the room sat Gabriel's desk. The tycoon's eyes narrowed and

Jacob could almost detect the slightest smile creep across the man's lips. He placed his hand on Moira's back and motioned her forward. Jacob kept his gun trained on Gabriel Grant.

"Well, well, well–look what the cat dragged in." He walked towards them, "Preacher, I have to hand it to ya, I didn't think you had the guts to kill a man. All that shooting."

Jacob stilled his body and tightened his jaw. He stood face to face with his family's killer. It wouldn't take more than a trigger pull to end Gabriel Grant's pathetic life. The desire to kill crawled back into Jacob's mind like a spider searching for his next meal. A bead of sweat rolled down his temples and Jacob pulled back the hammer, arming the gun. Momma's voice crept over his senses. *Be like Joshua. Be strong and courageous. Put on the armor of God so you can withstand the evils of this world.* Gabriel was evil and he didn't deserve to die at a disadvantage. Jacob saw the man didn't have a gun strapped to his hip, but the internal war raged on, ripping his soul in half.

Just pull the trigger.

Gabriel should be arrested, not killed.

He deserves to die for killing your family.

God is a God of justice and mercy. *Vengeance is mine!*

Jacob decided and lowered the hammer, "Gabriel Grant, I'm here to take you in for the murder of my family."

Laughter ripped the cold silence of the room, "And who, pray tell, gives you the authority to *take me in?*"

"Judge Talbert deputized me."

He cackled, "Judge Talbert, that no good fat sonofagun… Listen, if the Sheriff would have just listened, I would have not put a bullet in his gut."

"You killed him because he arrested you and you despised that he turned to follow the law."

Gabriel walked closer until Jacob could feel his breath, "I

will speak slow so you understand me, Preacher." He poked his finger at Jacob, "The only reason we're in this little predicament is because you couldn't let things be and got your family killed."

A low growl escaped Jacob's lips. His face warmed and his ears grew hot. He steadied his breathing. The gun's wood creaked against his tightening grip, then he pushed all thoughts from his mind except one, justice for Sarah and Virginia. God or not, Gabriel Grant would feel Jacob's wrath! A stick of dynamite exploded in Jacob's soul before pain rippled his hand as it melted against Gabriel's face. Gabriel flew backward and fell against the desk. Jacob lunged forward and drove another fist into his face.

Gabriel growled and tackled Jacob to the ground. Moira yelped somewhere behind him and the gun clattered against the floor.

Jacob peeled himself off the wooden floor and grappled toward the gun. A vision-shattering blow to his ribs sent waves of searing pain through his body. They hadn't healed, and now the bones crunched under a second blow. Jacob screamed and wrapped his hands around his lower chest, protecting them from another blow. He glanced over to see Gabriel reach for the gun—his foot couldn't reach to kick it away.

"Stop it, both of you!" Moira shrieked.

"What did my family have to do with any of this?" Jacob winced against the pain burning in his chest, like a lumberjack sawing down a tree. With each breath his vision clouded, pulling him deeper into a pit of darkness that had no bottom and no way out, knowing he'd be the next Creek to die by Gabriel's hand. Maybe it was best. Surrender and let him be with Sarah and Virginia. A tear slipped from his right eye and fell like a single raindrop looking to make its tiny splash in the world.

Gabriel pulled himself up from the ground with Jacob's gun in his hand. "You needed a lesson and they got in the way. Your daughter was not supposed to run into the building."

Jacob stood, holding his ribs tight. Tears continued to pool in his eyes, "That didn't stop you from killing Joe's family and beating my wife." That last word bit hard and the sight of Sarah's bloodied face flooded his vision. He should have been there, not sitting in Sheriff Ballot's office.

"I have the upper hand, Preacher."

Moira walked forward, "Put the gun down, Gabe. We don't need anymore bloodshed."

"She's right. Enough people have died."

Gabriel stood like a statue and Jacob couldn't make out his thoughts. He knew the tycoon had the upper hand. The sound of the hammer clicking filled the quiet room. Jacob steeled his body. He exhaled through his nose. Moira's hand reached toward her husband. Gabriel's arm reached forward. The world drew still.

"Time to meet your Maker, Jacob Creek."

This was it–the moment Jacob would meet God. Darkness encroached upon his vision and he was ready to accept the bullet that would send him straight into Sarah's waiting embrace. Then like a match going out, he saw Sarah's body burning against the demonic fire that had claimed her life. The nightmare of Virginia coloring a picture filled with fire erupting from a schoolhouse just before her flesh blackened and turned to ash. And a single bullet fired from Gabriel's gun, snapping Bill's head back, taking his friend's life.

One thought sat in the open like a trapped rabbit raced

through Jacob's mind—Gabriel Grant killed his family—they needed justice.

Jacob dug his boots into the wooden floor and sprung forward. He thrust his hands out and fastened his fingers around the barrel of the gun. The two men grunted.

BANG!

The sound of gunfire split the room and nobody moved.

"Gabriel…"

Gabriel dropped the gun and rushed to his wife's side as she collapsed into his arms. "Moira…! Don't…I'm so sorry." He looked at Jacob, "What have you done?" he growled.

Jacob watched Moira's color turn pallid. What had he done? This was not supposed to happen. Her eyes glazed over. She exhaled and fell limp. She was not supposed to…this wasn't his plan. *No!* He was now Gabriel. Moira was dead.

Gabriel looked up at Jacob and laid Moira's limp body on the floor. Gabriel reached down for Jacob's gun and stood, pulled back the hammer, and aimed the weapon at Jacob's chest. "You…you killed my wife." Gabriel's face twisted in anguish.

A lump formed in Jacob's throat and this time he didn't push it away. Thoughts of his family rifled through his mind as a single tear slipped and fell from his eye. Every good memory flashed through his mind. The moment he fell in love with Sarah or the day they married. Her tender kisses and the day Sarah said she was pregnant with Virginia. The day Virginia arrived into the world with tiny feet, hands, and dimples filled his heart like refreshing water. Jacob closed his eyes and waited for the bullet to send him to heaven to be with his family. He deserved to die. Moira wasn't supposed to die, nor was his family.

"God, forgive me," Jacob whispered.

"Take it."

Jacob opened his eyes. As quickly as Gabriel aimed the gun, he flipped the six-shooter around, and grasped the barrel.

Jacob's feet rooted themselves into the wooden floor. He wiped clammy hands against his pants and looked into Gabriel's eyes. The man's face was wet with tears and for the first time since coming to Purgatory, Jacob saw Gabriel's brokenness—maybe he'd always been broken. Jacob's fingers crawled around the wooden handle. It wouldn't take but a simple squeeze of the trigger to put an end to everything—to Gabriel.

Eternity passed and Jacob released the hammer and slid the gun into the waiting holster.

"Now, go before I change my mind and choke the life from your righteous body."

Jacob winced against the pain shooting through his ribs as he picked up his hat, "Gabriel, where does this leave us?"

The man shuffled his feet back toward Moira. He stared at his fallen wife for a moment before their eyes met again, "Leave. Me. Be. Preacher. You wi…" A sob choked his throat, "You win."

Jacob limped toward the door and gripped its frame. How could he arrest Gabriel now? Justice was served. Gabriel lost his wife and Jacob's heart shattered into a thousand pieces. For the first time, he understood how Gabriel Grant felt. A chill ran down his spine; maybe they weren't that different.

"Gabriel, I'm sorry about Moira."

Gabriel nodded and Jacob left.

CHAPTER SIXTY-SIX

JACOB STOOD at Sarah's grave, empty on the inside. His life had been squeezed like an orange with nothing left to give. The days since her death caused more pain in his life than anything he'd experienced, not even losing his father ripped at his soul as Sarah and Virginia's. A raw emotion he couldn't name fluttered through his heart as the heat from building tears warmed his cheeks. His knees plunked into the fresh dirt. Thunder rippled in the distance and rain soaked him. A waterfall formed over the brim of his hat and for the first time, Jacob allowed himself to cry. He couldn't feel the tears through an already wet face, but his chest heaved against the vise that gripped his heart. Each convulsion pulled him deeper into the mud. He craved to be close to Sarah and if he could claw his way through the earth just to feel her embrace, he wouldn't stop himself.

"God, I've been so far from you. I've lost so much of my faith and I've been so blinded by rage that I couldn't see." He dug his fists into the earth, squeezed the mud, and watched it ooze from his clenched fingers. They're gone, he couldn't change that, but he could move forward and be the man Sarah believed in–it's why she said yes all those years ago. "How do I move forward? What's next for me?" sighing, Jacob plopped his butt into the mud, praying that God would answer, if not for Jacob to figure out God's will through blind faith and trusting that would lead in God's own timing for the future.

But God wouldn't answer–not today.

He placed his hand on Sarah's tombstone and sighed. So many years stolen. She'd never be there as he grew old. The talks, passionate kisses, and gentle touches were no more. He'd looked over at Virginia's grave. A fresh volley of tears poured down his cheeks. He'd never walk her down the aisle on her wedding day and never see God's plans unfold on her life. "I'm so sorry, my Love," Jacob said.

Everything he'd fought for, since bringing his family to Purgatory to take over the church, was gone. Now, the only person left to fight for was Momma. Nothing else mattered and Purgatory deserved no more of his time or of his family. It was time to pack up and leave. He'd try to convince Momma to leave, but knew she would never leave, she cared too much about her life here, but Jacob couldn't stay. The memories, the pain of losing everyone–his father, wife, daughter, and future father all lost their lives–gave enough reason to ride out of town. The question that plagued his mind: *where?*

Jacob peeled himself off the muddied ground. He bent over and kissed both headstones. "Goodbye, my Love. You will always remain in my heart, but I can't stay. It's time I find my way in this world without you." Then a thought levered like a bullet in his mind, "There's a place for me in Cedar Grove. You always said that God would provide a way. He has and I know where."

Jacob mounted his waiting horse, "Bill, take care of them in heaven, will ya?" Jacob clicked his tongue and edged the horse toward Creek Ranch to pack his things. He'd leave the ranch in Freddy's capable hands–the man would do a good job running things.

WHEN JACOB ARRIVED at the ranch, he caught light emanating from the house windows. Jacob pulled his revolver and slid off the horse. Was Gabriel here to finish the job? Peeling off his rain slicker, Jacob gingerly laid it on a nearby rocker and wiped his wet face. Steeling himself, he pushed open the door and cocked the gun. He stopped cold.

"Jacob Elliot Creek, put that gun away."

He slid the gun into place, "Momma? What are you doing here?"

"I'm about to fix you some dinner. Lord knows after your day, you need a good meal." Momma wiped her hands and continued placing chicken into the waiting pan. The moment the meat hit the oil, it spat and crackled. "And look at you, you're a mess. Go get cleaned up. Dinner will be ready soon."

The aroma washed the weather from Jacob's mind as he walked into the bedroom to change. It would be nice to have one last meal before heading out of town. Momma never condemned him for going over the edge and losing himself in the sorrow of his heart. He knew full well she didn't approve, but would never say such things to stir him deeper into anger. Only the Lord knew what Jacob had become.

"Thank you," he called out as he shoved his wet and muddy clothes against the wall.

"For what?"

Jacob pulled on fresh pants and a shirt, walked to the kitchen and sat in a chair. "For not giving up on me." He ran fingers through his wet hair, "I had every intention of putting Gabriel Grant in the ground tonight. I used Moira as leverage. Then I remembered your words, *Vengeance is mine saith the Lord.* I know he deserves to die for what he did to our family–what he did to Sarah and Virginia, to Bill, but I also know that God stopped me from making a mistake that I would regret for the rest of my life. I know I'll never forget how Moira looked as blood soaked her shirt." Jacob buried his knuckles into his head.

Momma placed an arm around him and hummed the hymn from the night his family died, "I heard about Moira."

Looking up, he saw sadness creep into her eyes, "I keep telling myself it was an accident. I got angry and she died because I lost control. If I never would have involved her, she'd still be alive and Felix would have a mom to raise him. Now, he's got no one to look after him with Gabriel on the run."

"Well," she patted his arm, "don't worry about the lad. I'm sure some nice family will take him under their wings. He'll be just fine."

"Perhaps you're right." The moment lulled and they both instinctively knew he wouldn't stick around. He let his eyes fall to the floor–Momma, once again, would be alone in this town. No family to care for her needs and Bill–he squeezed his eyes shut.

"You're leaving, aren't you?"

He looked up. "I am."

"Where'll you go?"

"Clyde Heller left his ranch with no one to run the place. I will head down to Cedar Grove and talk it over with the bank and use the money he gave me as the down payment."

"Jacob, wasn't that ranch worth a lot more than this piece of land? I'd sell it all just for you."

Jacob nodded ,then walked over to a chest that sat under the window and pulled out an envelope, "Found this in my saddle bag."

He handed the envelope to Momma. She peeled back the flap and her eyes widened, "Where did you get this?"

"Clyde must have left it before confronting Gabriel Grant. He must have known things wouldn't go the way he planned. I don't know if he planned on dying, but maybe this was his contingency plan, that I would take his ranch."

"Jacob, this is seventy-five thousand dollars."

He pulled Momma's hands into his chest, "and this will satisfy the bank, along with the money I made from Clyde in the cattle sale. This money will begin a new life for me in Cedar Grove."

She turned away and dropped her head into her floured hands, "You know my life is here, right?"

"You can come with me."

"What about the Lodge?"

He sighed, "Momma, there's nothing left for you here. Bill's…" A lump lodged in his throat, "All I'm saying, you're more than welcome to follow me out there."

Momma pulled the pan off the stove and arranged the pieces of chicken onto a platter. She poured the potatoes and carrots into another dish and set them down on the table. They pulled up chairs and said a tearful grace before Jacob pulled a chicken leg apart.

"I need to stay. But don't let my decision stop you from finding yourself. I know losing Sarah and Virginia left a sour taste for you to remain here, and I don't blame you, but me, I know nothing different. And who will look after all my other boys who work so hard in the mines?"

Jacob smiled and took her hand into his, "Momma, sell the ranch, take the money and take care of your boys." Sometimes life gives you a fire that seems to consume everything in its grasp. The fire took his barn, his father, his wife, and child. The fire consumed Moira and claimed Bill. Gabriel's thirst for vengeance led him down a dark road of no redemption and now he had to live with those choices, no matter where he ran.

So many died by Gabriel Grant's hand that nothing seemed resolved by him losing his own wife, and for the town of Purgatory, maybe no one even cared. Jacob's heart felt sorry for the man. Fire and vengeance consumes a person and they never can find their way back.

Momma smiled at Jacob as a tear slipped down her cheek, "Remember, son, God always makes a way where there seems to be no way. Trust him, and you'll always find your way home."

He looked up at Momma and smiled. There had been only two constants in Jacob's life, Momma and God. Without their unwavering love–Momma was right–he never would have found his way home again.

EPILOGUE

Six Months Later

THE SALOON doors swung wide, then flapped shut behind him. His boots clacked against the rough wood, pitted from years of men coming and going from the establishment. Several eyes lifted from the cards being dealt and others stared, then nodded. He found the nearest stool and pulled himself onto its round seat and pushed his long rain slicker aside, letting it fall like a cape. Peeling off his hat, he flicked a finger toward the nearest bottle of whiskey. The Barkeep pulled down the bottle and poured a short glass.

"There ya go, Jake. Opened her this morning," he wiped his hands on a towel and moved to another gentleman who walked in and sat in the next stool.

"I'll have what he's having." Turning, the man asked, "How are you, Jacob?"

Jacob sipped on his whiskey, sighed, then extended his hand toward Tan Bennington, "Howdy, Marshal."

The large man downed his glass and tapped it against the

counter for another round. "I heard you're running Clyde Heller's place."

"Yep."

"Good for you. I'm sorry about your family, Jacob. I am. Never meant for them to get in the crosshairs. Talbert should have never released Gabriel from prison. And I'm awfully sorry I took so long…maybe things would have been different. After what happened, I felt responsible and couldn't face seeing you after Moira's death. But Talbert is in jail awaiting his trial. You did good, just not the outcome we were hoping for."

Jacob looked up and ran his fingers over the seven-day stubble. He pulled at the mustache corners and tried to push Sarah and Virginia from his mind. "Thank you, Tan. That means a lot," Jacob swallowed another sip, "and now Gabriel Grant is on the run. There's nowhere in this great territory for him to go that I won't find out about." He smiled, "Besides, he won't find me here. As far as Gabriel's concerned, I went back north and left Wyoming."

"How ya figure?"

"Let's just say, Jacob Creek is gone."

The Marshal laughed, "Seems like you're going to need more than facial hair to keep him from knowing who you are. You realize Gabriel has business in Cedar Grove?"

Jacob swallowed another glass, "Like I said, he's on the run. Don't think he'll be doing much business anywhere." He held his glass up for another round.

The barkeep refilled Jacob's glass, "There ya go, Mister Callihan."

"Callihan?"

Jacob smiled. He'd been in Cedar Grove six months. They never knew Jacob Creek. "It was my wife's maiden name."

"I'm sure she's honored."

Jacob nodded, "I'll drink to that."

They clanked glasses and drank.

Tan set his glass down, having enough, "What's next for Jake Callihan?"

Jacob stood and pressed his hat onto his head, "We wait, Marshal. We wait."

"For what?"

"For Gabriel to make his next move."

With that, Jake Callihan walked out the way he came.

ABOUT THE AUTHOR

JASON (J. B.) SISAM is a professional blogger, pastor, and author. He helps writers and leaders stay motivated with clear thinking so that they are equipped with tools to find their voice and succeed in their family, business, and life. he creates believable characters that connect and delivers stories that resonate with truth. Jason lives in Minneapolis with his wife, Kari and their two children, Amelia and Aaron. Learn more at JasonSisam.com.

facebook.com/jbsisam

twitter.com/jbsisam

instagram.com/jbsisam